The Blazing Unicorn

ALICE HEMMING

SCHOLASTIC

To Claire, James, Jack and Isaac

PROLOGUE

Shadows stretch as night draws near;
Little treasure, do not fear.
Twilight is the magic hour
When torches blaze and moonbuds flower;
When fairies dream and nightjars cry
Beneath an ever-darkening sky.
Take my hand and hold it tight;
Embrace the magic of the night.

ONCE, LONG AGO

DEEP IN BRUME FOREST

CHAPTER ONE

FOREST TWILIGHT

Quessia was a fine kingdom, with a grand sandstone castle at the centre of a thriving city. Outside the city walls lay undulating green fields, and beyond them, quaint villages, dotted amongst leafy forests. Brume Forest was one of the largest, just a few miles from the main city of Quessia. Nestled in its depths, near the point where two tracks met, was a single wooden cottage. It had once been a pretty, happy home, full of love, but over the last few years it had fallen into disrepair and laughter was rarely heard.

The cottage was home to twelve-year-old Marie, her older brother Wyll and her father, Jacob. One evening, Marie and her family had finished supper. Although it was autumn and getting cold, it was still dry, so they cooked and ate outside. They had eaten pottage as they did every day: boiled-up barley with some greens from the garden and scraps of ham. Marie had made sure that most of the ham ended up in her father's and brother's bowls. She was adept at going about her day ignoring her hunger pangs, whereas her brother needed the energy for his work, and her father … well, she wanted to keep her father in a good mood.

They had eaten barely an hour ago and scraped their bowls, yet they were all still hungry. Marie's father and brother had been arguing ever since. She'd taken the pots and plates to scrub clean in the nearby stream, hoping the argument would dry up in her absence. When she returned, her brother was working on some bowls at the lathe. The carpenters' work area was set up under a shelter just outside the cottage and Wyll had retreated there to make the most of the daylight. But the argument continued.

Marie wished they'd stop.

Her father was a small man, but when he grew angry, his

eyes bulged and his face turned red and he looked as though he might explode. "All I am saying is the city folk have taken our work. People are too lazy to come out to the forest to find real craftspeople any more. They visit the carpenters on their doorstep, even if they charge twice as much for shoddy work." He had been carving detail on to a wooden figure – a soldier about the size of a clothes peg. He waved the figure in the air as he spoke, pointing it towards Wyll to emphasize his point. "When I was younger, there was enough for everyone. Now it's a daily fight for survival."

A rhythmical scraping accompanied their conversation as Wyll's foot worked the treadle, sawdust collecting on the ground beneath him. The cottage and its surroundings all smelled of sawdust: dry sawdust in summer and damp sawdust in winter.

"I know only too well about our fight for survival, but it's easy to blame other people," said Wyll. "We should do what we can do to improve our own situation." Her brother had a calmer outward appearance than her father, but from his high chin and the urgency in his voice, it seemed that he too was losing patience. She ventured up to the lathe and put her hand on her brother's arm, but he either did not notice, or chose not to respond.

"What do you mean by that?" said her father, leaning forward in his chair.

"Just what I say," replied Wyll. "I'm the only one who has worked at the lathe in weeks. People in the villages still need cartwheels and chair spindles. They might not pay the handsome prices you yearn for, but they would give us food."

"Food!" said her father, dismissively.

"Yes. Right now, butter or cheese would be worth more than any gold. The work is there but I can't go out to find it *and* continue doing all the carpentry on my own. If you spent less time on your toys and more time looking for work, then there would be more to go round."

"*Toys?* These are not toys!" Jacob looked at the carved wooden figure in dismay. He threw it to his son, who caught it in one hand. "Take a proper look. These are collectable figurines – valuable items. If I manage to find one affluent buyer, then word will get around. All the rich families will want them, and we will make our fortune."

Wyll looked at it briefly, shrugged and tossed it back to his father, who failed to catch it. Jacob picked it up from the ground and cradled it as though it were a wounded child.

"You've been saying that since I can remember – fifteen

years or more – the same excuses over and over," said Wyll. "You are a carpenter. Why not build useful things like tables and chairs? Or bowls, like these I'm making now. Surely the rich families you speak of will pay for useful items too?"

Their father looked as if he were about to reply but changed his mind. He patted the stool next to his.

"Come here, Son. Sit here with me. Have a drink."

"I can't – I'm *working!*" said Wyll, with an exasperated sigh.

Her father checked his empty cup. "Marie! I need more ale."

Marie ran to get some. Even when the food supplies were low or non-existent, they were always able to get ale, which they brewed from the barley water drawn off the cooking pot. She returned with a jug. Wyll shook his head. "You don't have to get it for him, Marie – you're not his servant."

"It's fine, I want to," she said, topping up her father's cup. She did want to. As long as she could keep her father happy, then he and Wyll wouldn't argue. And if they didn't argue, then she could pretend they were a happy family.

"Of course she doesn't mind. She's a good girl and, unlike you, she does what she is told," said her father, patting her arm but missing and patting the table instead. He had drunk a little too much ale. He was still cradling the wooden figure in his other hand. "The city carpenters are taking all the work. The nobles don't want their carpentry done by the likes of us, living out here in the forest…"

On and on he went, the same old complaints they'd heard before. But her brother would keep arguing back, his retorts fuelling her father's fire. This would go on all night if no one intervened. At any minute, Wyll would mention their mother, and then Jacob really would get angry. She couldn't let it escalate to that point, as it had so many times before.

Marie ran to check the woodshed. Supplies were low – perfect. She did what she always did. She distracted them both.

"Speaking of wood," she said loudly, breaking up her father's rambling, "we're nearly out of firewood. Wyll, we need kindling for the morning fire. Will you come with me to fetch more?"

Her brother looked up in surprise, as if he was reluctant to break away from the argument. "Do you truly need me to come with you?"

"Oh, yes. It will soon be dark and the wolves come out in these twilight hours. I'm … afraid to go by myself."

"You've never been afraid before." It was true. Twilight

was Marie's favourite time of day. Just like her mother. *The sky turns my favourite colour in the twilight*, her mother used to say. *Pink*. When Marie thought of her mother, she always pictured her in a pink dress, with flowers in her hair. She could see her now, laughing and spinning Marie around. She said that twilight was the gateway to the magic hours. She even sang about it sometimes.

Twilight is the magic hour
When torches blaze and moonbuds flower

But Marie wasn't going to remind her brother of that now. She just wanted to get him away from her father before this argument erupted into something more.

"Please, Wyll."

He sighed and stopped working, leaving his half-turned bowl on the lathe. He grabbed his warm cloak. "Come on then, Marie. Let's go before it gets dark."

They left their father staring at the dying embers of the evening fire and walked out into the forest.

THE ENCHANTING SOUND

"I know what you are doing," said her brother. They left the cottage and followed the stream deeper into the forest, the smell of damp leaves growing stronger. "You were putting an end to our argument. Do we even need firewood?"

"Yes, we do. And there *are* wolves. But of course I wanted the argument over. You two would go around in circles like that all night."

Wyll ducked to avoid an overhanging branch. "You agree with me, though, don't you?"

"Yes." Marie sighed.

"So why don't you *say* something? You always smooth things over, placate him, when you could make a point instead. You could support me, especially when you know I'm right."

"But where would that get us? You know what Father's like; he will never see things from your point of view. And none of those arguments put food on the table. We should be trying to help him. If we had just a little more money and food, then maybe he would be happier and not so angry all the time—"

Wyll laughed. "Happier! When have you ever known our father smile?"

"He used to smile sometimes when Mother was alive." She spoke quietly, hesitantly, not wanting to upset Wyll even more. She thought of an autumn evening like this one, several years ago. Wyll had been around the age she was now and had been learning to play the fiddle. He'd squeaked out a jig, while Marie had sung along enthusiastically. They had no neighbours to disturb out in the forest, apart from the bemused birds, who had watched from a safe distance. Afterwards, the children had come into the forest for firewood as they were doing now. Their parents sat together, wrapped in a single shawl, watching the sky turn rose-coloured.

Wyll was quiet for a moment. She wondered if he was remembering the same evening. Maybe they were both hoping in their own way for that father – a once happy man – to come back.

"He did sometimes smile back then," conceded Wyll.

"We all did when Mother was here," said Marie, stepping over a gnarled tree root. Wyll stared into the distance, and she thought, not for the first time, how much he looked like her mother, with his fine features and thoughtful expression. No wonder her father could hardly bear to look at Wyll sometimes – these similarities must be a constant reminder of her. Marie knew she was more like her father herself: shorter, pastier, rounder.

When Wyll looked back at her, his eyes were a little red. "Father never smiles now. He knows it was his fault. He could have saved her if he hadn't been such a skinflint."

Marie sighed. When her mother had first succumbed to her illness, Wyll had begged Jacob to pay for a healer. He had refused, had kept telling them she would get better on her own. Until it was too late.

"We don't know a healer would have made any difference. Perhaps she would have died anyway," said Marie.

"Perhaps, but I don't think she would, and I'm pretty sure our father doesn't either. *That's* why he can never forgive himself and *that's* why he will never be happy."

They walked on for a few moments, where the trees grew close together and less light filtered through. They had discussed this before, but not often. Wyll was just so negative about their father, whereas Marie still hadn't given up on him. She tried to think of a time recently where Jacob had smiled or been pleasant company to be around.

"He seems content when he is working on his little figures."

"Yes, you'd think they were his actual children, not us! You just have to face it: Jacob Woodman is not a kind man."

"Not a *happy* man," said Marie.

"Not happy *or* kind. He never really was, but Mother brought out some good in him. The best of him died with her, and now he blames everyone else for his own misfortune. You have to stop trying to please him. He's the one who needs to change his ways, and he'll never do that now. I tell you, as soon as I can, I'm getting as far away from this place as possible. I'm going to make my own way in the world."

Marie lowered her eyes. The thought of Wyll leaving was too much to bear. She couldn't imagine it just being her and Father, and having to do all the work she and Wyll usually did together. If they had some neighbours it might have been a more tolerable prospect, but there was no other dwelling for miles around. An occasional traveller would pass through in the old days. Their generous mother would hand them a bowl of broth as they shared their stories. Otherwise, Mother had liked the solitude. "We are part of the forest; we don't need anyone else," she'd said. But now they never handed out broth to anyone, and Marie felt a desperate need for other people. Wyll couldn't abandon her.

She looked up at him with wide eyes, and, sensing her mood, he flung an arm around her shoulder. "Don't worry – I'll come back for you when I've made my fortune, but in the meantime, you must learn to speak up for yourself. I won't always be around, and if you aren't a bit more confident with Father, then he'll walk all over you. You'll be nothing but his servant."

Tears pricked at Marie's eyes. Wyll was older. She had always known he would leave home before her and that she wouldn't be able to go with him, but she didn't want to think about it any more that evening. "Let's just find some firewood and go home," she said.

They walked a little further, concentrating on the ground, but the forest floor was stripped of windfall. The onset of the cold weather must have sent folk from the villages deeper into the forest than usual in their hunt for fuel. They left the stream for where the trees were thicker. "I'll break some branches off that birch tree," Wyll said. "You find tinder."

He flung down his cloak, grabbed one of the lower branches, and swung himself up into the tree, disappearing from view. Marie gathered dry leaves and feathery bracken, stuffing it into the pocket of her apron. She could hear her brother's voice above.

"There's some deadwood in the middle of the tree. I'll throw it down and you bundle it up."

Sticks began raining down from above, and Marie moved out of the way. Before she went to gather them, a strange sound made her stop and listen.

It was like the echo of a bell, but softer, and it didn't die away like a bell ring, but kept going steadily, moving higher and lower like a song. It was an enchanting sound, filling her heart as well as her ears with wonder. She looked around but could see nothing out of the ordinary. Marie knew this forest well. She knew the eerie churring of the nightjar, the screech of the barn owl and the howl of the wolf, but this was different to anything she'd ever heard.

She called up to her brother. "Can you hear that?"

"Hear what?" The leafy branches rustled as he stuck his head out and looked down at her. "Aren't you going to pick up the wood?"

Marie didn't reply. She stood, listening. Wyll darted back into the cover of the tree and carried on snapping off branches, grumbling to himself about dreamy little sisters.

The sound rang on. She tried to imagine what might make a call like that. It wasn't a bird, or an animal she knew, but it couldn't be anything man-made. She felt an overwhelming desire to follow it.

She left the sticks scattered on the ground beneath the birch tree and walked away, her brother calling after her.

The firewood could wait, whereas this sound… It was just beautiful.

She walked a few steps back down to the stream, in the direction the sound was coming from. It grew louder. She walked quicker. She pushed through some bushes and stopped again, listening. She followed the stream down a slope. Orange sunlight fell in irregular patterns on the crisp dry leaves at her feet. She hurried along. She had the feeling whatever it was wanted to be found – as if it was calling her. "I'm coming," she whispered.

Marie knew the stream narrowed and met a waterfall just around the bend. She'd heard that magical creatures like water sprites sometimes played near waterfalls. Maybe they were singing. The flowing water rushed and churned white in the twilight, and the soft ringing grew harder, louder, until it was almost unbearable.

Just as Marie was about to put her hands over her ears, the sound stopped. She had nearly reached the waterfall. She ran the last few steps and then peeped around the trees to look. A bright flash made her blink. When she opened her eyes, she could hardly believe what was standing before her on the rocks next to the waterfall. Not water sprites, but something she'd never seen before.

THE BLAZING UNICORN

It was a unicorn.

The flash faded a little but didn't disappear, and Marie had to squint to see. The unicorn's bright white body was shimmering in the fading sun. Its tail and mane seemed to be made from long, flickering orange flames, rising upwards and outwards. Marie's first thought was to try to help, to gather some water to put out the fire, to push the unicorn under the waterfall. But she saw that the creature stood calmly: it was not distressed. The fire belonged to the unicorn; was part of it.

The sound began again, loud and clear, and Marie realized the unicorn was singing.

All she could do was stare.

This time the singing didn't last long, and as the lingering notes died away, the fire vanished too, until not a glimmer remained. The unicorn's tail and mane were now white and silky, matching its body. The only part that wasn't white was a wide black stripe down the centre of its face. The wild ponies that grazed in these parts sometimes had similar markings, although they were the other way around: white on brown. *A blaze*, that's what they called such a mark. The creature was beautiful, and

Marie shook her head in wonder. "Who are you?"

The unicorn took a few small steps down from the rocks, splashed through the shallow waters and trotted towards Marie, tail swaying. Then it stopped. She wasn't expecting the unicorn to answer, and it came as even more of a surprise than the flames or the singing.

"I am the Blazing Unicorn. You may call me Blaze. Who are you?" The voice sounded like a woman's: clear and sweet.

Marie took a step back.

"I am Marie," she said timidly. "I am here gathering firewood with my brother, but I live nearby, in the cottage just over yonder."

The unicorn – Blaze – bowed her head towards her. "Mistress Marie, are you a good listener?"

A good listener? Marie was surprised by the question. She thought of her father and her brother arguing around the fire. They were certainly the ones who did all the talking in her family. "I suppose I am," she said.

"You must be, for not everyone can hear me. Only those who listen can hear my cry."

So the unicorn had been crying? The poor creature. Marie stepped a little closer. "Blaze," she whispered, laying her hand gently on the side of the unicorn's face. Her coat felt soft, more like a person's than a horse's. Marie breathed in the scent of roses and summer and magic.

"I am an enchanted unicorn with great power." Marie stood back as Blaze spoke again. "Now you have followed my song and gazed upon me, I am your servant, and some of this power may be yours. You are granted three wishes."

Could this really be true? Marie had always known there was magic in the world – her mother had told her often enough – but she had difficulty believing this magic might be for her. Marie looked around for her brother – for anyone – to help her understand what was happening, but there was nobody else around.

She gazed into the unicorn's eyes. They were blue, like the water in the stream behind them, darkening in the twilight. Three wishes. But she only needed one. She closed her eyes and thought of how her family once used to laugh and joke together. How happy they were.

"May I wish for anything I choose?"

"Almost anything. I cannot bring people back from the dead, or turn back time. But I can bring you riches or great beauty or fame. Choose wisely and be clear – for once you have spoken, the wish may not be reversed."

Marie lowered her gaze. So, her only wish couldn't be granted. She couldn't bring her mother back, or return to the way things were. She might have known it wouldn't be that simple. She began to wonder if these wishes could really be possible, anyway. Perhaps she should be wary. Mother used to read her stories of young maidens making deals with magical creatures, only to be tricked in the end.

"Why me? The wishes, I mean?"

Blaze made a low sound, somewhere between a horse's neigh and a sigh. "My previous master died and I have been looking for a new master. You had the good fortune to follow my song and find me. Now I will answer only to you unless you yourself die or you bequeath my power to another. Please make your first wish."

It was all happening too quickly for Marie. "I want to know more about you, to understand. Who was your master? Why are you standing here, in Brume Forest?" She wasn't a silly girl like the ones in her mother's fables. "I wish to know everything I can about you."

The unicorn blinked her large eyes. "I see you are curious as well as kind."

There was a sudden blaze and bright orange fire sprang up

around the unicorn once more. Marie stepped back in surprise, although she felt no heat from the flames.

"Your wish is granted," Blaze said, as the flames died away. "You may ask me whatever you would like to know."

"Oh," said Marie. She hadn't expected to use one of her wishes in that way, and it took her by surprise. What a waste. But it didn't really matter; she still had two wishes left, and she did want to know more about this magical creature.

"Where do you come from?" asked Marie.

The unicorn spoke slowly and softly so Marie had to listen very carefully. "Before this life of servitude, I knew another life in a kingdom far from here. It was such a very long time ago that my memories are fading. I was a mother, with a family. I had a daughter, younger than you are now." The unicorn paused, dipping its head low. "I remember it only like a dream."

Marie understood that. She remembered her own mother like a dream. Fleeting images in her mind – little scenes that played out over again.

"What happened?"

"I was enslaved by an evil king, who trapped me in a form that was not my own. I swam like a fish in the water, hidden from those I held dear. For a long time, I answered to him alone, but after his death, I was found by another, a sorcerer, who put me under this spell. I have gone from one master to another until I hardly remember my real life any more."

Marie felt tears of sympathy welling up in her eyes. "How many wishes have you granted?"

"Too many to say, though I remember every single one. I have always hoped one day I will find someone who is kind and unselfish enough to use one of their wishes to set me free and let me return to the person I was before." Marie reached out to the beautiful creature before her. She wanted to help her if she possibly could. Surely there must be a way by which she could improve both their lives. "Would it be possible to have my own wishes but also help you?"

"Of course. But you must be prepared to sacrifice your third wish." The unicorn breathed out slowly through her nose, like a soft sigh.

Marie thought she was lucky to have any wishes at all. Of course she could help Blaze with one of them. "One or two wishes should be enough for anyone, shouldn't they?" she asked.

"Yes, Mistress Marie. I can change lives for the better with just one wish. If only people could think through what they are asking for. Yet I seem to bring nothing but unhappiness. People always want more. More wishes. More things. In the wrong hands wishes are hurtful and destructive and bring out the worst in people."

Those words hit Marie hard.

"I'd never want to hurt anyone." She only wanted to help her family. And she felt for this creature, who had never had the freedom to make decisions for herself. Marie had two wishes left and she would use one to free the unicorn. She just had to make sure she used the other one wisely.

She thought of their meagre supper that evening and the friction between Wyll and her father. This would be a chance for her, for them, for a different life. She was not able to bring back her mother, but perhaps they could still be a contented family. She pictured their little rundown cottage and their father sitting miserably by the dying fire. He had known only brief happiness, with Mother. Since she had been prematurely taken from them, all he had known was poverty and hardship. If Marie could only make his life better, maybe the father she remembered from her younger years would return. She knew that would make her life, and her brother's life, happier too.

She smiled at the unicorn, just thinking about it, and took a deep breath in preparation. This time she wouldn't rush her wish. She spoke slowly and formally.

"Dear Unicorn," she said (for she felt such an important wish required an introduction), "I wish for you to help my father, Jacob Woodman. Give him anything he desires."

She looked to Blaze for confirmation she'd done the right thing, but there was disappointment in the unicorn's eyes. She bowed her head and blinked as she had with the previous wish and fire ignited around her. A sign, perhaps, that the unicorn was working her magic.

"So be it. You have bestowed my power upon another. Your wish is granted."

"Oh!" Marie hadn't meant to bestow the unicorn's power on anyone else. "I didn't mean to give the power away... I only meant to help my family!" she cried, but she knew it was too late.

This time the unicorn began to fade along with her flames; flickering like a dying candle. She was leaving Marie – going to her father, she supposed.

"My father will help you," Marie called. "I'll ask him to set you free just like I promised." But the unicorn didn't reply; she was disappearing like the forgotten dreams they'd discussed.

A cold tingle of regret spread from Marie's chest out to her fingers and toes. She had given away her power to free the unicorn or to make any more wishes. What a stupid thing to have done. If only Wyll had been with her. If only someone else had been with her, then she would have thought things through. But she had done it all wrong – failed.

The unicorn had gone. Water continued to gush noisily over the rocks and everything looked normal, as if Blaze had never existed. Marie sighed. There was nothing to do but turn back, find Wyll and go home.

She trudged back along the side of the stream, her regret turning to worry. Would her father use the unicorn's power for good? Or was he one of those types Blaze had spoken of? The type that would become greedy and selfish, and cause harm and destruction? Every part of her froze. She already knew the answer to that question, and fear overcame her worry.

She quickened her pace. She had to reach her father before the unicorn, to warn him and tell him how easy it would be to make a mistake with his wishes. Perhaps she could persuade him to use this new power for good. She picked up her skirts and ran, following the winding stream. She found the spot where she'd left her brother. He'd climbed down from the tree, and she ran into him at full pelt, knocking the bundle of firewood out of his arms.

"I'msorryI'msorryI'msorry!" she cried out, bending to pick up the sticks and sobbing as she did so.

"Marie! Whatever is the matter?" he asked. "Where did you go? I thought you were playing some kind of game."

But Marie couldn't find the words. She clutched her chest, trying to catch her breath.

"She was here in the forest, by the waterfall," she gabbled. "Right here in a blaze of flames. She was magic, and if I'd have said what I meant to say, she could have helped us. I could have solved all of our problems, but I sent her away to Father and now I'm worried about what he might do—"

"I don't understand, Marie," said her brother. "Slow down and I'll help. Whatever it is I'm sure we can—"

"—No! There's no time to explain. Come home, quickly!" she said, tugging on his arm. "Then you'll see."

Wyll tucked the recovered firewood under his arm, and they ran home to their cottage as darkness descended.

BY THE EMBERS

Marie and Wyll arrived back at the cottage red-faced and out of breath. It seemed nothing had changed. Smoke spiralled from the embers, silver in the moonlight. Their father sat on the same stool, his back to them. There was no sign of a unicorn. An awful thought struck Marie, that maybe she hadn't sent the unicorn back to her father at all. She had said the wrong thing all together and sent her away. Her face must have fallen, for Wyll looked at her inquisitively. She couldn't explain in front of her father. If she'd lost something as precious as a magical unicorn, then she couldn't risk her father finding out; he would be so angry.

They walked up behind him. He was still. For a few moments, Marie thought he was asleep, or worse. Then she saw he still held the carved wooden soldier and was turning it over and over in his hands.

He span around; all trace of anger gone, his eyes bright and his teeth showing in a full grin. The skin on Marie's arms prickled. She'd never seen him smile like that.

"Look," he said as he placed the two-inch figure on the wooden stump in front of him.

Then Marie saw this model wasn't the soldier after all, but a young man, in peasant's clothes. Jacob pulled two more figures from the pocket of his apron. A girl, and a man. Then she knew who they were supposed to be. It was her father and the two of them.

Marie and Wyll exchanged silent glances. This was unexpected.

"Where would you place these figures if you could put them anywhere? What would you give them? Treasure? A crown?" He placed a tiny wooden crown on the father figure's head, then, when they didn't respond, he leaped to his feet.

"Well? Well?" he shouted. "Aren't you going to say anything?"

Wearing the same disturbing grin as before, he looked at their stupefied faces. Then he picked up the little wooden version of himself and held it aloft. He brought it to eye level and spoke again, as if addressing his toy.

"Things are going to be very different from now on."

Marie looked around for Blaze. Her father's rantings must be connected to the unicorn – yet Marie couldn't see her anywhere. Had her father made the same mistake as her, and given away his power? From the look on his face, she didn't think so; his eyes were glittering as though he'd unearthed a great treasure.

"What do you mean, things are going to be different, Father?" Wyll's frustrations from earlier were still visible in his tense stance. His cheeks were flushed from the run back home and his brow was furrowed. He looked confused at his father's behaviour; confused Marie had dragged him back here; confused at everything.

Marie put her hand gently on his arm, but he shook it off and continued.

"Things look exactly the same to me as they have always done. I worked all day, Marie cooked our meal and cleared up the dishes, and we've been to collect firewood. What have you done? Nothing! That's what. Just played with your toys as you've always done." Wyll knocked the three figures off the stump.

"That's what you think," said their father, smiling knowingly. He picked up the father figure, with its crown, and the figure of Marie, but left Wyll's figure lying on the dusty ground.

Wyll looked like he was going to boil over with rage. He threw the firewood down.

"How can it possibly matter that your figures now have their own adornments? You'll never find anyone to buy them all the way out here, in the middle of nowhere. Why can't you make a stool or a cabinet, or anything half useful? You taught me my trade and now you seem happy to sit back while I do all the work."

Wyll may have been growing increasingly angry, but Marie kept watching her father. He seemed calmer than before. Worryingly calm.

"That's where you're wrong. I don't need you to do anything for me at all. If you dislike being in the middle of nowhere, then perhaps you should leave. Go and make your fortune in the big city."

Marie tensed. This was the moment she'd been dreading.

"Fine! I shall! I'll be better off without you! It's time for me to make my own way in the world without you dragging me down. I'm going." Wyll stormed into the cottage, leaving their father sitting by the dying firelight and Marie standing uselessly alongside him.

There was a moment's silence, and then her father spoke.

"If he knew what I'd found, then he wouldn't be so quick to leave."

"I know," whispered Marie. "I met the creature out in the forest. I sent her here. Where is she?"

"Does Wyll know?" demanded her father.

Marie shook her head.

"Then keep it that way. Not a word, do you understand?"

His eyes were threatening and Marie was scared. She nodded. "Where is the unicorn?"

"It is safe."

Wyll emerged from the cottage, belongings thrown into a bundle over his shoulder. It had not taken him long to pack, but his possessions were few. None of them owned much.

"I am ready."

His father looked him up and down. "So, you really are going. But you are young and foolish. When you see how my fortunes change, you will be back begging forgiveness."

Wyll stood before him, clear-eyed and stubborn. "I will not be back. I will make my own way. Marie, will you come with me?"

Marie looked at her father. He would never plead for her to stay – he never showed his feelings like that. But if she left, who would sweep out the cottage or wash the clothes?

"If you are wondering how he will look after himself, then don't. He is a grown man and if all those who wait on him disappear then he would manage," said Wyll. He knew her well enough to know exactly what she'd been thinking. How would she ever live here without him? But on the other hand, how could she follow him into the forest as night was falling? They had nothing. Where would they go? What would they eat? Her brother at least could offer a trade, whereas she could do nothing; she would only hold him back. And there was something else now, too. Something holding *her* back. The unicorn. She didn't know where Blaze was, but her father did. She had to check that he treated her properly and he used her power for good. With three wishes, he could do so much.

She wanted to tell Wyll. If she shouted it out, he would know what to do. He would be on her side and help. But her father's cold eyes were upon her and the words dried in her mouth.

"I cannot come," was all she could manage to say.

Wyll nodded. He stepped towards her, put his arms briefly around her and spoke in a low voice. "I will return for you," was all he said, then he turned away and didn't look back.

Marie watched him walk away until he was lost in the shadows of the forest. It was possible he would change his mind, or her father would, that he would jump up and shout to his son. But neither of these things happened. Her father sat on his stool like a king on his throne, his grinning face lit eerily by the flickering fire. He didn't move a muscle.

Marie kept looking into the trees, but Wyll did not return. And the longer she watched, and the darker it grew, Marie realized he never would.

IN THE WOODSHED

Her father seemed unmoved by Wyll's departure, as if he had other things on his mind. Blaze. Where was she? Marie didn't dare ask, so she busied herself around the cottage as she always did, closing up the shutters and putting the cover over the hearth. Jacob continued to sit outside, staring at his wooden figures, shadows from the fire dancing around the tiny toys. Only when the fire had died away completely and there was no light save from the moon above did he stir.

Marie joined him out in the dark, bending down to gather the wood Wyll had scattered. She bundled it back together, careful not to leave any twigs behind. She would no doubt be gathering firewood on her own from now on, so she didn't want to waste any. She would put it in the woodstore as they always did. But as soon as she moved in that direction, her father sprang to his feet.

"I'll come with you, Marie," he said, following her. "There is something I'd like you to see." Her heart beat faster. Did he have the unicorn hidden away in there? Or was he just going to tell her to store the kindling in a different spot, that he'd reorganized things? That would have been unlike her father, who had little interest in the day-to-day running of the cottage.

No, this sudden interest in the woodshed was out of character. She held her breath as the creaky door swung open.

It *was* Blaze in there, looking like a shadow of the creature Marie had seen by the waterfall. Her mane and tail were no longer blazing, but barely glowing with a pale-yellow light. Her eyes, that had looked so proud and magical, were now half-closed and, worst of all, she had a filthy rope around her neck.

"Oh!" cried Marie, at the sight. "You didn't have to tether her!"

Her father's eyes bulged in astonishment. "I think you will find the unicorn is mine now, not yours, and I decide what to do with it. You would let a valuable creature like this run free?"

Marie lowered her eyes. "Yes, for she is bound to you anyway until you have used all your wishes. Isn't that right, Blaze?"

Jacob began to laugh. "Blaze! You've named it. And to see you talking to a horse! An hour ago, I'd have thought you mad!"

The unicorn ignored him and responded directly to Marie's question. "You are correct, sweet girl. I answer only to my master, Jacob Woodman, until his death or until he uses all three wishes." Her voice sounded duller and less musical than it had before.

Jacob laughed again, wiping his eyes with his hand. "And the horse speaks back! 'Until I've used all my wishes', the animal says. That's just what it told me when it appeared by the fire. I wondered if I was imagining a talking unicorn, but we can't both be imagining it, can we?"

Marie shook her head sadly, more worried about the glee on her father's face than she'd ever been about his bad moods. He stopped laughing and rubbed his hands together. "If the talking horse thinks I'll be happy with just three wishes then it doesn't know Jacob Woodman." He looked at Blaze with a nasty sneer on his face. "Oh no, I'm too clever to stop at three wishes. I am going to keep on wishing until I have everything I want."

Tears welled up in Marie's eyes. Not only had she failed to free this beautiful creature, but she had passed all its power to her father. That had been a foolish mistake indeed.

FIVE YEARS LATER

QUESSIA, IN THE

RULE OF KING JACOB

CHAPTER TWO

THE CAMP
Banes

Banes had walked through the night. She'd trudged away from her village, over the hills and towards the dark mass that was Brume Forest. Not stopping, not talking, just walking. Brume Forest had changed greatly in just a few years. Once, it had been a place for nature, not people, and there were few houses to be found. But under the rule of King Jacob, people could no longer afford to pay the rising taxes, so they fled the towns and villages for makeshift dwellings in the forest. Some were basic wicker-and-leaf shelters and flung-together shacks, but in the west of the forest, a sizeable settlement was growing. It was mainly young people who stood together against the new king. They had begun to think strategically, to train and to organize themselves.

It was to this settlement that Banes headed. She had a small bundle of possessions on her back and was hoping to leave her old life behind and start a brand new one. The journey had been at first exciting, then desperately tiring, then exciting all over again.

She had reached the forest at sunrise and found the camp by breakfast time, as it was beginning to come to life, plumes of smoke rising above the trees. At the outskirts of the settlement, she was pleased to find someone straight away. A tall young man stood chopping wood, sleeves rolled up to reveal slim freckled arms. He looked approachable. Banes cleared her throat and he stopped his work. He looked up at her, eyebrows raised.

"What do you want?" he asked, kindly.

Banes ran her hand through her short, curly hair and tried not to look as though her eyes were about to shut through exhaustion.

"I'm here to offer my services in the fight against King Jacob."

He smiled. "You don't look like the usual type we get around here. You will have to speak to Commander Flint."

Usual type? She wasn't sure how she differed from the usual type. Younger? Smaller? But it didn't matter, anyway. She'd speak to the people in charge and see what they said. "Commander Flint?" she asked.

"The boss. Used to work for the King's Guard in the old days but defected and has brought some much-needed organization to the place."

Banes started to feel a bit out of her depth. "I didn't know there would be commanders and officers and what-not here. I thought there would just be ... people."

He smiled. "Most of us don't bother with the ranks and titles but she's keen to make us into a proper army. He paused. "Anyway, she's the one to impress if you want to join the camp. We don't let just anyone in."

Banes looked away. She hadn't realized she would have to impress anyone, and had no back-up plan if they didn't want her.

Maybe this woodcutter sensed her anxiety. "Don't worry," he said, "I'm sure you'll be fine. Come with me. I'm Woodman, by the way."

Woodman. Of course he was. He offered his hand and she shook it with what she hoped was a firm grip: a grip worthy of a rebel fighting against the king.

"Ow," he said, wincing. "Perhaps you should be a little gentler with the commander – you don't want to break any bones."

THE COMMANDER

The camp was full of people, mainly men, ambling this way and that, yawning and rubbing sleep out of their eyes. Banes felt better about being so sleepy herself. Woodman guided her through the animal pens and rebels' tents.

"Do I see pigs? And goats?" asked Banes. Woodman nodded and Banes continued. "We had goats back at the inn where I come from. I was fond of them. They have a reputation for stubbornness, but I found them sweet-natured. I wasn't as fond of the chickens, though. It's funny, I wasn't expecting to find animals here but of course, everyone needs to eat, don't they?"

"They do," answered Woodman, as they passed a group breakfasting around a fire. "Do you always talk this much?"

Banes laughed. "No, normally much more, but I'm tired from my long journey."

Woodman led her up to a large table, where a woman sat

studying a map. Unlike many of the other people around camp that morning, she was fully dressed and looked alert, as if she'd been up for hours. Banes guessed straightaway it was Commander Flint. She was younger than Banes thought a commander might be, and beautiful, with arched brows, and impeccable hair. Banes resisted the urge to scrub at herself with a handkerchief. Instead, she stood straight, arms by her sides, looking as she thought a rebel soldier might.

"A new recruit, Commander," said Woodman.

"Thank you, Woodman," she said, and he walked away, smiling encouragingly at Banes.

The commander didn't shake her hand, so Banes was spared any worry about the strength of her grip. Instead, she looked Banes up and down from her seated position.

"Name?"

"Cassandra Edyth Banes, Madam," said Banes, in an official voice.

"Commander."

"Pardon?"

"I am Commander Flint, not Madam."

"Sorry, Mad— Commander."

"Age?"

"Nineteen, nearly twenty. My birthday—"

"—Please try to keep to the question." The commander looked Banes up and down once again. It was not an encouraging look. "We are not in the habit of providing shelter for any vagrant or runaway. What is it you feel you can you bring to our group?"

Banes's tongue felt thick in her mouth. She was aware of her own unimposing physical presence (just over five feet tall and slight in stature) and wished she'd prepared an answer. Her brain felt sluggish before such an authoritative person. But one thing Banes knew she could do was talk. So she began a speech without knowing where it was heading, hoping it might make sense and even convince the commander of her worth.

"It's funny you should ask that, Commander, because on my walk through the forest I was thinking about what I could bring to the camp, and I know I'm small but I'm able of body and of mind and I did walk here all in one night from the village of East Heath, which must be two score miles away, and I think that tells you something about me. And I was on my own and I kept going despite the blisters, and I wasn't frightened of the dark or the animals, which I think tells you something else."

"It does, Banes, yes." The commander smiled a very small smile. "And what was it that you did in the village of East Heath?"

Banes took a breath.

"I'm an innkeeper's daughter, Madam. I mean Commander. I've worked in an inn for most of my life and I know how to handle myself. The other thing you should know about me is that I know people. These people around the camp may be tough, but I'll fit in. You wouldn't have to worry about me. I'm loyal. I work hard. I've been working since I could walk. And I can be persuasive too. My ma always says I could talk my way into the king's treasure chamber or out of his dungeons—"

"—I can well believe it!" said Commander Flint, raising the palms of her hands to stop Banes in mid-flow. "And may I ask what you think of our current king?"

"Him? You don't want to know what I think about him. Well, you probably do, which is why you asked, but I might find myself using a few choice words. I picked those up at the inn, too. Anyway, I think he's a Very Bad Man. He's responsible for all the poverty we see today, and the disease, not least my own predicament. Would you like me to tell you about that?"

The commander stood up from behind her desk.

"As much as I would love to hear your story, Banes, it might have to wait for another day. I have important planning to be getting on with."

She called out across the camp,

"Woodman, come back here. I would like you to show Banes where she might find a tent."

Woodman, who had been chatting to some men nearby, strode back. Banes grinned at the commander. "Does this mean I can stay?"

"Yes," said the commander. "You have impressed me with your drive. Passion and drive are two of the most important qualities here. There are opportunities available for those with ambition."

The commander thrust out her hand, and Banes shook it firmly but not too firmly. "Oh, thank you, Commander Flint. You won't regret your decision!"

The commander was studying her map again. Without looking up she said, "I hope you're right, Banes. You are dismissed. Now go and get some sleep – you look fit to drop."

CHICKENS

Banes was never sure why the commander had found her a place at camp. It might have been her powers of persuasion, or that

Commander Flint had taken pity on her, or they were desperate for numbers. But whatever the reason, she was now a rebel and the camp was her home. She spent the next few days trying to determine what it was she was supposed to be doing.

Everyone else seemed to have an important job. Groups were assigned to sourcing and making weapons, training and fighting, or planning with maps and compasses. Banes wondered how a person could join one of those groups – no one seemed to explain these things. She didn't see Woodman again for days and was eventually shown her role by a scruffy, unassuming man called Robertson, who led her out to the animal pens with a basket of grain.

"Chickens?" asked Banes.

Robertson nodded. "They're all yours now. I'm going to be working with the blacksmith."

Banes sighed. She didn't particularly like chickens. "What are they called?" she asked.

Robertson shrugged. "I don't think they have names," he said, and hurried away, keen to be anywhere else. So Banes named them. Her favourites she called Annie, Flora, Elsie and Bet after her troublesome younger sisters. The fussy, preening cockerel, she called Frederick. He was not her favourite.

Chickens were not her only responsibility, it turned out. She also helped tending to the other animals and growing basic crops. It was difficult to see how this would lead to opportunities, as the commander had said, but Banes still completed her tasks with enthusiasm. She tried to learn everyone's names and get a sense of how the community worked. She wanted to prove her worth, and she hoped she would not be feeding chickens for ever.

When the evening came, they were all ready to eat, drink, relax, and share their thoughts on the world.

TALL TALES

One evening, when she'd been at the settlement for a couple of weeks, Banes sat with a large group of camp members, all deep in conversation around a blazing fire. Discussion had turned to height, prompted by the fact one of the men, Cotter, stood a head taller than all the rest, with a broad back and prominent ears.

"I've been this height since I was fourteen," he shrugged, almost apologetically. "You should see my older brother. He is almost seven foot and has to duck through every doorway."

"My second cousin on my father's side is seven foot one,"

said Woodman, who was sitting to Cotter's left. He was tallish himself and a little more reserved than some of the others, but quick-witted and funny when he did speak. Banes hadn't seen him much since their initial meeting, but she liked him and had a feeling he would be an interesting person to get to know. Before he could give any further details about his second cousin, she spoke up with a swift rejoinder.

"When I used to work in the inn, I knew a man who was eight foot two." All eyes swivelled in her direction. She took a swig of her drink and checked everyone was listening. "He was broad, too. He couldn't fit through the door either height- or width-ways. He would duck and breathe in at the same time, which isn't as easy as it sounds. We used to call him the Jenny Wren Giant."

Woodman smiled and said nothing but Cotter raised a suspicious eyebrow. "The *Jenny Wren* Giant?"

"The Jenny Wren was the name of the inn," explained Banes. "We attracted all sorts of customers, large and small, each with their own story to tell. Luckily, this particular giant was a friend of ours. If we had any problems with customers not paying, then he would sit on them until they begged to settle the tab and buy us a drink as well."

The others all collapsed with laughter as she'd known they would. If Banes knew anything, it was how to tell a story that would make people laugh.

"He never had to pay for a drink in the Jenny Wren," said Banes, solemnly.

"That's what you call a *tall* tale," said Woodman.

She grinned back at him. "Every word is true."

"Well, why don't you go back and call on your giant friend?" suggested Cotter. "It sounds as though he would come in very useful in our fight against King Jacob."

"I would, but sadly he died before I left, from a severe case of vertigo."

Everyone laughed some more and Banes grinned again. "No, we don't need my giant friend to defeat King Jacob. We could do it by ourselves if we could find his weak spot."

She took another swig of her drink and one of the young men, Ford, nodded slowly with a mocking smile. "Oh, I see. Armies have tried to fight him, whole kingdoms have set themselves against him and failed, but Banes here knows what to do. We should have asked Banes all along!"

They roared with laughter and Banes tried to protest, but her shouts were drowned out. They were happy to listen to her humorous stories, but less interested when she had a serious point to make. Woodman stayed quiet, examining the bottom of his cup, and Banes wondered why. He must have an opinion. Everyone here had an opinion.

In the midst of the noise and laughter, another figure appeared at the fireside. It was Commander Flint, her expression unreadable. Banes had seen during her time at camp how she noticed everything that was going on and made swift, rational decisions.

"You seem to be having a heated debate. What's the issue of the hour?" The hubbub died down a little, as if the teacher had just walked into the schoolroom.

Cotter put down his drink and smiled. "Banes here thinks she knows exactly how to overthrow King Jacob."

"That's not what I said!" Banes protested cheerfully, shaking her head. "I was saying he seems like an impossible foe, and when someone seems like an impossible foe, then it's time to do things differently."

The commander smiled and squeezed into a gap in the circle next to Banes. "Go on, Banes, and the rest of you, share your thoughts with me. This is why we have joined together here, to share our knowledge and our skills, at the expense of our common enemy." Someone passed her a cup of ale and she took a sip.

Banes was less confident than she had been earlier with just her peers as audience. Still, she took a deep breath and continued.

"I was saying King Jacob cannot be an invincible foe – there is no such thing—"

"—and I was saying everyone else has failed," interrupted Ford. "I don't know how many armies, but lots. Others have tried stealth. They've sent spies, secret armies, all have been captured and jailed for treason. Or disappeared."

"Yes," joined in Cotter. "Only last autumn Prince Arie from Larendale led his men through the city walls, victory all but his. Then a thunderous roar deafened all those within a square mile. Only the prince's horse was spared…"

"…and the prince and his soldiers were never seen again – I know!" joined in Banes. "And what about all those other armies? They weren't defeated in battle. Quessia has never been known for its fighting prowess."

"This is true," said Commander Flint.

Banes had followed all the gossip at the inn. She listed the stories of grave defeats.

"Shellgard lost three ships at sea on their crossing, in a freak storm, despite unusually clement weather. Wareland set up camp on their journey here and were wiped out by a mysterious plague overnight. The Elithian Royal Knights turned back when there was a sudden crisis back in the city. Shall I go on?"

"What's your point here, Banes?" asked Ford, draining his drink.

"None of King Jacob's armies have even reached the castle. My point is that unless we believe all these armies were unlucky, then there must be sorcery involved."

"But King Jacob doesn't use magic. He doesn't even have a court sorcerer," said Cotter.

"That's what we *think*," said Banes, "but I am suggesting there is some hidden magic at work."

Woodman nodded. "Some hidden magic," he repeated. "But what?"

"This is why they've sent spies," said the commander, quietly. She didn't have to speak loudly to get people to listen to her. "But no one has discovered a thing. What are you proposing that is any different, Banes?"

"I think the spies have been looking for the wrong thing. The hidden weapon. The magic. We're never going to find that, are we? It's obviously too well hidden!"

"So what should we be searching for?" asked the commander.

The fire was dying down a little and Woodman poked at it with a long stick. Sparks flew up into the night.

"The love of his life. The thing he cares about more than anything."

There was laughter around the fire. "No offence, Banes, but King Jacob doesn't strike me as the caring type," said Ford.

"He certainly doesn't," agreed Woodman, with a bitter tone to his voice.

Robertson nodded in agreement. "The reports from the castle say he treats his servants dreadfully. They never have a day off, even if they are sickening for something. They can be sacked for the smallest misdemeanour and they work as hard as can be: there is no room for recreation."

Banes waved her arms excitedly. "But that's why reports from the castle are of limited use. How much does anyone there really know about him? I've never spoken to anyone who even knows where he came from, which strikes me as suspicious."

At this, everyone began speaking at once, their voices merging. They each seemed to have heard a different rumour about the king.

"Wasn't King Jacob the second cousin of the queen?"

"I thought it was on the old king's side?"

"He was definitely the closest heir that could be found. And he was overseas when the rest of the royal family died."

"I heard he was in the Western Isles."

Banes laughed loudly, breaking through the noise. "Do you see what I mean? A mysterious illness wipes out the entire royal family and all the heirs to the throne, but no one else seems to be affected? All highly suspicious. Kings don't appear out of nowhere. They have long and colourful histories. Normally, people know everything there is to know about their royal families, especially the stories they try to keep hidden. Servants are keen to share their gossip. But not with King Jacob. Does anyone even know his family name?"

The group was silent. They shook their heads and shrugged.

The commander smiled. Banes was sure she agreed. But Ford remained sceptical. "So you think you know better than everyone else, do you, Banes?"

"No, I don't, but we should all make it our job to find out. We need to get to know him better than his servants. Better than anyone."

"And how do you propose we do that?"

"I've already told you – we need to find out what it is he really loves."

"We all know what that is, don't we?" said Ford.

"Money!" replied the voices in unison. Different voices piped up around the fire:

"The castle vaults are reported to be stuffed full of gold and jewels."

"King Jacob commissions fine art and eats great food—"

"— yet his taxes are so high, the poorest are barely getting by..."

"Just think of it!" said Robertson. "He could feed his kingdom and beyond!"

"And he would still have enough left over for personal wealth. A crown and a golden goblet or two. That's what I'd do if I were king," said Cotter.

"Good idea, but I'd favour an amethyst necklace," said Ford.

Banes fell quiet as the others struck up a conversation about their preferred royal treasures. Commander Flint didn't join in; she studied Banes in the firelight, until Banes started to wonder if she had some food on her face.

"You have some original views, Banes, and a good grasp of other people. You learned all this working in an inn, you say?"

"Yes," said Banes, in her usual light-hearted tone, "I have

been known to eavesdrop on the odd conversation." She wished she could say something a little more impressive. But it didn't seem to put the commander off.

"Very interesting," said Flint, gazing at her quite seriously. The only other person still paying attention – from the other side of the fire – was Woodman. Even though he was looking off in another direction, as if in a world of his own, Banes knew he was listening to every word. She wondered if Flint had noticed.

"Is the inn also the place where you learned to tell your tales?"

Banes nodded. "It was important for us to keep the customers cheerful."

"You are good at entertaining people, but there is also a skill to stating your opinion without hiding behind humorous stories. You are an intelligent woman, I can tell. Have confidence in that."

The flickering firelight reflected in the commander's eyes, which fixed on Banes. Banes felt the colour rise in her cheeks. This was partly from embarrassment at being observed so closely, but it was also partly with pride: this impressive commander thought she, Banes, an inn-keeper's daughter, was an "intelligent woman". She searched for the right response. "Intelligent! Me? I'm not sure my mother or anyone in my family would agree with that—"

"Banes!" interrupted the commander, before she could launch into another story. "Remember you don't always need to reply. Silence is a valid response."

"Oh. Yes. Silence. Of course." Banes grinned.

"Tell me, if you worked in the inn, and were good at what you did, what was it that brought you here? I understand, of course, if you would rather not share the personal details."

Banes lowered her eyes. She hadn't shared her story with anyone else at the camp but she felt the commander would understand. She took a sip of her ale and began.

BANES'S STORY

Back home, she had always been busy. As well as working in the inn, she'd looked after her younger brother and sisters and tended to the animals. She loved the inn and had thought one day it would be hers. Then her parents had shared the bad news. Quessia was no longer a wealthy kingdom. People had less money to spend in the inn. This, combined with the high taxes, meant the family were struggling to survive.

"I'll do anything I can to help," Banes had said. "Anything at all." She meant it, of course. She would have worked through the night for the inn to survive. She would have eaten half her usual portions of food. Anything. But she wasn't expecting the blow her parents delivered.

"The best thing you can do for us is to marry," her mother had said.

One of the customers, Frederick Fogg, had shown an interest. As if she were a cow at the market. He was twenty-nine years old: ten years older than her, a widower with small children. "He is a kind man and would treat you right," her mother had said. Banes knew him from the inn and it was all true. He was a mild-mannered, if somewhat fussy man who didn't swear or drink too much. He had commented on her curly hair and winning smile. She was happy to serve him drinks and chat about the weather, but she didn't want to *marry* him.

"If I marry Frederick, and go to live with him, then who will look after the inn?"

"Your brother will." Her younger brother, Fin, had never shown the slightest interest in working in the inn, but he couldn't be married off like she could.

You could talk your way into the king's treasure chamber or out of his dungeons, her mother always said. Banes had hoped it was true, but she couldn't talk them out of this.

"I can't marry him," she'd said. "Tell me, what else can I do? What other choice do I have?"

But her parents fell silent. No other option was suggested. There were too many children and she was just another mouth to feed.

So she made her own, alternative plan. She had heard customers talk about the settlement in Brume Forest, and she made up her mind to go.

She left in the night. First, she cut off her long curly hair, leaving the locks on her bed along with a note sending her apologies to Mister Fogg. If he liked her hair so much, he was welcome to it. She gave her family no idea where she was heading. It was better that way.

LATER

The commander listened carefully without interrupting. When Banes had finished, she held her gaze as if she understood. "It sounds as though you made the right decision, Banes. You will be well looked after here and if you show potential, then you will find plenty of opportunities."

Opportunities again! Intelligent! Banes was full of pride. She opened her mouth to thank the commander profusely, but then remembered the advice: sometimes silence was a valid response. She closed her mouth and nodded sagely instead.

"One more thing," said the commander. "Tell me, if you were to find this precious thing – the thing the king loves – what would you do with it?"

"I'd take it, of course. I'd take it and I'd let the king come and find me. We might discover that, away from his castle and his secret weapon, he's not quite as powerful as he appears."

The commander nodded and seemed about to reply, when someone called her name.

"Excuse me," she said, and moved further around the circle, leaving Banes staring into the fire. For the next hour or so she stayed quiet, listening to the others. Eventually, the temperature dropped, the barrel of ale was empty, and the conversation dwindled. The last stragglers set off for their tents.

Banes found herself walking alongside Woodman. He walked slowly, despite his long legs, and she found she had to adjust her naturally quick pace to match his rhythm. Now they were away from the easy group chatter of the fire, Banes was at a loss for something to say. She went back to one of the stock questions they called upon here in the settlement.

"What did you do before coming here?"

Woodman looked at her sideways and smiled a little. "I'd have thought my name was a giveaway. And the work I was undertaking when we first met."

Banes thought for a second. "Ah, of course. Woodman! You were a carpenter?"

"I *am* a carpenter," he corrected. "From a long line of carpenters."

"Must be useful here," mused Banes, wishing she could offer such a valuable craft.

Woodman seemed to read her mind. "There is a role to play for everyone here, even if it takes a little while to identify."

Someone called out from behind.

"Banes!"

Banes turned. It was Commander Flint again, quickening her pace to join them.

"Looks as though someone might have found that role for you already," said Woodman.

They stopped to wait for her to catch up. "Banes, may I have a quick word?" She glanced at Woodman, who took the hint and strode off to his tent, wishing them both goodnight. It was a shame: Banes had been enjoying their conversation. But she was interested in what Flint had to say. Perhaps Banes was going to discover where she fitted into this fight.

CHAPTER THREE

IN QUESSIA CASTLE

Marie

Princess Marie sat in the chair by her bedroom window. She was supposedly working on her tapestry, but she had gone wrong somewhere and it was tangled at the back. Anyway, she found the sights and sounds of the city too distracting. From where she sat, she could see a cart winding its way down the street, no doubt on its way to market. In the back, bundled in with the baskets of vegetables, were two little girls. They were laughing at the way their voices changed as the cart bounced over the cobbles – laughing so much that they rolled around in the back of the cart. Marie smiled.

The cart passed and Marie saw another child – a boy this time – who was older. He was daydreaming as he walked and didn't seem to notice a couple of friends waving to him from across the street. She waved to get his attention, but he was too far away, would never see her. In the end, his friends jumped on him, one with their hands over his eyes, and all three of them laughed.

So much laughter. So much love. How she wished she had a friend to talk to and giggle with. If she did manage to speak to any of these people, they would no doubt curtsey politely, but they would never share a joke. However strange it sounded to her ears, she was a princess. Princess Marie.

She gazed around her bedchamber. It was decorated in shades of sky blue: her favourite colour. Her large four-poster bed was surrounded by thick curtains and piled with thirty or more cushions. Pretty tapestries and a carved looking glass hung on the walls and rugs made the floor soft underfoot. At her dresser, where she now sat, a silver-backed hairbrush set was laid on a tray, the hairbrush, comb and hand mirror all with a matching floral pattern. Perfect. Yet it felt like somebody else's bedchamber. Somebody else's life. It always had.

Marie had everything a person could want and those people

playing in the streets would no doubt think it strange that she, a princess, envied them.

Yet at times she would do anything to replace the scent of lavender with the leafy smell of the forest. It was strange: her brother had always worried she would end up as a servant to her father but, as a princess, she never had to lift a finger. She was a prisoner in a beautiful castle, with no laughter at all and no one to love her.

As if in response, her little kitten, Twitch, weaved around her skirts, looking for attention. She should have said no *person* to love her; she and her kitten loved each other very much. Fern, her ladies' maid, had brought Twitch to Marie when the kitten was just a few weeks old. Fern's mother's mouser had begun to rear a litter, but rejected this one as too feeble and scrawny. Fern had saved him and offered him to the princess for her amusement. That was what Fern had said, although Marie had always wondered if she had really brought the kitten along to save Marie from being so lonely. Twitch had never seemed the remotest bit feeble or scrawny to her.

Twitch put up a paw and caught one of the tapestry silks, batting at it excitedly.

Marie laughed. "That didn't help, but thank you anyway."

She pushed the tapestry away and stroked him. He stuck his chin up, stretched out his front paws, and made a u-shape with his back. He was such a bendy kitten. Marie stooped to pick him up, but he sprang away. He was in the mood for playing, not petting.

"I know what you want," said Marie, standing up and crossing the room to her dresser. She found her cameo brooch in her jewellery box. The back of the brooch was concave and as shiny as a looking glass. Perfect for catching the light. She angled it so its surface caught the sun streaming through the window, and a little patch of reflected sunlight appeared in the room. Twitch leaped upon it, as if it were a mouse or a bird. Marie laughed and changed the angle of the brooch again and again, sending the light around the room. Twitch proudly showed off his developing hunting skills, springing and pouncing every time.

Her mood was instantly lifted. She didn't even mind when Twitch climbed up the drapes around her bed; Marie could live with plucked fabric. She didn't mind the litter tray in her dressing room or his food bowl at the foot of her bed. These quarters were Twitch's as much as hers.

After a time, there was a knock at the door and Fern walked in, her arms full of recently pressed robes.

"Good morning, Your 'ighness. Shall I 'ang these in your dressing room?"

"Thank you, Fern. I would appreciate that, but can you please close the – Twitch! No!"

Fern had only left the door open a crack, but Twitch needed no further encouragement. He sprang to the opening, put one crafty paw around the door to pull it wider, then was halfway down the corridor before Marie had even crossed the room.

Marie lifted her skirts and ran, with Fern following behind, calling, "I'm sorry, Your 'ighness!"

Twitch darted along the short passageway without looking back and turned left into the main corridor. They would never catch him in a chase, so Marie dropped to her knees and made a kissing, coaxing sound that occasionally piqued Twitch's interest. But not today. He stopped momentarily and looked back at his desperate owner, but the wide corridors of Quessia castle were much more interesting than anything Marie could offer, and he soon darted off again.

Marie watched as he ran past a number of closed doors, then stopped at the end of the long, straight corridor, looking at his options: left and right. If Twitch turned right, then everything would be fine. That corridor led to the almost empty east wing, where bedrooms were kept for non-existent guests. But if Twitch turned left, he would be entering forbidden territory: it led to her father's quarters. King Jacob would most definitely not welcome a feline visitor.

"Please turn right, please turn right," whispered Marie.

She and Fern had nearly reached Twitch now, treading slowly and softly so as not to startle him.

The kitten looked right and left again, back at the princess and the maid, then made his decision.

He turned left.

THE STRATEGY ROOM

Few people were welcome in the king's quarters. His valet attended to the king in his dressing room, and housemaids saw to the fires and cleaning duties, but only when requested. He had a reading room, which was rarely used, and a treasure room, where he kept some of his favourite possessions in locked cabinets. At the end of the corridor was a room which Marie herself had rarely set foot in. His favourite room. He referred to it as his "Strategy Room", but Marie privately thought of it as his Nursery.

Twitch was heading straight for the strategy room.

With any luck, her father wouldn't even be on the second floor. He was a later riser than Marie and might still be in the Great Hall, finishing his breakfast. But luck wasn't on Marie's side – she could hear some movement from within. A tin lid clattered, and the king muttered to himself. He was in there.

The door to the room stood open. The servants knew this room was strictly out of bounds, so there was rarely any need to lock it. But Twitch didn't know about the rules, and *of course* he darted inside. Marie followed. She turned to Fern before she reached the door, hoping for a bit of moral support, but the maid hung back. "Are you coming with me?" asked Marie, but Fern shook her head. "Pardon me, Ma'am, but it wouldn't do for me to come into the Strat'gy Room. The king would be quite displeased. So if it's acceptable to you then I'll stay out in the corridor in case I'm needed."

"That's fine, Fern," said Marie. The maid bobbed a little curtsey and looked quite relieved she didn't have to face the king. Marie wished she could do the same. She stood outside for half a moment more, then she steeled herself and stepped through the doorway to rescue Twitch.

The Strategy Room was both wide and long, with two high

arched windows on the wall furthest from the door. Marie didn't know what the room had been before they'd moved to the castle (she tried not to think about the previous royal family). The master bedroom, perhaps. It was bigger than her own quarters, but with a similar layout: a large chamber for sleeping and a smaller chamber for dressing and bathing. There was no bed in it now, or any of the other furniture that one might expect to find in a castle's chambers, like dressers or cupboards. Instead, the walls were lined with shelves and the central space was crammed full of tables for the king's toys.

The distinctive woody smell of sawdust and varnish transported Marie back to her early childhood: not a place she wanted to revisit. Wooden figures like those Marie's father had enjoyed making back in the old days had taken over this room. Over five years, he had spent all his free time (of which he had a lot) hidden away up here, carving and painting. There were rows of model soldiers like the one he'd shown them by the fire that fateful evening. Armies of soldiers, painted in different colours to represent their kingdoms. Civilians too: peasants, farmers, dancers, schoolchildren, going about their daily lives in miniature. The tables even stretched around the corner, to the part of the room Marie couldn't see. They represented different areas of the kingdom – the islands, the coastline, the forest and the mountains. On the central table was a perfect replica of the city in miniature, with Quessia Castle and all its grounds.

Marie had never ventured this far into the room before, although she'd hovered in the doorway. She couldn't remember whether she'd ever expressly been forbidden, but she knew that, like the servants, she wasn't welcome. This room was her father's alone. He would certainly not appreciate a cat's presence. She looked around to survey any damage. She'd pictured scattered soldiers and scratched varnish, but from what she could see, Twitch didn't seem to have been up to any of his usual mischief. Marie breathed a sigh of relief.

The king was at a side table, paintbrush in hand, six small wooden horses lined up in a row in front of him. He was staring at the kitten as if he were a rat or a spider, or another unwelcome pest.

The models were unfinished but it looked as though the king had been daubing them with glossy back paint, slicking it on thickly from nose to tail. To Marie, this showed a remarkable unoriginality. She would have chosen to paint each one a different colour, and given them individual markings. A white coat with brown patches, or a blaze down the middle of a face. Her throat constricted a little at the thought of *that* blaze.

Her father didn't acknowledge Marie's arrival and he moved on to the final horse, painting it the same as the others. He must have been aware of her presence, though, because he began to speak.

"What is that creature doing in here?"

Twitch knew when he wasn't wanted and crouched back under one of the central tables, front paws outstretched, fur sticking up, hissing at King Jacob. His little kitten mouth was a perfect pink semicircle as he tried to defend himself. Marie crawled towards him, slowly, slowly, speaking soothing kitten words and being careful not to make any sudden movements. She didn't want to upset Twitch or any of her father's models. Finally, she reached him, scooped him up in her arms and managed to extricate herself from under the tables. For once, Twitch didn't squirm, and Marie stood up, still holding him close to her chest

"Horrible things, cats," said King Jacob, inspecting the little horses for imperfections. "They appear out of nowhere and seem to do as they please. I wonder if we could rid the kingdom of them. Drown them all."

Marie wasn't sure if he was serious. He had made stranger laws, after all, including banning anyone in Quessia from wearing the colour pink, or flowers in their hair. She didn't like to test his anger by questioning him, but she did wonder if she could talk him out of it. "Cats are useful rat-catchers, Father. You might find if you rid the kingdom of cats, then the rat population increases."

"Hmmm," said the king.

The smell of paint in the room was overpowering and Marie felt a little sick. Her father held one of the freshly painted horses in his hand and scrutinized it, sneering when he spotted something not to his liking, although from Marie's position it looked as plain as the other five. He flung the carving to the floor, where its head broke off and left a black streak of paint on the stone. Marie glanced at it, feeling even sicker at the sight of the decapitated animal, even though she knew it was just a model.

Twitch began to twitch his tail. At any moment he was likely to wriggle free.

"Fern," called Marie, around the doorframe, "could you please take Twitch back to my room and make sure the door is closed?"

Fern scuttled into the room, eyes averted from the king, and prised Twitch from Marie. The kitten's paws scrabbled at her front, but Fern held him tightly, clearly keen to get out of the room. She bobbed her usual curtsey and fled.

"Very wise," said the king. "Make sure the animal does not return. I will not tolerate its presence in here again."

Marie nodded, fear for her kitten gripping her insides. Drowning cats! She wouldn't put it past her father. She would make sure she told all the maids to close her door whenever they visited.

But, with Twitch out of sight, her father seemed to have forgotten all about cats.

He left the horses on the table to dry and picked up a pile of wooden soldiers. He crossed the room and, like a child playing with his favourite toys, he lined them up on the other side of the mountain as if they were advancing on Quessia city. "Well, what do you think?"

Marie was surprised he'd asked her. She'd expected him to dismiss her as soon as Twitch had been taken away; not for him to ask her opinion. She looked at the wooden soldiers with their motionless faces. The carvings were intricate but the faces were all painted in the same way, with crude red slashes for mouths and black dots for eyes. "They seem very … lifelike," she said, although it was far from what she felt.

Her father grinned, his eyes wide and bright. "Oh yes, they

can be realistic in life. Or in death…" He laid one of the soldiers on its back. She shuddered.

"Tell me, Marie," he said, tapping his fingers on the soldier's chest, "if you discovered an army approaching, what natural disaster would you wish for? A flood, a fire, a plague?"

It was a strange question, and Marie did not enjoy her father's games, but she knew he expected an answer.

"I suppose…" She tried to think of what would be better for those poor little wooden soldiers with their fixed expressions. "I suppose I would send an army. Maybe when they saw it … they'd see how powerful you are and would be so afraid they would retreat."

Jacob laughed at that as if he enjoyed the thought. "Yes, yes, I suppose they would." He stared at the figures a little longer. His eyes glinted. "No, not an army. A nasty illness, obliterating the lot of them." He swept his forearm across the table so the soldiers all fell with an alarming clatter, some flying off the table and bouncing off the hard floor.

Marie winced.

"That's better, isn't it?" asked Jacob, with a smile.

She didn't know if his question was rhetorical this time, but she answered automatically. "Yes, Father."

He sighed as if her very presence was boring him. "You may leave. Remember, if I see the cat again, I'll drown it."

Marie felt shaky. She'd thought his soldiers had distracted him from thinking about cats. She lowered her gaze.

"Yes, Father." She curtsied and left the room, finally able to breathe again.

It was a relief to be out in the silent corridor, away from those unblinking figures. She didn't know what they were *for*, or if they served any purpose at all other than for her father's amusement. Deep down, she knew it must have something to do with the unicorn, but she didn't know what. For the past five years King Jacob had kept Blaze hidden away, and Marie could only sneak the occasional visit. Marie wished she could see her more, but she didn't dare ask – her father's unpredictable moods and whims scared her.

Wyll had told her she would need to fight for herself, but he was no longer around. How she wished he would return to her. Why hadn't he? Surely wherever he was, he knew she was now a princess and their father was king. He must see the way their father treated the people of Quessia and wonder why she did nothing to intervene. After all, at seventeen, she was no longer a child. Maybe that was why he didn't return, as he had promised.

He was ashamed, and wanted nothing more to do with her.

She reached the door to her room and opened it carefully, in case Twitch was waiting to spring out again. But Twitch was curled up under the bed, recovering from the adventure.

Marie stepped into the room, shut the door behind her and leaned back on it with a sigh. How she regretted her actions on the night she met Blaze. She should have thought carefully about her wishes, or told Wyll about the unicorn, or run after him into the night. How different her life, all their lives, would be now if only she had been a little braver. Now she was stuck here in the castle, with no way of knowing where her brother was, and as scared as ever to stand up to her father.

CHAPTER FOUR

A SECRET MISSION

Banes

"Just past the old carpenter's cottage, where the two … I can't read the next part." Banes slowed her horse to a near standstill, attempting to scrutinize the commander's directions as she did so. She and Flint had talked for a long time the other night. The commander had followed up their conversation with these clear instructions, but now a fat raindrop had blurred the ink, and it was indecipherable.

"It's no wonder when you're trying to read and ride at the

same time," grumbled Woodman, who was following along behind. He had a point, as the rain continued to pour down and the parchment was at risk of becoming a soggy, inky mess. He looked over her shoulder. "Where the two tracks meet," he read.

Banes laughed. "I don't know how you managed to read that, but this track does seem to meet another up ahead, look. If you're correct, then we're heading in the right direction."

They trotted a little way further. The road through the forest was wide and straight, its bare earth strewn with leaves and trampled by horses' hooves, deep grooves from cartwheels on either side.

"Look, there is a cottage just behind those trees. I'd wager it's the one the commander mentioned," said Banes, brightly.

She urged her horse further on, to investigate. The cottage was old and run down, and a wooden pole lathe stood under a shelter outside. A carpenter's cottage. Or it had been, once. There was no longer any sign of life. A pile of rotting, half-turned bowls littered the ground beneath the lathe and the front door swung open. Someone had walked away in a hurry.

Woodman drew up next to her, staring at the door of the cottage as if he expected the carpenter to emerge at any minute.

"It's a funny sort of place, isn't it?" Banes said. "Shall we stop and shelter for a few moments? We can eat something and check our location."

Woodman flicked his gaze upwards. "I thought you said we were nearly there? And that we couldn't be late? Why would we stop *here*, of all places?"

He was getting irritable. In fact, he had grown more irritable as this journey had gone on. He'd been quite sprightly when they'd set off. Perhaps he was hungry. Or tired, or both. What he said was true, though: they *were* nearly there.

"You're right. It was just an idea!" she said, amiably, then hugged her horse with her legs as a signal to move forwards. The horse set off obediently. It was a shame they didn't have time to investigate, as she would have quite liked to poke around inside the cottage. You never knew what you might find in these abandoned places. There might even be something in storage that was still good to eat. Her stomach rumbled at the thought. She hadn't eaten any breakfast that morning because of the excitement. She'd thought they'd stop on the way. But they hadn't found an opportunity and had been travelling eastwards through the forest for almost two hours without a break.

As they continued along the pathway, Banes looked back

over her shoulder.

"There's nothing wrong with the old place that a good clean and a bit of patching up wouldn't fix. I'm surprised no one's plundered the wood stores or moved themselves in, as it's obviously stood empty for some time. I suppose this is such an out of the way location that no one in their right minds would live here. Although I think I would like to live in the forest one day. In the future, I mean, when all of this is over. Wouldn't you? It's so leafy and fresh and never gets too hot—"

Woodman shouted back through the rain.

"Can we stop talking about the cottage? I don't care about it! I don't care who lived there, what they did or when they left. It's just a house!"

Banes moved her gaze from the cottage to look at him. He was no longer just irritated; he was now red-faced and glowering. She was surprised, as he didn't seem the irrationally angry type (she'd met plenty of those at the inn). Maybe it was the hunger. Or he was cross she hadn't revealed the nature of their mission. He had asked first thing where they were going and what they were doing, but Banes couldn't tell him. Maybe he was the type who didn't like not knowing what was going to happen. Banes wouldn't have minded, herself. She liked surprises. Life was all about surprises.

She consulted the directions again. "*Follow the track in the direction of Quessia*, it says, and then *find cover by the big tree stump*. Hmm, fair enough, but I wonder how we judge when a tree stump is really a *big* tree stump. That one over there, for example, is big, but hardly notable. And that one there is a medium stump, wouldn't you agree?"

Woodman didn't reply.

They continued along the track, the rain slowing to a light drizzle. Banes spotted at least three more biggish tree stumps, but she decided not to mention them to Woodman. She just muttered under her breath, "Big, but not big enough," each time. After a couple more miles, they encountered an enormous tree stump to their right.

"Now, that is a stump worth mentioning! I know I'm not the tallest person in this forest, but I could use that as a bed. It must be the base of an oak, do you think?"

Woodman shrugged.

"Well it means we've arrived!" she said, and they both dismounted. *There is thick tree cover nearby – use it!* the commander had said, so Banes led Woodman and the horses off the well-trodden pathway, and into the leafy part of the forest. It felt good to be out of the saddle at last, and Banes stretched out the sore muscles in her thighs. Woodman tended to the horses, attaching nosebags full of oats to each to enable them to feed.

Although the rain had stopped, water still dripped through the quivering leaves and seeped up from the ground itself. Banes would have quite liked to sit and rest but she kept moving to stay warm.

She glanced over at Woodman, who had said nothing since his little outburst about the cottage. This wasn't going to work if the two of them weren't on speaking terms. Perhaps the whole endeavour was a bad idea. Still, she continued with the plan, kneeling on the ground and sorting through the kit she'd brought along in her leather drawstring bag. A rope. A pocketknife. A roughly drawn map, a handkerchief.

Woodman left the horses and stood by her side. He stamped on the leafy ground and blew into his hands. "I can't feel my toes. I hope there's a good reason for all this. Are you ready yet to tell me what we're doing here?"

Banes was pleased, in a funny sort of way, that he'd been the first to break the silence. A sort of apology. She looked up and faced him.

"We're on a *top-secret* quest." She whispered the words

top-secret and he rolled his eyes.

"That much I know, but you still haven't told me what we need to do."

"Only because Commander Flint told me not to. She said it was *top-secret*," Banes whispered again.

"Oh, really? Is that because she thought I wouldn't agree to it?"

"Maybe." Moisture from the soggy ground was soaking through the knees of her leggings and Banes stood up. "But we're here now so it seems reasonable for me to tell you what we're doing. Promise you'll listen and not instantly dismiss it as a bad idea."

"That sounds ominous. I promise nothing."

Banes guessed he was being humorous. It was hard to know. Either way, she was going to have to tell him. She checked nobody was listening, although the likelihood of anyone else being out in the forest in these wet conditions seemed slim. "Well... Princess Marie comes out riding this way each morning, before luncheon, whatever the weather. She always takes the same route." Banes pointed to the path leading back to the carpenter's cottage.

Woodman said nothing but gazed in the direction she

pointed.

"She's always on her own," Banes continued. "No guards. Which will make things easier for us."

Another pause, then Woodman turned back to face Banes, an incredulous look on his face. "Are you suggesting we *kidnap* the princess?"

When he said it like that, it sounded preposterous. Dramatic and bigger, somehow, than when Banes and the commander had discussed it the other night. But he was right, and she nodded. "Yes."

Woodman stared at her as if she were talking a different language. He slowly shook his head. "No. Absolutely not."

Banes was beginning to wonder herself why she'd thought this mission was such a good idea. It had made perfect sense when she was discussing it with the commander. Still, it was too late to back out. She would have to convince Woodman (and herself) it was a rational thing to do.

"I knew you wouldn't want to do it," she said.

"It's not that – I mean, it is that – do you realize what the punishment is for kidnapping a member of the royal family?"

"Death, I should imagine."

"And that doesn't bother you?"

"No. Because I don't intend to fail."

Woodman rolled his eyes. "I wouldn't want to offend you, Banes, but you don't look like the most obvious kidnapper in the world."

Anger rose up inside of her. "I'm sure if I were six-foot-tall, and a man, you wouldn't be so disapproving."

"That's not actually true. I happen to think the whole plan is ridiculous, no matter who executes it." He crossed his arms and glared at Banes. "I can't believe I came all the way out here, thinking this was a valid mission approved by Flint. She would never allow this—"

Banes put her forefinger in the air to stop him. "Actually, that's where you're wrong. It was her idea – well, my idea, that she sanctioned. The other night, after the fire. She liked my suggestions. She said they were refreshing … and original."

Woodman laughed. "Unbelievable. For months we've all been coming up with well-thought out strategies, which the commander completely ignores. The first time she takes any advice, it's from you! You've only been here for five minutes. What's so special about you?"

"Ooh, I don't know…" Banes grinned. "Wit? Intelligence? Charisma?"

Woodman made a noise somewhere between a sigh and a growl. "In that case, I should be asking what's so special about me? Why exactly am I here with you?"

Banes's grin faltered a little. "Well, I couldn't do it on my own, could I? The commander said I could take one other person and I suggested you."

Woodman scrunched up his eyebrows in disbelief. "*Why?*"

Why. It was a good question. The real reason was, Woodman had intrigued her – she knew he had an interesting story to tell – and she thought she might hear more about him on this mission. And, importantly, he seemed like someone she would be able to count on. But she was too embarrassed to say any of that. Besides, she was beginning to think that she'd been wrong about him. He was being highly disagreeable. She felt her cheeks redden. "Well, I wasn't going to go with Ford, was I? Ford hates me."

"Ford hates everyone."

"But you can see why I didn't invite him. And Robertson is a bit ... well, he's not the most cunning fox in the forest."

Woodman nodded. "That's true. Why not Cotter?"

"Cotter's too ... tall."

"Too *tall?*"

"He'd struggle to hide away, wouldn't he?"

Woodman glanced around him as if expecting Cotter to leap out from the bushes. Banes had had enough of this conversation. Besides, the princess would be here soon, and she wanted to be prepared. She picked up the handkerchief she'd brought to use as a mask and folded it into a triangle.

"Look, I can tell you're not keen on the plan, but you don't have to actually do anything. I'll do the risky part." She sighed. She'd thought, at least, that Woodman seemed the brave type, but clearly not. "You hide away and keep a lookout for any danger. Take care of the horses and get ready to ride off with her when I say the word."

"I see my part is all planned out." Woodman raked his fingers through his hair, looking suspiciously at the handkerchief. "What's that for?" he asked.

"It's a mask. I've heard all infamous criminals wear them. I can make you one if you'd like?"

"No! I won't need one, will I, if I'm hidden away in the trees?" He looked around anxiously, as if he was already seeking out a hiding place.

"If I'd have known the whole thing would scare you so much then I never would have asked—"

"I'm not scared! I just think you should have checked with

me. Even without the threat of the death penalty, capturing the princess is a bad idea in every way. What is the point? It's not the princess we have a problem with."

"Isn't it? I have a problem with the whole royal family," said Banes.

"But she's not … I don't think she's like her father."

"Why?"

Woodman was talking about the princess as if he knew her. It was odd. Banes knotted the handkerchief at the back of her head, a fiddly manoeuvre, but she didn't want to ask for help. Woodman didn't meet her gaze. He was looking out in the direction she'd pointed earlier – where the princess was supposed to appear. "I don't know," he said eventually.

"Well, it doesn't matter if she is like King Jacob or not. The whole idea is we use her to get the king to come to us."

"And we look after her?" Woodman's eyes showed something like panic.

"Of course we look after her. We're not brutes."

"But what if the king doesn't care about the princess? What if he only cares about himself?"

"He must care a bit. She's his daughter!"

Woodman snorted. "Not all relatives care deeply for

one another."

Banes shrugged. She knew that as well as anyone, but still, they shouldn't assume anything about the king and his daughter. They might have a normal, functional, relationship.

"From the way you're talking, anyone would think you are a royal expert. This is a good strategy, approved by Commander Flint. And on this occasion she's the one whose opinion matters."

"That may be, but she's not the one standing out here on the drippiest of wet days waiting to kidnap a—"

"Shhh!" Banes put a finger to her lips. She could hear a thundering sound in the distance. Coming from the direction of the palace.

"What is it?"

"A horse. It's her – the princess!"

PRINCESS MARIE

Woodman ran back under the cover of the trees and began untying the horses. He was going to hide as Banes had instructed. Still, she felt disgruntled he'd needed no persuasion to leave her. She stepped a little way out into the open, towards the road, and crouched low so she wouldn't be seen as the princess approached. She quickly rehearsed what she was going to say. She and the commander had planned it out. *Stop in the name of Quessia's people. You are now our prisoner. No harm will come to you if you do everything I say.*

The handkerchief was loose around her nose and slipped down a couple of times, but Banes couldn't adjust it when the horse was nearly there. She pulled it up so it rested on her nose and clutched her bow in her hand.

Banes had good vision from her position, which gave her a couple of seconds to assess the situation before jumping out. Was this actually the princess? And was she travelling alone? Banes could answer the second question easily: she could only hear the hooves of one horse, trotting steadily. But as the horse appeared around the corner and Banes got a proper look at its rider, she was left unsure of the answer to the first question. *Was* this the princess? The person astride the horse didn't look as Banes expected. Weren't princesses fine-boned with alabaster skin and golden crowns? Didn't they ride side-saddle in stiff frocks? This girl was little more than a child, rounded and sturdy, with wavy mid-length hair, a plain dress and no expensive jewellery. Normal. Like any girl riding a horse.

Still, Banes had to make her decision quickly, and she chose to act. If she hijacked the wrong person, she would release her, make her excuses and run away into the trees.

She leaped out on to the track, drew back her bow and aimed an arrow at the rider. Up close, Banes was even more doubtful she was targeting the right person, until she saw a small royal crest on the panniers.

It was a relief. The princess – Banes was now pretty sure that's who she was – gasped with surprise and drew back on the reins, bringing the horse to a sudden stop.

"Stop!" Banes shouted, somewhat unnecessarily. She forgot what came next, so she stood on the spot, trying to hold her shaking weapon steady.

The princess seemed to recover quickly from the shock of someone jumping out at her. She looked down at Banes with interest, taking in the bow and arrow, and the makeshift mask.

Banes tried again to think of the next part of the speech, but the words escaped her. "Stop," she repeated eventually. "Stop in the name of Quessia's people." She felt pleased with herself for remembering, but the princess raised her eyebrows, eyes wide.

"I have stopped," she said.

Banes flushed. She was beginning to wonder if she was any

good at this. Princess Marie was looking at her intently, which was unnerving. Banes knew the princess was seventeen, just two years younger than her, but her round face made her look much younger. Their eyes met. Marie's were a grey-blue. "Is everything well with you?" she asked. It was such a strange question to put to a masked attacker that Banes was thrown.

"Yes," she said, speaking in a deep voice she hoped sounded serious. "Everything is well with me. Thank you. It's you who should be worried."

It didn't sound quite how Banes intended. More like she had a sore throat. She hoped that, wherever Woodman was hiding, he couldn't hear her.

The princess frowned. She didn't look scared; more puzzled. "I see," she said.

Banes tried again, in a more natural voice. "I mean, there is no need to be worried if you do everything I say. Get down from your horse." It wasn't quite what she'd planned to say, but the meaning was the same.

Banes watched as the princess followed the instructions, hoping she wouldn't try to run away or call for help. Luckily, Marie was obedient and, although Banes kept her bow and arrow trained upon her, she thought it was unlikely she would have to shoot.

Banes was growing hot. It was not a warm day, but the handkerchief was keeping in the heat, like a scarf. Her cheeks were burning and her nose felt sweaty. The handkerchief kept slipping out of position. Banes's hands were occupied with the bow so she had to keep jerking her head back to avoid it sliding down her nose.

"Turn around," said Banes, and the princess did so, holding on to her horse's reins with her back to Banes. Banes had planned to bind the princess's arms as soon as she was off her horse, but that was proving to be more difficult than she'd imagined. She held the princess's wrists and rummaged for the rope in her bag. As soon as she found the rope, she dropped it and it pooled at her feet. She tried to pick it up while still holding her bow, but it was difficult. Why had she insisted Woodman keep hidden away? She would benefit from a bit of support, but if she shouted for him he'd think she couldn't manage this by herself.

The princess looked over her shoulder. She still didn't look particularly frightened – more concerned. Banes was very close to her now – she could see the flecks of her irises and a cluster of spots on her forehead.

"I don't have many valuables," said the princess,

matter-of-factly. "All the real treasure is back at the castle. But I am wearing a pearl hairpin and there may be a gold coin or two in the pocket of my dress."

"I don't want your gold," said Banes, hoping she sounded more imposing than she felt. "Hold your hands together." She wound the rope around Princess Marie's wrists but struggled to knot it. "Blast!" she muttered as she failed a second time. The rope was too thick and slippery.

"The only thing you can't have is my brooch – my kitten loves it," said the princess, who still seemed to think Banes was a highwaywoman.

"Your cat?" Banes was confused now. Why were they talking about cats?

"The brooch sends little diamonds of sunlight dancing around the room and Twitch – my kitten – loves to chase them…"

Banes tried to concentrate on the rope rather than Princess Marie's dreamy ramblings but she couldn't help glancing at the brooch at her throat. It looked fairly simple for royalty: a white head in profile set in a shiny surface surrounded by pearls. Round, like a tiny shield. Banes pictured a royal kitten dressed in a cloak, the brooch fixed to its collar. She found herself wanting to ask more about this pet but stopped herself; the aim for the morning was not to befriend the princess. "I don't want your brooch or any other valuables," said Banes, finally managing to tie the rope in a bulky knot, which should withstand a bit of wriggling.

Luckily, the princess didn't wriggle. She stood there, as instructed, and jerked her head in the direction of the panniers at the back of the horse.

"There's some fruit in there. If you're hungry," she said.

"I don't want…" began Banes, but then she stopped. She still hadn't had a chance to eat and now was as good a time as any. She put down her bow and arrow and unbuckled the panniers, which were stuffed with fresh fruit and vegetables. She'd just pulled out a ripe-smelling pear when Woodman shouted out from the bushes. "Banes!"

She still couldn't see him, but his voice sounded urgent. "The soldiers are coming, Banes!" As soon as he said it, she heard hooves. No wonder the princess had seemed so relaxed; she must have known her bodyguards were following behind. Banes stuffed the pear into her bag.

Her first thought was for Woodman, who had been right after all: this whole mission had been a terrible idea. The last thing she wanted was for him to try any heroics and for both of them to get caught.

"Don't worry about me. Go, Woodman! Get away! Quickly!"

"I'm sorry! I'll get help!" he called and was up on his horse and away before the king's men burst into the clearing. He was doing exactly as she'd asked, but Banes still couldn't help feeling a bit let down.

Two armed men on horseback thundered into the clearing.

The princess glanced over her shoulder at them, looking more frightened than she had before, which was strange. Weren't they supposed to be on her side?

"Oh, thank goodness you've come!" she cried, in a dramatic voice.

The guards dismounted. They looked remarkably alike, with the same dark hair and heavy brows, but one was a good twenty years older than the other. Father and son, perhaps.

"What's going on here?" asked the younger one, grabbing Banes and twisting her arm painfully behind her back. Banes said nothing and looked over at the princess. She was completely free of the rope, which spooled on the ground at her feet. The knot must have been even worse than Banes had thought.

"This, this ruffian, accosted me. She tried to steal my brooch," said the princess, pointing to her brooch, which lay on the ground, clasp undone, glinting in the sunlight.

"I didn't!" shouted Banes indignantly, but the guard holding her only bent her arm back a little more. The older soldier picked up the brooch, the dainty object looking comical in his heavy black glove. Marie took it from him and fastened it back by her collar. She gave Banes a strange, pointed look as she did so, eyebrows raised, which Banes couldn't interpret.

The older guard prowled around the site as if searching for clues, while the other looked at Marie suspiciously.

"Why are you out in the forest again, Your Highness?"

"I come out for a daily ride. Nobody can stop me doing that," she muttered.

"You haven't been feeding the poor again, have you, Ma'am?"

"No!"

"Because you know how your father feels about that. We would be obliged to tell him, I'm afraid."

The princess lifted her chin. "So that's why you're here? You're spying for him? I haven't been feeding anyone! You can search the panniers, if you like."

The younger guard looked as though he would have gone ahead and done that if he hadn't been holding Banes, but the older one stepped in. "No, no, Ma'am, that won't be necessary," he said.

Banes was surprised to hear this exchange after seeing the panniers stuffed with food just a few moments before. Princess Marie must have called their bluff. Quite successfully, as well, thought Banes, impressed. But why was she feeding the poor? Woodman had thought she was different from her father. Maybe he was right.

The older soldier continued to look around. "What's this, Your Highness?" he asked, kicking at the uncoiled rope which lay at Princess Marie's feet.

"It's mine. I dropped it," she said.

It was then Banes realized she was lying to protect her. Holding up a stranger was a grave offence but less so than kidnapping a princess.

The second man turned and looked around in the bushes.

"Was it the one thief or was there a band of them?"

Banes bristled at the word *thief,* but again, it was probably better than *kidnapper,* so she kept quiet.

"Just her," said the princess, pointing at Banes.

"I'll have a check in case there are any more of them hiding," he replied, hacking his way into the bushes with his sword in a futile display of gallantry. He must have known any other bandits would be halfway home by now, as Woodman surely was.

Banes glanced at Princess Marie. She was talking quietly to the older guard and giving a good impression of a delicate princess recovering from a hold-up. She'd known Woodman was there – she'd heard Banes call to him – yet she'd lied to the guards about that too.

The lies benefited Banes, but why would the princess try to help her? Of that, she had no idea.

DOWN IN THE DUNGEON

The jailer was about three times the size of Banes, with a big, square head and hands to match. He riffled through the contents of her bag, sniffing and wiping his nose with the back of his hand. He unfolded her pocketknife and ran a finger along the sharp edge of the blade.

"Careful! It's a good knife, that one. You don't want to cut those delicate little fingers of yours," said Banes, although his fingers were the same approximate diameter as her window bars. The jailer stared at her but didn't respond. It wasn't clear whether they shared the same language. He folded the knife back in on itself and stashed it in his pocket. Next he shook out two folded white handkerchiefs Banes had packed as back-up masks.

"They are clean, I can vouch for that," said Banes. "They might come in handy for mopping up all the blood when you slice your finger with the knife."

He discarded the handkerchiefs on to the floor without saying a word, but Banes kept chatting. If she was going to be down here for a while, then she would try her best to get on good terms with the jailer. In her experience, it usually helped to be friendly with anyone who was responsible for bringing you food. But this character was proving to be a challenge.

"Are there many people down here?" she asked. On her way to her cell they had passed numerous wooden doors, each with a barred viewing hatch, but she hadn't been able to get close enough to see in.

The jailer only grunted and pulled the princess's pear out of her bag.

"I didn't hear anyone, but I'm guessing the walls are quite thick, am I right?" Banes kicked at the wall with the toe of her boot, which actually quite hurt. "Ow!" she cried.

He still didn't react. He was too busy sniffing the pear, which seemed unnecessary, as she could smell its ripe greenness from the other side of the cell.

"Oh, please let me keep the pear!" cried Banes. "I haven't eaten since last night and I'm so hungry!"

He bit into it and juice ran down his chin.

"Is it good?" she asked. "It should be – it's a royal pear, after all."

He grunted and continued munching, throwing her empty leather bag on the floor with his spare hand. Then he left, without so much as a wave goodbye, locking the door shut behind him.

"Rude." Banes sighed.

She moved over by the wall nearest the door, where she had a view out of the window and sat on her bag, rather than the cold floor. The jailer didn't appear to be the friendliest type, and so far, there was no cellmate. She didn't know how long she was going to be down here but it looked as though she was going to have to get used to her own company. And that was something which, up until now, she'd been very careful to avoid.

CHAPTER FIVE

AFTERNOON TEA

Marie

Every afternoon, tea was served to Marie on a tray in her room. She'd never asked for it, and it wasn't something she'd ever had in the old days, but at the palace it was part of her usual routine. On the table before her stood tea in a pot, with a matching cup and saucer and a stiff white napkin folded in the shape of a swan. A tiered china cake stand was laden with delicacies fit for a princess. Soft watercress rolls, devilled quail's eggs and dainty bitesize jam tarts with three different colours of jam: yellow, red and deep purple. The spread looked and smelled delicious, as it always did, but Marie had no appetite.

She thought she should eat something – it seemed only polite to the cook who had prepared it – so she placed half a quail's egg on the fine white plate. She turned the plate around in a circle, lost in her thoughts. Twitch approached, rubbing against her skirts, and Marie stopped plate spinning and broke off some egg white. She threw it to the floor and Twitch pounced on it as if the egg were a mouse. Marie ate a bite too, barely registering the flavour. It seemed wrong to nibble on an array of treats she didn't want, when a girl her age lay cold and hungry down in the dungeon.

Thoughts of her would-be kidnapper danced in her mind. That spark of energy, of passion, and the look of want in her eyes. Out in the forest, something about the girl had grabbed her attention. She hadn't been sure what, but now she thought about it, she knew. Marie had never had a friend, had never been to school, and never saw anyone her own age apart from Fern, who was a little bit younger than she was. And although Fern knew everything about Marie, from her shoe size to the temperature of her bathwater, she knew little about her maid. They weren't proper friends.

If Marie could choose a friend for herself, she thought it

might be someone like the girl in the forest. She supposed she'd wanted to take her prisoner for the ransom money. Having been in that impoverished situation herself, she understood how desperate a person could become.

She tossed another morsel of egg to Twitch.

But maybe there was another reason. Maybe the girl despised her father and the way he treated their people. Marie supposed she could understand that too.

There was one more thing that had piqued Marie's attention: just before she was arrested, the girl had called to someone in the trees. It had sounded like she'd said, "Woodman." Marie's thoughts had, of course, immediately turned to her brother, whom she hadn't seen since that evening so long ago. Could he have been there in the forest earlier, hiding in the trees?

It may have been wishful thinking on Marie's part. Maybe the girl had said "Woodham" or "Goodman" and Marie had heard what she wanted to hear. Even if the girl *had* called for Woodman, it didn't necessarily mean anything: there must be numerous people out there with that surname.

Marie would dearly like to speak to the girl: to find out. She could ask her father for permission to visit, but he was likely to say no, and she didn't want to have to explain the reason for her curiosity. She started spinning the plate again, rotating it in the opposite direction.

As a rule, Princess Marie tried not to do anything to displease her father, but on this occasion, thoughts of the prisoner conflicted with her good sense. If only she could find a way to talk to her…

"That's it!" she shouted, spinning the plate so forcefully it nearly flew off the table. She looked to the doorway, hoping no servant had heard her outburst.

She had a plan.

She would take some of this food to the prisoner. If the girl's eyes had lit up at the sight of a single ripe pear, then this array would be cause for celebration.

So it didn't look suspicious, she took a bite out of one of the jam tarts on the top tier and left one tart on her plate. The maids would assume she'd been hungrier than usual and polished off everything else on the stand. She unfolded the white napkin, scooped the contents of each tier into the centre, wrapped it up and tied it with a bow. She tucked it inside the folds of her dress, between her inner and outer robes, without it bulging too noticeably.

Next, she took her basket of tapestry wool and upended it on to the floor. Twitch sprang at it in delight, his little claws out. Marie knew when she returned, the wool would resemble a bird's nest, but it would ensure Twitch was distracted and didn't follow her. Marie left her room, closed the door firmly behind her, walked down the corridor and turned right, towards the staircase that led to the dungeons.

$\mathcal{C}$HAPTER SIX

HUNGER

Banes

You could talk your way into the king's treasure chamber or out of his dungeons.

Once again, Banes thought of her mother's words and wished they were true. But there was no one here to chat to. No one to persuade, or even to argue with.

Banes had been so confident out in the forest, telling Woodman she didn't intend to fail. In all honesty, she hadn't expected to. When they had planned it, the commander had made the mission sound foolproof, and they hadn't discussed the possibility of Banes ending up in a cell. It was easy to be brave when she was riding through the forest with the wind in her hair. It was far more difficult here, locked up in the dark, damp dungeons.

She was hungry. She lay on the hard floor, wishing again she'd eaten before the kidnapping expedition. She'd expected to be back at the camp with her prisoner by now.

It struck Banes that, although she wasn't in a particularly favourable position at the moment, at least she was close to the king. Closer than she would ever be able to get under normal circumstances. This might be her one chance to find out more. She sighed, glancing around the tiny cell. If only she weren't locked in a dungeon. And if only she weren't so *hungry.*

She tried to think of something else, to take her mind off food, but she didn't like the places her brain wandered. Would she have to stand trial for her crime? And if so, would she be found guilty? What would the punishment be? Woodman seemed to think the death penalty would be imposed for the kidnap of a princess. The king might be more lenient when it came to a simple robbery, but maybe not.

Banes stood up and paced around the perimeter of her cold cell. On tiptoes at the door, she could just about see through the square hatch, but her only view was of the grey wall opposite. She listened but could only hear her own breath, which sounded loud in the empty, echoing room. She'd imagined a dungeon to be filled with the noise of prisoners shouting.

"Hello?" she called out, experimentally, but there was no answer except her own voice echoing back. Perhaps all the cells were empty. The only other sound was the breeze from outside, coming through the small oblong window, with its three metal bars.

She walked to the window, which was even higher than the hatch in the door; the only way she could reach it was on tiptoes, her hands stretched above her head. Not for the first time, she wished she were a couple of inches taller. She tried pulling at the bars but they were, unsurprisingly, well-secured to the brickwork. How many others had tugged in the same desperate way, hoping for freedom? Many, if the reports about King Jacob were to be believed. All she could see out of the window was a grassy slope and a patch of sky above.

The sky was bright blue, but the wispy clouds with their touch of orange hinted at the late hour. It would soon be getting dark, and on such a clear night she would be able to see the stars. The single scratchy blanket she'd been given was thin and she wasn't looking forward to the night ahead. Would she get any sleep? Would it be cold? Would little creatures crawl through the bars in search of a warm place to sleep?

Suddenly, she heard a sound in the corridor: footsteps.

QUAIL EGGS AND CONVERSATION

Banes crept back to the door and heard voices. One was deep and gruff – a man's voice.

"She's in this cell here."

It could be the jailer, although she'd never heard him speak so it was hard to know for certain. The other voice was higher. "I won't be in there long. I just want to hear an apology."

Unless she was mistaken, it was a voice she knew: the princess! She was sure of it. And the princess was saying she wanted an apology? Well, that could be arranged. Banes could apologize most eloquently if they granted her freedom in exchange. Hope made her smile to herself. Perhaps she didn't have to worry about trials and punishment after all.

The voices in the corridor continued.

"Of course, Yer 'ighness. Leave the door open. I'll be along the corridor if you need anything."

If it was the jailer, he'd managed to string a whole sentence together. Maybe he saved his words for people he wanted to impress. And he'd said *Your Highness.* So it *was* the princess, since the king had no wife.

Banes hurried back to the other side of her cell to sit as she had before, leaning against the wall. When the door to her cell creaked open and the princess walked in, Banes looked up with wide eyes, feigning surprise.

The princess pushed the door shut behind her, against the advice of the jailer, Banes noted.

"Hello, Banes," she said. "Your name is Banes, isn't it? I heard someone shouting it out in the forest."

Banes nodded, confused, and the princess put her finger to her lips. She brought something out of the folds of her skirts – a linen-wrapped bundle, which she unwrapped and passed to Banes. This time Banes was genuinely surprised, but she didn't ask questions, she took it gratefully and spread it out on her lap like a tablecloth. The princess seemed to have brought her a picnic, which was a strange thing to do if she was seeking an apology. Still, from what the guards had said, she already had a history of bringing food parcels to the less fortunate.

"Why have you brought me this?" Banes asked.

"I couldn't stop thinking about you. I was worried you'd be hungry."

"Hungry doesn't begin to describe it," said Banes. She examined the unfamiliar food. There were tiny, halved boiled eggs. She held one up in the palm of her hand. They had the same pungent smell as regular chicken eggs.

"What are these – sparrow eggs? Or do you have miniature chickens?"

The princess smiled. "They're quail eggs."

"Quail eggs? I wouldn't know a quail if it flew into me."

"I don't think they fly."

"What do they do, swim?"

The princess shrugged. "They walk, I think. Unless they are startled, then they flap about."

"Ah, like chickens." Some of the yolk had fallen out of the white and Banes squished it back in with her finger. It was speckled with some kind of pepper or sauce.

"These aren't poisoned, are they?" asked Banes, cheerfully. At least it would be a quick way to go, and at least she wouldn't die hungry.

The princess smiled again and shook her head, and Banes

popped the egg into her mouth. It was delicious. Creamy, but spicy too. Marie averted her eyes as if she could see something interesting outside the barred window besides blue sky. Maybe it was impolite to watch one's prisoners eat.

Banes shrugged and finished her mouthful. She examined the rest of the food – the rolls and the jam tarts. They were about a tenth of the size of what she would usually eat, but looked strangely perfect. The rolls were white with a glossy sheen to them, like play food for small children. Quite unlike the rough floury bread she was used to. Maybe this was how they always ate at Quessia castle. The only bit she didn't fancy was the leaves inside the roll, which looked like wild clover.

"Is all your food *small*?" She didn't wait for an answer but removed the leaves and put them in the napkin. "I suppose the pear was normal-sized but I never got to eat it – the jailer stole it."

"Sorry," said Marie, "I did mean for you to have it."

Banes shrugged and stuffed the bread into her mouth, wondering again why the princess cared so much. She gulped it down more quickly than she should. It was delicious: whiter and softer than she was used to. *Royal* bread. She took a swig from the cup of water on the window ledge and gazed back up at the princess, who continued standing awkwardly in the middle of the cell. She did look genuinely sorry about the pear, which made Banes uncomfortable.

"I didn't say it so you'd feel sorry for me," Banes said. "You weren't to know he'd take it. This tiny food makes up for it. There's plenty here. It's just, I'd have thought royal food would be big. If I were a princess, I'd eat ostrich eggs and jam tarts the size of my head!"

The princess laughed. "I don't think we keep ostriches in the castle. Although I'm sure my father would find some if he heard the eggs were good."

"I'm not saying this food wasn't nice," said Banes, eating the last of the buttery, crumbly pastry. "It was lovely, in fact."

She bundled up the napkin and handed it to the princess. It was probably impolite to hand old napkins to princesses, but she couldn't leave it on the cell floor: the jailer would ask questions. As Princess Marie stared bemused at the crumpled linen, Banes realized she was sitting at the princess's feet as a servant or a dog might do. She was too proud for that. She stood up and brushed the crumbs from her lap. "Thank you."

"You're welcome," said the princess. "You looked hungry out there in the forest."

"I was," said Banes, intrigued again by the princess's interest in her wellbeing. She'd imagined what a daughter of King Jacob might be like – spoiled, vain and arrogant – but this girl appeared to be none of those things. She seemed kind, curious, intelligent.

"Does your family know you are here?" she asked. "Will they be worried?"

"They don't live anywhere near here," said Banes, shortly. She didn't want to talk about herself, or to give anything away about the settlement. She wanted to know about the princess: why she was here, pretending to the jailer she wanted an apology and yet bringing her secret rations. She wanted to know why she lied to the guards about what had happened in the forest. She wanted to know exactly what it was the princess wanted from her. And in her experience, the only way to find out was to ask. Again, she was probably breaking all sorts of rules of royal etiquette, but the princess seemed relaxed … quite normal.

"Why did you tell the guards I was trying to rob you?"

The princess looked at her with wide eyes. "My father… He is a stern man…"

"You're telling me!" said Banes. "I've seen how he's wiped out whole invading armies before they reached the city gates."

Marie looked at her quizzically for a moment, then continued. "Anyway, in my father's eyes there would only be one punishment for a kidnapper – a public hanging – and I could not have that on my conscience."

Banes felt relief flood through her at the thought she'd escaped death. And she could understand only too well how a young girl might want to rebel against her parents. After all, that was exactly what she'd done herself when she'd left the inn, and Frederick Fogg, behind. "But you didn't seem at all scared. Didn't you wonder why I was tying you up, or where I was taking you?"

The princess smiled. "Not really. You mustn't be offended when I say this, but you aren't very frightening."

"Oh." Banes *was* offended. It wasn't her fault she was small and slight. It didn't mean she couldn't fight better than most other people. And she was brave. Woodman had been too scared to even approach the clearing.

The princess seemed to sense her mood. "You mustn't mind. I suppose I saw myself in you. I knew you must be seeking a ransom from the king, and you were only doing that because you were poor and hungry. I have known what it is like to go hungry myself…"

She trailed off and Banes studied her face. What did she mean? Surely a princess's only experience of hunger was if there was a delay at the dinner table. But they had discussed King Jacob's questionable origins around the campfire, hadn't they? Banes had said then, *"Kings don't appear out of nowhere. They have long and colourful histories."* But not King Jacob, it seemed.

It was conceivable their background was a humble one, but that didn't feel like the whole picture. There was something more.

Banes wanted to grill the princess, to ask question after question, but the commander's words played in her mind.

Remember you don't always need to reply. Silence is a valid response.

So she said nothing. She shouted the questions in her mind – *Why are you here? What do you want from me?* – but she bit the inside of her cheek and managed not to voice them.

Silence hung between the girls for a minute or more. Princess Marie paced around the cell, glancing occasionally at the door. Then, just when Banes thought she might burst from not talking, Princess Marie spoke again.

"Out there, in the forest, the person who shouted your name… I heard you calling back to them."

Banes cheered internally. The commander's strategy had worked! Maybe silence was the way forward if she could manage it. Now they were getting to the real reason for the princess's visit.

"I don't know what you mean," said Banes. Was the princess trying to gather information? To get her on side and arrest two people for treason rather than one?

"I don't mean the person any harm. I just want to know – it matters to me. I thought I heard you call 'Woodman'?"

Banes shook her head. She wasn't taking any chances.

"Tell me his first name," said the princess, almost desperately. "Is it … Wyll?"

Banes had no idea. She didn't know the given names of any other members of the settlement and they didn't know hers. Even if she did, she wouldn't reveal that kind of information to the princess. She wouldn't tell her anything at all: she was not that easily bought by jam tarts. "I don't know any Woodman. The kidnapping was my idea alone."

Tears welled up in the princess's eyes and Banes started to wonder if she should tell her what she knew. After all, she didn't know much, and it wouldn't hurt to have someone on her side within the castle walls. She opened her mouth, but was interrupted by a girl's voice from outside the door.

"Your 'ighness?"

A face appeared at the viewing hatch. A young girl in a plain white cap, probably a servant, who ignored Banes and spoke to the princess. Her voice sounded high and anxious. "The king is looking for you, Ma'am. 'e's shouting your name and 'e'll be cross if 'e can't find you. I ran down 'ere as fast as I could."

The princess paled. "Thank you, Fern," she said. "Please wait outside and I will be there presently." Princess Marie turned back to Banes. "I must go. It was nice ... talking to you." She removed the wrap from around her shoulders. "Here, take this. It gets cold down here."

"Thank you." The wrap felt soft and warm, like a spring lamb.

Marie lowered her voice. "Despite the cold, these dungeons are not always the terrible place they seem, especially as darkness approaches. If you hear anything, or see anything unusual, then don't ignore it. *Follow the magic.*"

"Follow the magic? What magic?" asked Banes, but the maid's voice came from the corridor.

"The jailer's coming to lock up now, Ma'am."

"Coming, Fern!" called the princess.

The jailer's heavy footsteps sounded in the corridor.

The princess pushed the door open.

"I'll see you back to the safety of the castle, Yer 'Ighness."

"Thank you, Jailer," said the princess, but before she stepped outside, she turned and looked over her shoulder.

"I'll be back," she whispered. "I'll bring more food if I can. And if you remember any more about your companion – about Woodman – please let me know. You can trust me."

What an odd thing for her to say. The princess whom Banes had tried to kidnap that morning, and whose father had thrown Banes into the dungeon without a trial, was telling Banes she could trust her.

The strangest thing of all, was that Banes believed her.

STRANGE SOUND IN THE CORRIDOR

Banes was alone in her cell again and the light had grown softer. She walked back to the window and drew the princess's wrap around her shoulders. Its warmth and lavender scent felt comforting; somehow the prospect of a night in the cell didn't seem quite as daunting as it had.

Marie had told her of some magic down in the dungeons, but she couldn't see anything out of the ordinary. The night was coming as it always did. The sun had almost vanished below the horizon, leaving a beautiful twilight glow. Twilight. It was a magical time. When she'd been a little girl, she'd known a rhyme about it, but she could no longer remember the words.

The pattern of the sky was changing as she watched: the clouds drifting and the colours spreading as the sun sank lower. A single crow flew past. She tried to think of the last time she'd done nothing but watch the sky. If she'd tried that back at home her mother would have soon pulled her up on it. *"Are you waiting for the clouds to fall?"* she might have asked, and she would have given Banes a job to keep her occupied. At the settlement, it was the same. She was either working hard or socializing with the others; never idling the hours away on her own.

Banes didn't know how long they would keep her down here or if she would have a trial. She should have asked the princess some useful questions like that, rather than quizzing her about the food. But however long her sentence, as a prisoner of the king, she would have more time for indulgences like gazing out of the window: she'd get to know the sky in all weathers, at all times of the day and night. She laughed to herself. It was good to know there was a bright side, even down in the depths of the dungeon.

Thoughts drifted through her mind like the clouds in the

orange striped sky. *Trust me*, Princess Marie had said, but could Banes trust someone she didn't even know? Someone who lived a spoilt and privileged existence? Someone who was her enemy?

The princess should not have been visiting Banes in her cell this evening; that much was clear from her reaction when she heard her father's name. Yet she'd taken a risk. Why? She'd seemingly wanted to help Banes, but she'd also been extremely interested in Woodman. Woodman was a common name and it could be mere coincidence, but Woodman himself had acted strangely, hiding away in the bushes. At the time she'd put it down to cowardice, but he didn't seem to be the cowardly type. After all, he was happy to be involved with the secret mission until the princess was mentioned.

Woodman and the princess knew each other – Banes was becoming more and more sure of it. But what could the connection be between a carpenter rebel and a princess?

As if in response to her thoughts, a strange sound rang out, echoing in the cell. At first, she thought someone was playing music outside. A low stringed instrument, or a hand bell. Banes jumped to her feet and ran to the window. She stood beneath it, listening, but the noise was fainter there: it wasn't coming from outside the castle.

Banes turned. It sounded as though the music was playing here in the dungeons themselves. She walked slowly towards the door, where it grew louder, vibrating a little. Was one of the other prisoners playing a tune on a musical instrument? How strange, when she hadn't heard a thing from any of the other cells up until this point. Now the noise was so loud.

She stood on tiptoes and looked out of the viewing hatch. Once again, she saw nothing but the stone wall. She placed her hands flat against the heavy door and pressed her ear to the cool wood. To her surprise, the door shifted and creaked open. She took a step back. Impossible! Had the princess left the door open behind her? No – the jailer had locked up behind them both – she felt sure she'd heard the key turn in the lock. Still, it was open now and it was an opportunity to escape.

The sound rang out again, clear and inviting.

She looked up and down the stone corridor. Empty. There was no sign of the jailer. He had escorted Princess Marie and her maid back up to the main castle, but would surely be back soon. Banes couldn't let this opportunity pass her by: she had to venture out.

The windowless corridor was lit by flickering torches and, as she stepped through the doorway, she found it warmer than her cell had been. The ringing was much louder now, almost too loud, yet Banes had a strong urge to find out where it was coming from. Normally, Banes would have found the nearest exit, but the ringing was now echoing through the passages. It pushed out all thoughts of anything else. It was as if it was calling her name, willing Banes to follow. *Follow the magic,* the princess had said. It could be a trick, cooked up between the jailer and the princess, but Banes didn't think so.

She would follow the magic and find out.

Turning to her right, she followed it, unable to hear anything else, not even her own footsteps.

She walked past three cell doors, but she knew they weren't the right ones; the sound was coming from further along. Her curiosity was so strong she didn't even peep into the door hatches to check for fellow prisoners. She walked until she was sure she'd reached the correct door, then stopped.

Banes had reached the source of the sound. It was so loud now it felt almost as though it was part of her. It ran through her bloodstream and touched her heart. She knew whatever it was, the sound was not coming from a musical instrument. It was nothing to do with a fellow prisoner, or even another human. The sound was more powerful, more magical, than that.

There was no hatch in the door so she couldn't peep into the room. Instead, she raised her hand to touch the door, to test it. Before she even applied any pressure, she knew it would open for her, as her own door had. Maybe it hadn't been the jailer, or even the princess, who'd left it unlocked. Maybe something more magical was responsible. She pushed open the door. Maybe whatever was on the other side wanted to be found.

THE SINGING FIRE

It was a fire! An out-of-control fire blazing within the cell. Whatever Banes had expected to see, it had not been that. She hovered in the doorway, not knowing how to react. Maybe it was a trick, as she'd suspected. She had been lured here, and now someone was going to push her, lock her in the cell and leave her to a fiery fate. She grabbed hold of the door and checked over her shoulder, but no one was there. And this was no ordinary fire.

It was not crackling, or emanating any warmth whatsoever. Banes was close enough to feel it if it had been. And there was no smoke. It was not real fire at all, but only dancing, orange light. Strangest of all, whatever was making the ringing sound seemed to be within the fire itself.

The flames faded a little and Banes could make out the clear outline of a creature within. A swishing tail and mane, the curve of a long back, and a horn pointing to the ceiling. The bright, blazing, beautiful beast was a unicorn. It wasn't consumed by the fire but stood there, impervious, as if it had created the fire around itself.

It was magic – real magic – just as she'd thought. But a unicorn? She'd heard tales of these magical creatures but thought they hid away in forests, not castle dungeons.

The music died away until it was so low it was barely audible. The flames disappeared too, and the unicorn was completely revealed. It was all white, with a single black marking on its face. The unicorn fixed its blue eyes on Banes, acknowledging her for the first time since she'd walked into the room.

"Well!" said Banes. "I wasn't expecting a unicorn."

To Banes's surprise, the creature replied. "Tell me, what were you expecting?" Its voice sounded like a woman's but also somewhat bell-like, like its song.

Banes laughed. "I don't know. Something magical, definitely. I knew no person could make a sound like that. I nearly turned back when I saw the fire, but I knew it wasn't real fire because there was no smoke. You hear the phrase *There's no smoke without fire,* but I thought, *there's no fire without smoke."*

"Many who meet me are left speechless with wonder," said the unicorn. "But not you?"

Banes thought she heard a hint of amusement in the unicorn's voice. "That's not really my way," she replied.

The unicorn took a couple of steps closer. "I'm glad you found me," she said.

"You called me," replied Banes. "Didn't you? The music, I mean."

"I call every twilight, but it is rare anyone answers my call. Most people cannot hear me cry. But you listened, and you found me."

"You were ... crying?" Banes was confused. It was the most beautiful cry she'd ever heard. "Why?"

"I cry because I am trapped down here in the dark and the cold. I long to be out in the forest – to be free like the hares and the deer. I long for another form and another life I led long ago. I once came so close to freedom, and now it is all I can think about."

The unicorn gazed out of the window, with one hind leg resting on its toe, as if her thoughts were far away from Quessia castle. "There was a girl who was so kind of heart ... a bit younger than you. She wanted to help me, but she also wanted to help someone else, someone dear to her. In doing so, she inadvertently led me straight to a new imprisonment."

The flames had died away completely, and Banes questioned whether she'd imagined them all together.

"There's no need to be sad any longer. I'll help you," said Banes. She wanted to embrace the unicorn, to stroke her, but she wasn't sure if it would be welcome, so she hung back. She looked out into the corridor. It would have been difficult enough to escape by herself, let alone with a fiery unicorn, but she would try. "Come with me! We'll find a way to break out of here."

The unicorn shook her head. "You don't understand. I am bound by ties you cannot see. I must obey my master. Unless he bequeaths my power to another, or if someone kills him and takes that power, then I serve him until his death or mine. If I break these bonds, then I stay in this form for ever."

This raised so many more questions for Banes. What did the unicorn mean by "this form"? Who was her master? But Banes was running out of time for questions. She checked over her shoulder, aware the jailer, or even the king, could appear at any time.

"When you say, 'your master', do you mean King Jacob?" Who else would lock this magical creature in the royal dungeons? Not the princess, who had encouraged her to come here and find the unicorn.

The unicorn held her ears stiffly back and twitched her tail. "Yes, my master is King Jacob. King of the city and kingdom of Quessia. The most powerful king in the land."

Banes shook her head in confusion. "I don't understand … if he's so powerful and you must obey him anyway, then why does he keep you down here in the dungeons? You could have your very own forest in the castle grounds; he has the money to pay for it."

"Ah, but my master doesn't keep me down here for fear I will run away. It is for fear others might learn of my existence."

Banes wrinkled her brow. "But what does he want from you? What can you possibly do for the king—?"

As soon as Banes asked the question, she realized she already knew the answer. She gasped. "It's you! You are his secret weapon: the reason no one can overthrow him?"

The unicorn didn't answer her question but bowed her head again. "I grant wishes."

Wishes. Banes knew exactly what she would wish for if this

beautiful creature were within her power. She would go back to the inn, without the high taxes, Frederick Fogg or any other prospective husbands. Her brother would be happily employed elsewhere and she would inherit the inn and run a happy home and business.

She pictured it in her mind, as if it were real. She must have glazed over for a second. When she came back to reality, the unicorn's large eyes were looking straight at her.

"I sadly cannot grant *your* wishes," said the unicorn. "I may answer only to my master."

"I know," said Banes. "I was just thinking about what I would wish for if I could have anything."

"People always think they know what they would do, until it happens to them. There is one sort of person who thinks they would wish for peace across the world, or for the end of suffering. But somehow world peace is never the first wish on the list. They always plan to make that wish once they have sorted out their own problems."

Banes felt guilty, knowing her wishes were just as selfish. "Surely most people's problems can be solved with a bit more wealth?"

The unicorn shook her head, mane quivering. "It is never

that simple. People make their wishes without thinking things through. They could take their time, spend days planning their choices, but they never do. They wish as though they expect their lives to end in seconds. And that's where they get it wrong. So many people squander their chances."

Banes could well believe it. She thought of the people she'd seen lose their livelihoods gambling on the dice back in the inn. Rich men losing their fortunes and poor men betting everything they owned.

"But what about the king?" she asked. "He can't have made those mistakes. Not if you're still with him, granting him wishes."

The unicorn looked up with sad eyes, her mane lifting as she did so. "Oh no. My master is one of the other sorts of people. The sort who know straightaway how they can get the most from my magic. They are not content with three wishes. They want more. Far more. They crave power, wealth and fame, no matter if innocent people pay the price."

"Power, wealth and fame," repeated Banes, nodding. That definitely sounded like Quessia's greedy king.

Footsteps echoed in the corridor outside. The jailer! In her excitement over finding the unicorn, Banes had forgotten about him. Now he was back, and when he found her cell empty, he would not be happy. He would come looking for her.

She looked at the unicorn and back towards the door. "We need to get out of here," she whispered. "Perhaps when the jailer is searching my cell, we can sneak out of here and up the stairs. I don't suppose you know of any secret passageways or escape routes?"

The unicorn gazed at the window of her cell, at the one patch of sky she looked upon for most of her waking hours. "I am not allowed to help you; only my master. Yet, sometimes when I wish for something, particularly in the magic hour, then it becomes true, whether I intend it or not. Your way out may soon become clear."

Banes didn't understand, but she watched the unicorn, who lightly closed her eyes. Her breathing became so shallow, Banes couldn't see her chest move. Flames began to lick around her once more. Not quite the blaze Banes had seen when she walked in, but still impressive enough. The unicorn's eyelids fluttered open. She stared at the iron window bars and now the flames surrounded them too. When the flames died down and then vanished completely, the bars were left shimmering and glistening like a mirage in the hot sun.

"How are you doing this?" Banes asked, but the unicorn

didn't reply. Instead she continued to stare at the bars until they dissolved and left a square opening to the outside world. Small, but big enough for Banes to wriggle through. It was magic, real magic, and Banes wanted to whoop for joy. She grinned. "That was unbelievable," she whispered. "I'll thank you later – make it up to you somehow – but let's get out now, before the jailer arrives."

Banes assessed the window. It was way over head height, like all the windows around here, and there was nothing to grip on to. She looked around for something to stand on but, again, there was nothing.

"You can climb on me if you like," said the unicorn, kneeling.

"Are you sure?" Banes wasn't sure herself. What if the unicorn burst into flames with Banes perched on her back? But because there was no other choice, she climbed on. The unicorn remained steady, and Banes was able to kneel, then slowly stand, until she could reach her head and upper arms through the window.

As she was wobbling on the unicorn's back, Banes heard the jailer's footsteps again. They sounded more hurried this time. He must have found her cell empty and come looking for her. She had no idea if he knew about the unicorn, but she didn't want to stay in the dungeons a minute longer than she had to. Before she pulled herself through, she turned to the unicorn.

"How are you going to get out?" It seemed a redundant question. If the unicorn could melt iron bars then she could no doubt fly out of the room, or magic herself out in some other way.

But the creature answered in her smooth, sweet voice, "As I explained, I am not held here by bars but by stronger bonds of duty and magic. I will not be accompanying you."

"Really? Not even to the edge of the forest?"

The unicorn shook her head. "Not even there." She stepped away into the room, her hooves echoing on the stone floor, leaving Bane's legs flailing against the wall.

Banes pulled herself up with all her strength and wriggled through the window. There was no space to turn around, but luckily, after the ground dipped down into a deep ditch – the old moat perhaps – it sloped up again. Banes was able to reach for the grassy slope with her hands and fling herself towards its soft surface. She'd done it. She was free.

It felt wrong to be leaving such a sad and beautiful creature alone in the cell, but she truly couldn't think of anything else she could do.

"Goodbye, unicorn!" called Banes in a whisper, not wanting

to attract unwanted attention from any guards. "Until we meet again." She felt certain they *would* meet again. Banes would make sure of that. She would come back to Quessia and rescue her. There was no response from the cell. Instead, Banes heard the same ringing sound that had drawn her there. The unicorn was crying once more.

The cold nearly-night air hit her and she shivered. She'd lost the princess's wrap somewhere along the way, possibly when she'd been climbing on to the unicorn's back. But it was too late now to retrieve it. She had to get away from there as quickly as possible.

She scrambled up the slope to ground level into the darkening evening. Inside the castle she could hear the jailer's voice shouting, "Guards! Guards!" She guessed he had discovered her missing, but it didn't bother Banes. By the time the guards had assembled and come to find her, she would be long gone, over these hills and deep in the cover of the forest.

$\mathcal{C}$HAPTER SEVEN

CAT AND MOUSE

Marie

"That prisoner of yours is missing," said Fern, as she brought in Marie's supper.

The smell of grilled sardines wafted into the room ahead of the maid, who balanced plates of fish, bread and fruit on a silver tray.

Twitch was instantly there, rubbing around Fern's skirts, hoping for a fish supper of his own.

Fern busied herself arranging the cutlery, so Marie couldn't read her expression.

"The prisoner of *mine*?" Was it possible that Banes had escaped?

"The one you went to visit, I mean."

"How strange," said Marie, trying not to show emotion as her heart leaped. So Banes *had* escaped!

"How did that happen? The jailer is growing a little lazy," she added, picking up Twitch and moving to the window. In her heart, she knew it was not the jailer's fault. She suspected it had a lot more to do with the magic that was at work down in those dungeons, but of course she couldn't mention that to Fern. She must pretend, keep quiet as she always did.

Fern said nothing, but as she finished the job, Marie thought she detected a slight raise of her eyebrows. Did Fern think Marie had something to do with Banes escaping? That she'd smuggled a key in the quail eggs? She thought of Banes laughing at all the tiny food, and it made her smile.

"I've finished 'ere, Ma'am," Fern said, looking at Marie's smiling face even more suspiciously, although she wouldn't have dared ask her directly.

"Thank you, Fern," said Marie, and the maid curtsied and left the room.

Marie liked Fern and wished she could tell her about her lost brother, and about his possible connection with Banes, but she didn't dare. She didn't want to put Fern in a difficult position if her father ever decided to ask questions.

Marie gazed out of the window into the night sky. She held Twitch close to her chest with his little paws draped over her hands, so they could both see what was going on.

A group of guards ran past, holding flaming torches to light their way. They were heading in the direction of the main road. Marie nuzzled her nose between Twitch's ears and spoke softly to him. "Look, Twitch, see the guards? They are playing their own little game of cat and mouse, but this time, I think the mouse will get away, don't you?"

At the mention of mice, Twitch grew restless and wriggled to be free of her grasp. Marie placed him down and he sprang away to find something to chase. She returned straightaway to the window.

All those guards, for one girl. She tried to imagine herself in Banes's position. Would she have been brave enough to hold up a royal horse, to risk prison, and then to escape? She sighed, as she suspected she knew the answer. She wasn't even brave enough to stand up to her own father.

Banes intrigued her. A very small part of her wished she'd

not escaped at all, or that the guards did bring her back. She had felt they were becoming friendly, if not exactly friends. If she were brought back then Marie would gain her trust, she felt sure of it, and Banes would tell her everything she knew about Woodman. But on the other hand, if the guards did find her, the punishment would be severe.

Marie sat in front of her food for a good while. She was tempted to watch until the guards returned but there was little point. She knew they would be empty-handed – Banes was too clever for them.

FEELING ALIVE

After supper, there would usually be time for a little more tapestry, bath and then bed. But she couldn't eat or perform any of her usual activities; she felt too alive. Ideas fizzed in her brain, sending sparks of happiness to her fingers and toes. For once, she wanted to act, to do something. The attempted kidnap, Marie's visit to the dungeon and Banes's subsequent escape seemed to have triggered something new inside her. Something daring and adventurous.

Since meeting the unicorn in the forest and becoming princess, she'd made few decisions for herself; done as she was told and watched her life unfold. But life was going on not far from here. Real life was happening outside her window. Somewhere out there was Banes and, probably, her brother, leading their own lives.

She jumped up from her chair, disturbing Twitch, who had been near her feet, sniffing around for scraps. The kitten gave her a hurt look, and mewed for food. Marie stroked him and then sliced off a good mouthful of pink fish as a treat.

Outside, the market stalls and small businesses had shut up their shops, and people were scurrying past her window with earthenware pots, bundles of linen. Not for the first time, Marie wondered if, as a princess, she could use some of her privilege to touch those lives. It was already something she'd tried to do, by taking anonymous food parcels to people in the forest, but now she felt she could … no, she *must* do more. Her father's actions were causing people harm. Maybe, just maybe, she could influence his decisions. She'd never felt this daring before.

Fern would come back later to turn back her sheets and help her into her nightclothes. But, before that, Marie planned a different, secret expedition. She placed the plate of fish on the floor for Twitch.

"It's gone cold anyway," she said.

The kitten didn't have to be asked twice and sprang upon it.

Marie took a deep breath. Instead of working on her tapestry, she would go and see her father. She had a lot of questions about why he made the choices he did. If she could see things from his point of view, she could understand. Maybe she would also then be in a position to change things.

Marie took one bite of bread from the supper tray, then left her quarters, locking the door behind her so Twitch didn't stage another escape. She had a good idea of where she would find her father. He would be in the place where he spent most of his time.

TRESPASSING

Marie strode purposefully to the Strategy Room, trying not to talk herself out of her bold plan. She would speak to her father in a confident, but non-confrontational way. If he was in a good mood, then he might even admire her for it.

Out of habit, she stopped when she reached the door and knocked. There was no reply. It was possible he was still dining in the Great Hall. King Jacob ate alone down there, and sometimes worked his way through six courses. Marie had always taken her meals alone in her room. She didn't know who'd decided this, but it was the way it had always been since their arrival at the castle. One could almost imagine the king's routines were designed so father and daughter met as little as possible.

After making her bold plans, she felt deflated at the idea of returning to her quarters.

Marie looked down the corridor, but it was empty. She listened. Nothing. Only the sound of her own heart beating. If the door was unlocked, then she could take a little peek inside. The whole idea of speaking to her father was to get a better understanding of him, after all, and what better place to do this than the very room in which he did all his plotting, planning and thinking?

She couldn't bring herself to burst in so she checked through the keyhole, but she could barely see a thing. She put her ear to the door and heard nothing. After a couple of moments, she felt silly; there was nobody there. She slowly turned the handle.

Marie stepped inside, staying close to the doorway at first, not daring to move amongst his things.

Candles flickered in their chandeliers, but the room stood empty, apart from the hundreds – thousands – of wooden figures, their eyes tiny and unblinking. Marie almost expected them to turn towards her, but mercifully they stayed still. She walked tentatively at first, tiptoeing around the miniature forests and fields of their kingdom. Then she grew brave. First, she walked to the other side of the room, by the windows. She'd never been this far into the room, or explored around the corner, but she had a good look while she could.

Tucked away in the old dressing room was a carpenter's workshop, containing all the tools Marie remembered from her childhood. This must be where her father made the models. Stepping back into the main part of the room, Marie was able to see in detail the tables and models she'd only glimpsed from the doorway. There was a whole world in here. Rivers, mountains, houses. A whole kingdom, full of people. The shelves around the sides of the room were filled with half-painted figures and models awaiting finishing touches.

Dust had settled on many of the surfaces (the servants weren't allowed in to clean) and the atmosphere was thick, as if no air had ever entered the room. It tickled Marie's throat and she felt a sudden urge to cough, but suppressed it. How she would have loved to open the shutters and let a cool breeze blow through, but she suspected her father would have been outraged at such an idea.

She was here for a reason. She needed to understand why he was the way he was and how he did the things he did. Why did he spend so long surrounded by these life-like dolls? It had something to do with the unicorn, but she didn't know what. Her thoughts returned to something that Banes had said to her. *I've seen how he's wiped out whole invading armies.* Had he really done that, or was it just country gossip?

Her gaze flitted around the room and fell on Quessia castle. She moved towards it, admiring how similar it was to the real thing. It was like spotting the castle from a carriage on a journey home. Her breath the only sound, she crouched down to see the model at eye-level. Now she was really in their world.

How she would have loved to have a dolls' house like this to play with when she was little. Each room was perfect. She could see the banqueting hall, the treasuries, the kitchen. The tiny details, like bowls of fruit and shining clocks, particularly appealed to Marie. The castle was so much better in miniature than in real life, where she had to endure lonely rooms and the moods of an unpredictable king. Maybe that was what her father liked about his Strategy Room. He preferred to live in this fantasy world than in reality.

Inside the scaled-down castle, the colours and textiles in her bed chamber looked the same as the full-sized version. There was a dressing room annexed off the main room, with little frocks on hangers, identical to her own. The model of her – Princess Marie – was sitting on a chair, with a tiny replica hairbrush set on the dresser front of her. She picked up the figure and examined it.

It was a rudimentary likeness, so it was hardly like looking into a glass, yet there were clear similarities. The figure wore a crown upon its head and a fine gown of the sort she rarely bothered with, but her hair and face were plain. She swallowed. Even when he carved her image her father hadn't pretended she was beautiful. The little princess had her hands clasped in her lap, and her mouth was carved in a fixed, demure half-smile. How often she'd worn that exact expression, although she felt tormented within.

"Hello, small me," she said.

The figure, of course, did not reply. It looked meek, unthreatening and somewhat uninteresting. There wasn't even a miniature of Twitch to play with. Her father drew the line at models of kittens, even if they were part of the castle. If Marie were a child and this were her playroom, she would never bother with the princess sitting alone in her fine rooms. No, she would play with the soldiers or the villagers, or even one of the maids. Someone who was actually *doing* something.

She experimented with moving the princess figure into more exciting places. If she put it in the marketplace, or out in the hills, it might look ready for adventure. But wherever she placed the little figure, it was difficult to care about its fate. Perhaps it was the static position, or the expression on the model's face, but it didn't look as though it was capable of action. She even put the figure down in the dungeons, but it didn't look like a criminal, just a dull princess. She noticed that one of the cells was missing. The one that didn't have a viewing hatch. The one with the king's most valued treasure hidden away inside. It was as if it didn't even exist.

Marie left her likeness side-saddle on a horse and examined the tiny servants' quarters with their basic furniture. At least they were doing useful things, like making up fires and washing clothes. Seeing their area, hidden away in the corner of the palace, it seemed obscene they were given so little space when their work was done. There were so many: maids and footmen, cooks and gardeners, yet they disappeared into their tiny rooms. Marie and her father were free to call the rest of the castle their own.

She picked up one of the maids. "Hello, Fern," she whispered. It looked nothing like Fern, for the king hadn't differentiated between the servants: they were all the same height, with peach skin and brown hair. Still, she would pretend.

"You look tired, Fern. You've been working too hard. Time for a rest." She laid the servant figure on the bed in one of the unused visitors' rooms, on top of the pretty sheets, but it looked wrong, even to her eyes.

She placed the servant figure in the scaled-down kitchen. Then she noticed another couple she hadn't seen before, standing under the pear tree arch in the kitchen garden. They were touching hands. How sweet! A romance between two of the servants, perhaps. Then she noticed the fine robes. They weren't servants at all. She picked up the figure of the man. It was her father, in his purple cloak and finest crown. It was even a good likeness, if a little more handsome. It was also bigger than the other figures, and much more delicately carved.

How like her father to portray himself as bigger, more important than everyone else. But the woman figure was tall, too, and also more intricately carved. Who was she?

Marie picked up the figure and turned it over in her hand. Her dress was regal, robes laced at the bodice over a pink dress. Like the king, she wore a crown, and her hair was dotted with flowers. She must be the queen, although there was no queen at Quessia castle. Marie knew, of course, who it was intended to be. This figure had a curl of brown hair brushing her cheek and a mole on the left-hand side of her face, above her upper lip. Marie had forgotten about that small detail. It came back to her, along with memories of Wyll and of another life, a different life, she'd long left behind.

Her mother.

THE BOX

Marie's chest ached all over again at her loss and at the fact her father had spent hours creating this vision: a ghost of the past, living in the present.

He had everything apart from the one thing he wanted. Her thoughts returned to a particular conversation at twilight by a waterfall.

"May I wish for anything I choose?"

"Almost anything. I cannot bring people back from the dead, or turn back time."

Blaze made her father king. She could give him power and riches, but she could never bring back his wife or undo the mistakes he'd made.

Marie placed both figures back under the pretty archway, fingers touching, looking out at the colour and greenery. It was the exact spot her mother would have liked best.

She moved away from the model castle, thoughts of her mother still clear in her mind. How she wished her mother *was* queen at Quessia castle. How different their lives would be. But if her mother were alive, then they would not be here at all. When Marie met the unicorn, she would never have wished to help her father. She would have wished for a huge treasure chest, then she would have set the unicorn free and lived happily ever after in their cottage. But that didn't happen, and it was impossible to imagine it so.

"Focus!" Marie told herself, aloud. She was here to investigate the present, not to daydream about the past. She walked to the shelves, and found the horses her father had been painting the other day. There they stood, lined up nose-to-tail, ready for whatever adventure her father had in mind.

Next to them on the shelf was a box. It was a plain wooden box, over a foot wide with a brass clasp, that looked handmade. She reached up and slid it from the shelf. It was heavier than it looked and she had to be careful not to drop it, but she managed and placed it on the wooden painting area below.

An image had been burned into the lid of the box, the lines darker than the pale wood. She ran her hand across it, feeling the indentations. It was a crude picture of a person sleeping flat on his back. She couldn't identify the person: it was little more than a stick figure, in a similar style to the wooden figures. But then she saw the mound at its head. A gravestone. The sleeping figure was, in fact, a dead man.

THE OBJECTS INSIDE

Marie drew her hand back from the box. Why would her father show a picture of death on the lid? And what did he keep inside?

There was no question, she had to open it and find out. She turned to the door and listened for a moment, but there was nothing. She turned back, undid the clasp and, with both hands, lifted the lid.

Nestled at the top of the box was some light blue, gauzy material, almost silver in colour. Marie took it and shook out the folds. It was about the size of a neckscarf but was too lightweight for that. It reminded her of flowing water.

She put it to one side and reached for the next item. This one she recognized. It was a wooden tinder box, with separate compartments containing a flint, tinder and curved iron firesteel.

She felt somewhat relieved to see these normal-looking items; the image on the lid had led her to believe she would find something sinister. But when she took out the next object, she was less sure. It was a flat piece of hammered brass, in the shape of a zig-zag, like a lightning bolt.

Lightning? Fire? Water? What could these objects mean?

Then she remembered her conversation with her father the last time she'd stood in this room:

"If you discovered an army approaching, what natural disaster would you wish for? A flood, a fire, a plague?"

That was what these things were. That was why there was a dead man on the box. These objects were weapons.

She delved deeper, hoping she was wrong, but found only further evidence: a realistic miniature rat, a mosquito, a bottle labelled with a skull. Plague, pestilence, poison. Were these the items he used to defeat Quessia's enemies? Marie had thought it was a game of sorts, but now she wasn't sure. *Could it be real?* Banes had told her whole armies had fallen before reaching Quessia's gates. Surely not because of the contents of this box? And where did the unicorn fit into things? For Marie was sure she did.

Marie was so distracted by her discovery she forgot to listen out for footsteps in the corridor.

Until she heard them in the room itself, and the door to the Strategy Room slammed shut.

Marie jumped at the sound, nearly dropping the lightning bolt.

She swung around to see her father in the doorway, back from his supper and staring at her as though he wanted answers.

YES, FATHER

Marie's cheeks were hot. The way she jumped must have made her look guilty, and she held the lightning bolt behind her back like a pickpocket in the market square. She silently congratulated herself for restoring most of the figures in the castle – all apart from the princess – to their original positions. Her father wouldn't have seen her touching them … would he?

"What are you doing here?" asked the king, in a low voice.

Silence hung in the room as she searched for the right words to say, anything that wouldn't anger him. Her mind was blank.

He marched towards her and grasped her left arm. He discovered the brass shape clutched in her hand and snatched it from her.

He stood so close to her she could see the pores and little hairs at the end of his nose. Shaking, he held up the lightning bolt in front of her.

"Why do you have this?" he asked, icily.

"I… I…" Marie stuttered. She couldn't let him know her suspicions. "I found this golden hair decoration, and this beautiful scarf," she said, picking up the gauzy material. "I wanted to try them on. I wondered if they belonged to my mother."

"Your mother?" The king moved away from her, his eyebrows pushed together. He looked puzzled, but less angry. "No. These are nothing to do with her."

King Jacob placed the lightning bolt and watery fabric back in the box, closed the lid and replaced it on the shelf. "This is not a dressing-up box. And these are not dolls' houses for you to play with," he muttered, gesturing to the room at large.

Marie wondered what they were exactly, if not very elaborate toys, but she would never have dared to ask such a thing.

"Sorry, Father," she whispered.

He looked around, reassuring himself everything was in the correct spot, and then turned back to Marie.

"So you may have been examining pretty things, but I repeat my question: What are you doing here, in my Strategy Room, in the first place?"

All Marie's plans to question her father now seemed unwise, but she had no other suitable explanation for her presence. She thought of using Twitch as an excuse, but she hadn't forgotten her father's threat. She looked at her feet.

"I was just interested."

Her father plucked the princess figure from the horse. He held it at eye-level and addressed it, rather than her.

"You seem to have been most interested in a lot of things lately: interested in the paupers in the forest and interested in my war figures. Have you forgotten where you belong?"

Marie swallowed. He knew. He knew that she'd helped Banes and that she'd come here to try to influence him. She was sure of it. King Jacob put the tiny princess back where Marie had found her, at the dressing table in her room. His lips curled into a satisfied smile and he stood back from the castle, eyes darting around the room. When his gaze settled back on the real Marie, he tilted his head to one side, looking surprised to see her standing there. She wasn't sure if she should say anything.

"I have something to ask you," he said. "I will ask only once and I expect you to reply honestly."

Marie felt lightheaded in the stifling room. "Yes, Father. Ask me anything."

"The girl. She escaped. Do you know anything about this?"

He looked up and his eyes bored unblinking into her own, like one of his painted figures.

"Which girl, Father?" She tried to keep her voice steady.

"The girl. Your attacker from the forest."

"I don't know. I mean, I heard she'd gone, but I don't know how she escaped."

"And yet you were seen visiting her cell." His voice was cold, hard. The jailer must have told him. But perhaps she could convince him it had been idle curiosity.

"I wanted to look upon her, to ask her why she held up my horse. I wanted to hear an apology..." Marie trailed off. The story sounded unconvincing, even to her.

Her father drummed his fingers on the table. "You were seen bringing the prisoner food," he said.

She didn't look up. Curse that jailer. Or had it been Fern? Surely not her maid. Why did everyone have to report everything back to the king? Whoever it was, she knew better than to risk another big lie. "It was some ... leftovers from my tea tray. She is just a young girl and she looked hungry. You and I have known what it is like to feel hunger."

Jacob brought his fist down hard on the table. It seemed everything in the room wobbled. "Hunger? Yes, I've known hunger, but I had no princess bringing me bread. I had to pull myself up by the bootstraps and get on with it. We can't begin to feel sorry for criminals and down-and-outs, when they do nothing to help themselves."

You didn't help yourself. The only reason you became rich was because of a magic, wish-granting unicorn. If it hadn't been for the unicorn, then you would still be sitting by the fire, grumbling about the unfairness of the world while I worked away at all the household chores.

That was what Marie wanted to say. Instead she murmured, "Yes, Father. I'm sorry, Father."

He inclined his head. "And you know nothing about the cell door? The jailer found it unlocked."

Marie looked back up at her father, who seemed to be losing interest in the conversation.

"I know nothing of any unlocked doors. The jailer holds the keys to all the cells and I am certain he locked up behind me. Perhaps the girl managed to pick the lock. She is a thief, after all."

"A common thief. Hmm." This seemed to satisfy her father. "And you did not go into any other cell? Didn't try to meddle with anything that doesn't involve you?"

He was talking about Blaze, of course. Marie had been in trouble for seeking her out before, and now she hardly ever dared to visit. Her father had made his feelings about that very clear.

"No, Father. I wouldn't, Father."

He brought out a folded garment from under his cloak. She recognized it as the lambswool wrap she'd given Banes. She swallowed. She could try to lie, tell him she'd never seen it before, but he probably knew already. "It's mine," she confessed. "I left it in the prisoner's cell with the food, to keep her warm. I'm sorry. It was wrong of me."

He scrutinized her face and she felt herself redden, even

though she was telling the truth. "Yet the shawl was found not in the prisoner's cell, but in another cell. I'm sure you can guess which one."

The unicorn's cell. So Banes had found her! That was how she'd escaped. "I left it in the prisoner's room, I promise," she said in a whisper.

He nodded his head once. He believed her. She'd escaped his wrath, although she didn't know what that meant for Blaze.

"I'm sorry," she whispered again, although she meant it more for the unicorn than her father.

"You know how I feel about meddling," he said. "Meddling in here, meddling down there. I do not want to hear of you meddling again."

He didn't seem quite as angry as she thought he might. He believed her about not visiting Blaze, at least. Now that they were finally discussing these subjects, Marie wondered if it might be time to ask those questions to which she wanted answers. She took a deep breath.

"I'm not trying to meddle, Father. I just wanted to see what you do all day. I know you have great power throughout the kingdom and beyond. I also know that you spend many hours in this room. What is it that do you do with these models?"

His eyes bulged. She'd said the wrong thing, as she'd feared.

"It is not your place to question me!" he said, at volume. "I am the king and I make the rules. You are a princess and you follow the rules. You do not belong in this room. A new rule, in case you didn't understand before."

He grabbed her roughly by the upper arm and marched her across the room, pulling the door open with his free hand. He led her along the corridors, gripping her arm tighter. "That hurts, Father."

He said nothing. Tears pricked at her eyes. For a moment, she wondered if he was taking her to the dungeons, but he did not. He led her back to her room. He released her and she stepped inside, rubbing her arm.

"*This* is where you belong," he said, as if she were a small child. "You need to stop interfering in things that don't concern you and keep to your own pursuits. You have everything you could ever need in here – your reading and needlework and so forth." He gestured vaguely into the room as if everything that could be of interest to her was contained within.

"Your brother was always *questioning* things. Always wanting to know *why*, always coming up with clever ideas. Now he is the one 'making his own way in the world', no doubt destitute and alone, whereas we are the ones living in luxury."

He slammed the door shut, turned the key in the lock and shouted through the door. "I suggest you stay in here until you are a lot less interested in the running of my kingdom. If you can't do that, then you are welcome to go and find your brother."

Marie leaned her back against the door and slid to the floor, tears streaming down her face.

CHAPTER EIGHT

DISBELIEVERS

Banes

"A unicorn, you say?"

"And it was on fire but unharmed? A shame – I've heard grilled unicorn meat is rather tasty!"

All eyes were on Banes as they tucked into that night's supper. Someone had managed to poach a deer from the king's land and with the addition of vegetables, they would be eating venison stew for the next few days. It should have been the perfect welcome home meal, but Banes was not enjoying it.

Woodman had returned and told everyone at camp that she'd

been captured by the king's men. Apart from Commander Flint, that is, who was off on a separate mission to source weapons. Her comrades had been planning a rescue attempt that night, but Banes had surprised them all by appearing back at camp unharmed.

She had just shared her incredible story of escape from the castle dungeons, but it had not received the reaction she'd expected. Cotter grinned at her latest "tall tale", while Ford hid his smirk behind his hand and turned to whisper to his neighbour, loudly enough for Banes to hear what he said. "She's trying to draw attention away from the fact that she failed."

Banes flushed pink. Everyone seemed to find it difficult to believe.

The problem was, most of them were city folk. Where she came from, out in the country, folk knew of the fairies in the forest, hummingfish in the lake and strange creatures that kept away from humans. They didn't have to see things for themselves if others could vouch for their existence. Had Banes brought this news back to the inn, folk would have been curious to hear about the unicorn. They would have asked questions – too many questions – but they wouldn't have doubted her.

Here, it seemed everyone doubted her. For once, Banes

couldn't see the humour in the situation. Her cheeks grew hotter as she tried to convince them she was telling the truth.

"You're not listening. It wasn't like real fire. I couldn't feel its heat and I was able to stand close to the flames—"

"—So it was *cold* fire?" interrupted Ford.

The group laughed and Banes struggled to explain. She wished that Commander Flint was there. She would never have laughed at her like the others.

She tried to remember how the flames had looked. "They were like an image of fire, real but not at the same time…" She trailed off.

One of the young women in the group, Cobb, spoke more kindly.

"Look, Banes, you did a tremendous job. We all know you wanted to bring the princess back, but it was never going to be easy. You got closer to the king than any of us and you managed to escape. There is no need to feel you have to … embellish."

"Embellish? Lie, you mean? I am not lying!" She stood up, her cheeks now burning.

The woman continued. "I didn't say lying. Sometimes, in nerve-wracking situations, our minds conjure up all sorts of things—"

"I did not imagine the unicorn!" shouted Banes. She looked around the familiar circle of faces and saw a variety of expressions. Some incredulous, some amused and some pitying. But no belief. No trust. She was never going to convince them.

She pushed away the remnants of her stew and started to head back to her tent. As she left, she caught a different look. Only one person wasn't looking at her with a smirk, raised eyebrows or a curled lip. One person was gazing at her seriously, looking as if he believed every word she said. And that person was Woodman.

BELIEVERS

Banes stomped back to her tent, furious. She didn't know who she was more cross with: those unimaginative, smirking people; or Woodman for believing her but not having the courage to speak up. Stars twinkled above her in a cloudless sky. The unicorn constellation was particularly obvious, and she laughed to herself. Even the sky was mocking her.

She crawled through the flaps of her tent, put down her

lantern, and threw herself down on her cot. Woodman. He was the one she was the most cross with. The others couldn't help being stupid, but Woodman should know better. She wondered if he felt bad he'd abandoned her to be arrested by the kings' guards, but he'd barely said a word to her since she'd returned.

A few angry tears escaped, and she brushed them away. The flickering candle threw dancing shadows on the stained canvas and she watched them for a few moments. She'd changed her mind. The person she was most angry with was herself, for ever thinking of Woodman as a friend. Her eyelids began to close, and she didn't try to fight it. After all, she'd been up early that morning. It felt like days ago.

After a few moments, she heard the soft tread of footsteps outside and someone coughed. Her eyes snapped open. It wasn't her comrades returning from the fire: they would be making much more noise. She couldn't see much through the material of the tent but there was the suggestion of a light drawing closer.

Banes wondered if it might be Woodman, come to apologize, or to tell her he believed her story. She'd been angry, but if he said sorry, she would be gracious about it. It would be good to be able to share her tale and talk to him properly about it.

But when a voice came from outside, it was a woman's voice. "Banes? Can I come in?"

Commander Flint. What a time for her to return. Banes blinked vigorously and hoped it wasn't obvious she'd been crying: she wouldn't want the commander to think her weak.

"Come in!" she cried, more brightly than she felt, throwing some of her discarded clothes under the bedcover in a last-minute attempt to tidy up.

The commander poked her head into the tent and crawled through, holding out her lantern ahead of her. She put it by Banes's own lantern, increasing the light in the tent considerably, and sat down next to Banes. There was barely room for one person, let alone two, but they managed to squeeze in. It was strange to be sitting so close to someone, especially after all those hours alone in her prison cell.

"I hope you don't mind, but I overheard the conversation a few moments ago," said Flint.

Banes hadn't noticed the commander return, but she seemed to overhear everything. Banes guessed that was a useful skill to have when you were in charge of a group the size of this one. There was not much that could get past her. Yet another thing to be envious of.

"And what did you think?" asked Banes, twisting her hands together. If the commander laughed at her in the way the others had, then she might burst into tears in front of her.

The commander gazed at her for a couple of moments, and said, "I think you shouldn't have told them anything about it. But their reactions were as I would expect. Typical camp talk. You will get used to it." She spoke calmly as she always did, so Banes found it hard to tell what she was thinking. "Your comrades have a narrow view of the world and when someone comes to them with something a little … different, as you have done, it throws them. They laugh."

A narrow view of the world. "You believe me?" Her voice came out as a weepy croak. How she wished she could control her emotions the way the commander seemed to.

"Yes," said Flint. "Your story seems far-fetched, but that is one of the reasons I believe it to be true. In my experience, when a person lies, they often embellish the truth but try to keep it believable. Whereas this is so out of the realms of possibility, I suspect it must be true."

Banes smiled. She felt absurdly grateful to the commander. She sniffed and sat up straighter. "It *is* true."

"Yes." Commander Flint set her jaw. "And it is highly

important information. Information we can make use of. I need you to tell me everything you can remember. Where the creature was standing, what its cell was like, what it said to you – everything."

Banes nodded. She had gone from a laughingstock to being in possession of *highly important information* in minutes.

She began to recount her tale as she had at supper, but to a very different audience. Parts were hazy. Certain facts eluded her. When the commander asked the colour of the unicorn's eyes, she couldn't be sure. She'd looked straight into them, so she should know, but it was difficult to remember.

"Black, I think, or blue…"

"If you don't remember, then tell me that. It is better that way than making up something that isn't true. If you stick to the facts then you can't go wrong."

"But when I stick to the facts people don't believe me! Then I worry about what they think of me and whether they like me—"

The commander raised her hand to stop Banes mid-flow.

"All that worrying might make you a nice person, but if you are going to get on in life, to get what you want and make a difference, then you can't be everyone's friend. Sometimes you have to say what you think and do what you feel. Be ruthless."

Banes nodded. She would love to be like that and to not care what other people thought.

"I remember now," she said. "The unicorn's eyes were blue. They were so sad, as if she was really suffering. And she had a black marking on her face."

"Show me," said the commander, and Banes traced the outline of the shape on her own face with her forefinger.

In the flickering candlelight, Flint watched closely. Banes told the commander everything she could remember about the unicorn, and about the dungeons in general. The commander seemed even more interested in the princess than the unicorn: what she'd said, how she'd said it.

The only thing Banes didn't tell her about was the questions the princess had asked about Woodman. She didn't know why she held back, just it seemed to be breaking some agreement with the princess. Princess Marie had helped her, after all.

As she spoke, the commander didn't always give the impression she was paying attention. She didn't make eye contact with Banes, but looked off into the distance. Occasionally, she would make a comment, or ask Banes to repeat something.

She had a lot of questions, and she stayed in Banes's tent for a long time. Banes was tired. She wanted to sleep and found herself leaning further and further back. It would be so easy to curl up right there. Maybe if she stopped talking, the commander would think she'd run out of things to say. But Flint kept on with the questions for so long that the candle in Banes's lantern burned right down.

Banes thought the commander might leave at that point. Instead, she lit a fresh candle and continued, with more questions. Didn't the woman ever sleep?

"Tell me about the jailer," she said.

"There's not much to say," said Banes. "He was a big man, as jailers tend to be. He kept the keys on a ring at his belt. He didn't say much … or anything, actually, the whole time I was there. He went through my bag and ate my pear… I'm sorry, Commander, but I'm not sure how much of this you want to know; it doesn't seem very interesting to me."

Flint looked at her then, and smiled. "On the contrary, Banes. This is all decidedly interesting. Please continue."

When it had got to the point where Banes thought she might actually drift off mid-sentence, the commander said, "Banes, I can see you're growing tired – it's been a long day for you – but may I ask one more thing?"

Banes yawned and nodded.

"Can you please not mention the unicorn again? It actually helps our cause if as few people as possible know about this."

Banes sighed. If she never mentioned this again then the whole group would be sure she'd been making it up. But they thought that anyway, so what difference did it make?

"My lips are locked as tightly as a cell door. But one without a magic unicorn to open it," she added, and the commander rewarded her with another rare smile.

"Will we be able to help her?" asked Banes.

The commander frowned. "Help who?"

"The unicorn."

Flint looked away as she had before and said, "Maybe we will." Then: "I think I have all the information I need. I will go and make some notes now." She left the tent with the air of a person ready to go and do a few more hours' work.

Banes summoned all her remaining energy to snuff out the candle. Then she was finally able to close her eyes. It had been one of the longest days she'd known.

*C*HAPTER NINE

CHANGES

Marie

It had been a long day, and Marie's bed looked inviting. The curtains around her bedstead were drawn for the night and the covers neatly turned back. Fern would no doubt have slipped a softly wrapped bed warmer down at the foot of the bed and her toes would enjoy wriggling in between the warm sheets. But first, she had some thinking to do.

After her father had locked her in, she'd cried for a long time. That was what she got for trying to show an interest, for trying to speak her mind. She'd always suspected he would get angry but now she saw how far he would go. He had mentioned her brother for the first time since he left. Would he throw her out to find him? Leave her to make her own way in the world? She wasn't sure she would know how to cope out on her own. For the first time, she allowed herself to think he didn't love her at all.

She'd picked herself up and gone about her evening routine. Fern had filled her bath, not commenting on her swollen face and red eyes. And now she was ready for bed, with endless days of confinement stretching ahead of her.

Marie sighed and opened her shutters just a crack. Fern always shut them to keep the warmth in, but, on all but the coldest nights, Marie opened them again. She also left a gap in the drapes around her bedstead. On a clear night like tonight, she could gaze at the bright stars as she went to sleep.

She smoothed down her nightgown and sat on the bed, picking out familiar shapes and patterns in the night sky. How often she'd gazed up at these stars with her mother and brother. Her once happy family. She was a child of the forest, not the city, and she couldn't bear to be cooped up inside. She wondered if her father would soften, if she would be allowed out for her ride in the morning. If not, what would she do all day?

Twitch emerged from the dressing room and looked at Marie with big eyes. He seemed to know it was bedtime and curled up next to her, on top of the coverlet over the bedwarmer, and allowed himself to be stroked into a sleepy stupor.

"I suppose you're used to being stuck in here all day, aren't you? It's not so bad, is it, with your toys to play with and your food? The only difference is that I know what it's like to be outside; to roam free. Maybe that's what you were trying to do when you went exploring. Maybe it's a natural urge within us all."

Marie sighed. She still had that strong feeling that something had to change. She knew, since finding the box of death in the Strategy Room, that her father wasn't only neglecting his kingdom through inexperience. He was hurting people. She had to stand against him and make her feelings known.

Marie rubbed her hand all around the kitten's head and under his chin, just as he liked, then she clasped her hands in her lap. She realized she was in exactly the same position as her small wooden likeness when she'd found her in the Strategy Room: dormant and dull.

Marie clenched her fists, which was something the tiny carved princess could never do. She'd finally had enough of being dormant, dull and dutiful.

"Twitch," Marie said. The kitten lifted his sleepy head. "Up until now, part of me has been hoping three more wishes will come my way, but that will never happen. I had my wishes and I lost them. I am beginning to realize not everyone can rely on a magic unicorn to change their life."

She sprang up, shifting Twitch from his spot, and darted back to the window. She flung the shutters wide open, determined to let something of the outside world into her life. So what if she froze in the night?

The constellations shone up above: one that looked like a castle, and one like a unicorn, three stars in a row shining like its pointed horn.

Marie spoke directly to the twinkling unicorn as if it could hear. "Blaze, I love you, but I don't need you to make my wishes come true. I am going to have to make some changes myself."

She wasn't sure quite what those changes would be, but saying the words felt exhilarating. She smiled widely to herself for the first time in years. Change was coming.

CHAPTER TEN

PEACEFUL PROTEST

Banes

The next few days passed at a mercifully slower pace. Banes was back to menial tasks: the gardening, the cooking, the chickens; but this time she didn't feel the urge for something more interesting. Her failed capture and her time in the dungeon had worn her out, not to mention the late night answering Commander Flint's questions. She did what was required of her, with heavy eyelids and bouts of yawning.

"Oh, Annie," she said, to her favourite plump chicken, "I'm tempted to curl up in the hen house with you."

But Banes's energy levels were never depleted for long and when, four days after her return, Flint called a camp meeting, Banes was excited to find out why. Large meetings were not a regular occurrence, because the commander preferred to keep her plans on a need-to-know basis. The more people who knew about an idea, the more chance there was of an information leak back to the palace. Which is why Banes's and Woodman's kidnap mission had been so low profile to begin with.

Because of this, the whole camp knew this meeting meant the revelation of important news. Banes hoped it was linked to the information she had gathered during her arrest.

She found herself standing between Cobb and Cotter. She'd barely spoken to her comrades since the night of her arrest, but now her confidence had returned. She smiled and chatted as they waited for the commander's address.

Commander Flint spoke quietly, and as always there was a respectful hush as the crowd listened to every word.

"We are all here for different reasons: some have seen a family member wrongly imprisoned; others have found it impossible to pay taxes."

She paused, and Banes, along with (she guessed) many others, reflected on her own reasons for being at the settlement.

Without the high taxes, she would still be working at the inn and looking forward to taking over when the time was right.

The commander continued. "Whatever our reasons for being here, we are united against our common enemy: King Jacob. For a long time now, our mission has been at the preparation stage, but this cannot last for ever. We are going to turn preparation into action and we need all of us, working together, to make this a success."

It was coming – the plan. Maybe Flint would send Banes back to the castle on a new mission. Then everyone would take her seriously again.

But as Flint set out her plans, Banes's optimism faded.

"Now we are prepared to fight, our first act will be to make ourselves known to King Jacob. Others have tried to attack by stealth and it has worked against them, so we will try a different approach. We will give him every chance to put things right before we take to arms. We will gather together in the city square in a few days' time to stage a peaceful protest. We will shout our complaints and make ourselves heard. Our informants have told us the city folk will be on our side. When they know of our existence, our ranks will soon swell, and King Jacob will face the most powerful army yet."

As cheers went up from the rest of the group, Banes stood in silence, not returning Cotter's grin. She couldn't believe what she was hearing. This was a full rebellion. After everything they had discussed, the commander thought they should gather together in the castle square? Commander Flint was the cleverest person Banes knew, yet this was the most foolish idea she'd ever heard. King Jacob was hardly likely to stand around and justify his unfair treatment of his people. More likely, he would throw the whole lot of them into the dungeons. Or worse. With a magic unicorn under his command, he could do whatever he pleased.

Banes couldn't bear to listen to any more. She turned and pushed her way out of the circle, leaving the claps and cheers behind her.

THE SECRET

For once, Banes wanted to be alone. Despite the size of the settlement, this was relatively easy to achieve in Brume Forest, which stretched for miles. She soon left the main tracks behind her and pounded the ground angrily, trying to untangle the thoughts in her mind. After everything she'd risked, the commander was going to put the whole camp in danger; it didn't make sense.

The sounds of nature soon soothed her. She slowed down. Insects buzzed and leaves scrunched beneath her boots. The breathy coo of a bird sounded above. She didn't know much about birds but was fairly sure it was a wood pigeon. It reminded her of her very first walk to the camp, when she'd left the inn behind and come in search of a brand new life.

She sat on a fallen tree and breathed deeply. The earthy smell of leaves mingled with the scent of fresh ferns. She took off her boots and stretched out her feet, wiggling her toes and enjoying the cool breeze.

There was no rule that she had to stay at the camp: no one forcing her to stay. She could leave today and become a solo outlaw in the forest. Better than getting thrown back in the dungeons. She sighed. In reality, she knew she would never survive out here on her own. But she would never go back to the inn and Frederick Fogg either. She couldn't help thinking of that poor unicorn, imprisoned as she had been, but for months – years. Banes had promised to help, but that was looking unlikely. What was she going to do?

She sat for a few minutes hoping the answer might find her.

Then some sticks snapped nearby, and Banes looked up sharply.

"Banes?"

Commander Flint. She must have followed her.

The commander stood in front of her and smiled briefly. "You left abruptly."

It wasn't a question, but some response seemed necessary, and Banes wasn't sure what. She wouldn't normally dare to question a superior's decisions, yet she had to speak her mind.

Banes breathed in through her nose and spoke in a rush.

"Commander, with all due respect, I don't understand your plan. All these missions may be well-thought-out, but as minutely as you plan them, the king is always going to be one step ahead. He will stop the protest before it even starts."

Flint sat down next to her on the tree trunk. "You may be right, Banes," she said.

Banes didn't understand. She thought she'd made it clear to Flint that King Jacob was using the unicorn for his own purposes. She wasn't sure quite how, but wouldn't it be sensible to find out before rushing in? Banes dropped her voice to a whisper, as if anyone would hear them out here in the forest. "Look, I know you said not to mention the unicorn again, but it's important you know: King Jacob is using its powers. That's what makes him such a deadly opponent. Commander, if we carry on like this, everyone will be imprisoned. You are putting the entire camp at risk, not to mention the city folk. We will have no rebels left to fight."

The commander grew very quiet and looked Banes in the eye, as if she were about to share a secret.

"Banes, you made the point that the king always finishes off the armies before they even make it to Quessia city. But what if they were already there?"

"Inside the castle?"

"Yes. You got closer to the royal family than any of us have done. You came to me with the biggest piece of information we have uncovered in the five years Jacob has held the throne: his secret weapon. How was it you were able to do so?"

Banes furrowed her brow. "By luck! It was a happy accident."

"A happy accident. And tell me, where were you when this happy accident occurred?"

Was this a trick question? "I was in jail. In the dungeons."

"Exactly. We are going back, as you envisaged, to free the unicorn from King Jacob's power-hungry grasp. Without it, his power will be diminished and we can finally remove him from the throne. To do so, we are going to get as many of us arrested as possible, then we will be right under his nose."

Banes blinked. It made some sort of sense, she supposed.

"But why the secrecy? Why not explain the plan to the others?"

"For the same reason I asked you to keep quiet before. The more people that know a plan, the more likely it is to trickle down to the wrong ears. As brave and confident as our rebels are, they don't always have the sharpest military minds. Unlike you. You seem to be capable of strategic thought."

Banes felt all traces of anger disappear. "Really?"

"Really. You remind me of myself when I started out." Flint kept her voice low and her tone was conspiratorial. "You will go far if that is what you want. But there may be some of our number who don't like the idea of getting arrested. If they know this plan ends in the castle dungeons, then we may find our ranks smaller by dawn. There are always people who have their own agenda and something like this, that requires risk for the common good, would be abhorrent to them."

Banes thought of Ford and his snide remarks. She couldn't imagine him working for the "common good".

"When *will* you tell them?"

Flint tilted her head to one side.

"I'm not sure. In the meantime, I know I can trust you to keep quiet about this, as you have done on the other matter."

"Of course." Banes laced up her boots then stood up, energized at the new plan and at the thought of being able to help the unicorn, as she'd hoped.

Flint stood up too. "We should really head back to the camp now. Your comrades will no doubt be full of questions about this protest."

She strode off briskly and Banes had to run to keep up. "Let me know how I can help at the protest – if there's anything I can bring—"

"—Hold on, Banes," The commander interrupted, standing still for a second. "I'm afraid you won't be able to join us at the protest."

"What? Why not?"

"I can't send you out in broad daylight. The guards will recognize you and it may put the whole mission in danger; they will suspect we're planning something. From what you told me, the guards think you were working alone, and your kidnap attempt was a botched robbery. If you appear as part of an organized group, they may suspect something else is going on."

Flint strode off again and Banes tried to walk at her side this time. "I would be of use to you there. I can show you where everything is. I could go in disguise! With a hood pulled up." Banes pulled her cloak over her head to show how it obscured most of her face.

The commander set her jaw. "It's too risky."

Banes sighed, and Flint smiled. "I know this is frustrating, but you will be an important part of this mission; a vitally important part. Your role is just different to ours. I will brief you properly tomorrow, but here is the essence of it. You must stay away until the time is right, and then come around the back of the castle."

"How will I know when the time is right?"

"Wait until twilight. By that time, if the plan has worked, then we should all be down in the dungeons and ready for you. You will also have less risk of being recognized when the light is dim."

Twilight. She'd escaped from the dungeons at twilight, and she would be returning there at the same hour. Picturing it in her mind brought back the same feelings of fear and loneliness she'd experienced in her cell. She swallowed.

"You will need to bring some things with you," continued

the commander. "Will you be able to remember them, if I tell you? I don't want anything written down."

Banes nodded. "I have an excellent memory."

"Good. You will bring them to me in the dungeons, if you can find me, and I will be able to give you your next set of instructions."

Banes felt her pulse quicken again. She would be of importance to the mission after all. A vital player, in fact.

"Will I be doing this on my own?" Banes worried that might sound negative, as if she were scared of being left on her own. "Not that I mind!" she added. "But if I am found and arrested on my way to the castle then the plan fails."

"I understand," said the commander, "but you won't be alone; I will make sure at least one other person stays behind with you."

Banes felt happy at that; to have the whole mission resting on her shoulders alone felt like too much responsibility. The path narrowed and once again she was walking behind the commander.

"May I choose who accompanies me?" Banes asked the back of Flint's head. If so, she would ask to go with Cobb. They had a lot in common and it would be good to get to know her away from the rest of the group.

The commander turned and smiled in a way that made her

think she wouldn't be going with Cobb.

"I thought this mission would once again be perfect for you and Woodman."

Banes cringed. Not Woodman again! They hadn't spoken since he had left her alone to be captured. How was it he always seemed to be absent when any bravery was needed?

"Can I ask why Woodman?"

"We need craftsmen more than ever back at the camp while we are preparing for a big fight. And Woodman has a set of skills that complement yours. And I trust him to keep quiet where Cobb never would." The commander smiled. She knew Banes well enough to have read what she was thinking.

"Besides, I happen to think you and Woodman make a good team."

PERFECT TASK

The camp was a noisy place. During the day, there were always people talking, animals squawking, hammers on nails and axes on wood. Even at night-time, fires still crackled and low conversations bubbled away, about secret missions and who knows what else.

But on the morning everyone left, Banes found the camp eerily quiet. She'd kept a low profile for the past few days while everyone else was preparing for the protest. There was a buzz around the camp. Even though the commander had explained why she couldn't be part of it, Banes had the feeling she was on the outside looking in; left out of the main action.

And when the day came for her comrades to leave, she stayed in her tent after waking. They left early. She heard the build-up of excitement, the horses' hooves and cartwheels trundling away, and then silence. They'd gone.

She wandered around the deserted camp, trying to appreciate the absence of noise while she could, although she didn't much enjoy silence. On a normal day, it was virtually impossible to find any privacy, so she luxuriated in the time alone. She took her time bathing in the river. It was cold, but invigorating once she got used to it. She soaked her hair and scrubbed herself from head to toe. And she sang.

Next on her list were the chickens. She needed to let them out for the day and they were *never* quiet. As she neared the hen house, she heard a loud hubbub of squawking and flapping. But on this occasion, it wasn't just their usual noise. A four-legged visitor had taken advantage of the quiet morning. The distinctive brush tail and sharp orange features marked it out straightaway as a fox. A vixen, by the looks of things, and she was very interested in the chickens, circling the hen house on dancer's feet and pawing at the earth around it.

"You!" shouted Banes. "Get away from those chickens!"

The fox pricked up her ears, alert, and looked at Banes, her amber eyes assessing her without blinking. She turned, as if she were going to make her escape into the forest, but then jumped up on to the roof of the hen house, and continued to stare at Banes.

"Why, you impertinent animal," shouted Banes. "You're supposed to be frightened of me."

The fox didn't move.

Banes rushed towards her, squawking and flapping her arms like a chicken as the birds in the hen house all joined in.

This seemed to do the trick and the fox jumped down from the roof and trotted away, although she still didn't seem to be in too much of a hurry.

Banes looked around to check no one had witnessed her embarrassing chicken impression, but the place really was deserted. She would keep the chickens inside for one day. No doubt they would be cross with her by tomorrow, but it was for their own safety.

She fed them, checked for fresh eggs, then she thought she'd better go and find Woodman.

On the outskirts of their camp, there was a large, fenced off area they referred to as "the woodpile". As well as the actual woodpile – a giant stack of logs felled from the forest – there was a great mass of carpentry tools, wheels, nails and machines. Banes had never paid the area much attention before, but she knew that was where she'd find Woodman. She wandered over, enjoying the smell of sawdust, leather and linseed oil.

Sure enough, Woodman was there, standing on a long wooden beam, swinging an L-shaped tool at the timber, curls of wood flying. He looked lost in his work, as if he'd been there for some time. He wasn't much of a talker and rarely surrounded himself with people, so he was presumably enjoying his solitude.

"Good morning!" she said brightly, trying to put any anger towards him out of her mind. It seemed a good idea to leave the past mission behind them and set off on the right foot. After all, they would be spending at least another twelve hours in each other's company.

"Banes," he said, in brief greeting, stopping his work to glance up at her. He didn't look overly pleased to see her. "Bit early, aren't you? I didn't think we were required at the castle until twilight?"

"I thought I'd come and discuss our plans. Sorry to interrupt," she said. "Don't let me keep you from your ... whatever it is you are doing."

"Adzing," he replied, bending back over the beam.

"Axing?"

"Adzing," he corrected. "With an adze." He picked up the tool he was using, which did look a little like an axe. "This. I'm using it to smooth the wood."

Banes laughed loudly. "Well then, don't let me keep you from your adzing. I'm sure you can adze and talk at the same time."

She couldn't see if he smiled or not as he continued to swing the tool. The rough outer layer of the wood flaked away, leaving a smooth beam underneath.

"So you *are* a carpenter," she thought aloud.

Woodman stopped again, wiping his hands down the sides of his breeches. Now he looked amused. "Of course I'm a carpenter – I told you that."

"But you never know with people, do you? There's always two people: the person they choose to show you and the person they really are."

Woodman shrugged. "Perhaps."

"What are you making?"

"A catapult. Well, fixing it, although I have asked myself repeatedly whether it would be easier to start from scratch. I've dismantled most of it to finish the wood properly. This is the last big piece." He jumped off the beam and led Banes a few yards away to show her the semi-constructed catapult. It was quite a weapon: the size of a large cart, with wooden wheels at each corner. "The beam I am working on will attach in between those two, and then I need to fix the mechanism."

"What's the problem with the mechanism?" asked Banes.

"The problem is, it was built by people who didn't have a clue what they were doing," said Woodman, as if to himself. He peered into the middle of the machine then stood up, sweat at his brow. "Take a look in there." Banes looked at what appeared to be quite an intricate wound cog and wheel system.

"It keeps slipping, do you see?" Woodman demonstrated the problem.

Banes nodded. "Does it need some sort of stop?" she said, not sure if she had the right idea at all.

"Yes, that's it! See, you don't need to be a master craftsman to figure that out – just a couple of brain cells to rub together."

Banes wasn't sure whether to be pleased or offended.

Woodman was now inspecting the catapult frame, running

his hands along every surface and tugging and testing here and there. She'd never seen him quite so animated.

"Gah!" he exclaimed, making her jump. He wobbled the corner of the catapult. "This joint is not tight enough for my liking. I'm going to have to peg it. See that toolbox by your feet?"

Banes nodded.

"Can you pass me the awl and a couple of tapered pegs?"

Amongst the selection of tools in front of her, she saw an axe and a mallet, a chisel and a couple of knives. There was one tool she didn't recognize, with a sharp iron peg that it looked like it might be the right one to make a hole. The awl? She passed it to him and he seemed satisfied. Maybe the commander was right and they did make a good team.

She watched him digging away at the wood. He looked so content and she could imagine him happily working as the village carpenter, building chairs and cabinets. He could have a wife, children, a happy life. She wondered what it was that had driven him here. She thought of his strange behaviour on the morning of the kidnapping, and of the princess's questions down in the dungeon. Princess Marie had been very interested in Woodman. Or a Woodman, at least. Wyll Woodman.

Banes watched for a few more seconds and then asked

suddenly, "What's your first name?"

Woodman did a double take.

"My name?" he asked, as if she'd enquired about his bunions. "Why?"

"I thought as the commander has decided we'll be spending so much time together, then it might be interesting to find out a bit more about each other."

Woodman stood stock-still. "Oh."

He clearly didn't like sharing personal information about himself.

"Mine's Cassie," offered Banes. "If you're interested. I grew up in the village of East Heath, in an inn. I worked there and I was good at it. I was happy for a time. But my parents wanted me to marry an older man named Fogg who liked my curly hair. They thought it was a perfect solution to our money problems, despite the fact I'd practically been running the inn for years and all the customers – not just Fogg – were fond of me. It meant one less mouth to feed. They were happy to pass the business on to my younger brother who has never done a day's work in his life but was less of a marriageable prospect."

She stopped and smiled ruefully.

"Oh," said Woodman, again. "So do you want me to call

you…" He seemed confused, as if he'd forgotten her name already.

"Cassie."

"Yes. Am I supposed to call you that now?"

"No. I thought you might be interested to know, that's all. I'm making conversation."

"Oh." He brushed the wood filings away from the hole he'd made and then stood back and looked at her. "My name's Wyll."

QUESTIONS

Wyll. That was definitely the name the princess used when she was enquiring about Woodman. Banes tried not to look too interested but it must mean there was some connection.

He went back to the joint, fitting the peg into the hole, but Banes was now on edge.

Why would the princess have been asking about Woodman? She'd sounded as if she cared about him and wanted to know how he was. Woodman had also been cagey. He hadn't wanted the princess to see him, which is why he hid away in the trees when she appeared on horseback. They knew each other!

Banes had no doubt about this, but she would keep things light, wait and see how much he would tell her of his own accord – as a friend.

"Can you pass me the mallet?" he asked. She took the awl from him and handed him the large wooden mallet.

"There was something I wanted to ask you about," said Banes.

Woodman – Wyll – smiled. "Another thing? We're never going to get the catapult fixed at this rate."

"When I was in the dungeon, the princess came to see me."

His relaxed expression fell away and he looked at her sharply. "Why?"

"I don't know. I mean, she brought me some food, which was nice, but I'm not sure that was the real reason."

"Oh."

He knelt down by the catapult and picked up a mallet. Then he stopped and looked up at Banes, wrinkling his brow. "Did the princess talk to you at all? Did you get a sense of what her life is like?"

Banes shook her head. It was a strange question to ask.

"Why?" she blurted out suddenly. "Do you know her?"

"No, of course not!" he said, but he didn't meet her eye. He was lying.

"Are you sure?" said Banes, but Woodman didn't reply. He turned away, and began hammering in the peg. Hard.

Banes's heart was hammering just as hard in her chest. What was the relationship between Woodman and the princess? Were they sweethearts? Was he a spy? Had he been feeding information back to the king?

She wasn't sure what to do next. What was it the commander had said? *"…you have to say what you think and do what you feel. Be ruthless."*

Banes could be ruthless. Of course she could. She was still gripping the awl she'd taken from him and she felt the tip with her thumb. It was sharp. She didn't think it through – she didn't stop to wonder if Woodman was dangerous to her. Banes's face felt hot. She'd finished with the polite questions now.

AWL

Woodman had clearly decided their conversation was over and resumed his banging. Banes stepped over the catapult frame and stood beside him as he knelt, as if she was fascinated by his work.

Her heart still beating fast, she grabbed his shoulders and

held the sharp tip of the awl to his throat. He seemed confused at first, not scared. He stayed very still but his eyes glanced down at her makeshift weapon.

"Drop the mallet," she said, in her best ruthless voice. He did as she said and straightened up. She kept the awl at his throat.

"What are you doing, Banes?"

"I want answers," she said, trying to keep the wobble from her voice. "Tell me what the connection is between you and the princess."

"I don't know what you're talking about."

Banes pressed the tip of the awl into his neck. She could feel his pulse beating steadily under her thumb. She was close enough to see his hair, which was different shades of fair, from almost white to chestnut, like the wood he was working with. She knew she wouldn't be able to hurt him but she hoped he didn't realize that. "It wouldn't take much to kill you," she said.

"Oh. Do you think the commander would be pleased with you if you murdered me when we're supposed to be going on a mission together?"

Banes thought quickly. "No one would ever know. I would hide your body deep in the forest and tell them you'd run off. That you were scared again, like at the kidnapping."

"I see. You'll hide my body... But how would you get me to the forest on your own? I weigh about twice as much as you."

Banes hadn't thought about that. She looked around desperately for an answer.

"I'd put you on this catapult and wheel you."

"Then you'd project me off the trolley like a missile?"

"Maybe."

He was ridiculing her. Here she was, threatening to kill him and he was still mocking her.

"You've thought this through, have you?" he asked, and Banes felt any power she had slipping away. Why did she find it so difficult to be threatening? The princess had dismissed her efforts. Even the fox hadn't been remotely intimidated by her appearance that morning.

"Just tell me what you know about her. Are you reporting back to the royal family?"

"Reporting back? No!" He sounded genuinely surprised. That, or he was a very good actor. "Look, I'll tell you. I know I haven't been very forthcoming. I'm sorry you felt you had to attack me to get any personal information out of me. You'll see I have my reasons, but can you please keep them to yourself? I don't want the rest of the camp to question my loyalties."

She lowered the awl and moved around to face him.

"Tell me," she said.

Woodman closed his eyes for a second, then opened them. "My loyalty is with the rebels. To this settlement. Nothing I can tell you will make any difference to that. I'll carry out this evening's mission as planned."

Her hunch had been right. He had been hiding something.

"I understand. Tell me – please."

He looked at her and there was pain in his eyes. "Marie is my sister," he said.

WOODMAN'S TALE

Banes held the awl by her side. Her mouth dropped open and she sat down on the catapult frame.

"Princess Marie is your sister?"

"Yes."

He sat down next to her but a little way away, perhaps concerned she might attack him again.

"A step-sister born of a wicked stepmother?"

"No. She's my full sister. We grew up together. And our

mother was anything but wicked."

"So that means King Jacob is your—"

"—My father, yes." His face was steely.

"But how… I mean…"

Woodman smiled, looking more like his normal good-natured self. "I don't think I've ever seen you speechless before," he said.

Banes tried to grasp what all this meant. "All this time, when people have been gossiping about the royal family, around the fire, back home at the inn … nobody ever mentioned a prince."

Woodman raised a single eyebrow. "I'm no prince. I left before my father's change of fortune. Just before," he said wryly. "I had no royal upbringing. And he was no king. When I left home after an argument, he was a poor man. He was a carpenter. I learned my trade from him."

Banes looked at the toolbox as if it might provide her with answers. "A carpenter? Carpenters do not become kings."

"Not usually, but in this case that is exactly what happened. My mother died when I was young and I couldn't get along with my father. He was lazy, greedy and selfish, like the king we know now. I left one evening in anger, abandoning him and my sister."

"Princess Marie?"

"The very same, although she wasn't a princess then."

Banes tried to bring Marie's face to mind. They did have the same colouring and the same face shape, although Woodman was slimmer. He was speaking the truth. But a pauper to a princess? How was that possible? It must have been the unicorn. She dropped the awl on the dusty ground and turned to him.

"When did their fortunes change?"

Woodman stood, picked up the awl and packed it away in the toolbox. "That has been difficult for me to understand, although it is beginning to become clearer. I went back to my father's cottage in the forest, a few months after I'd left. Not to stay, but to fetch my sister as I'd promised. I arrived in the middle of the day and found my old home deserted. All their things were still there, as I remembered, but abandoned, as if they'd stood up and walked away."

Banes had no problem picturing a deserted cottage in the forest. "The cottage – it wasn't the carpenter's cottage we passed, near where we … I … held up Princess Marie?"

Woodman nodded and Banes stopped her questioning for a moment, trying to keep up with everything he had told her. She remembered Woodman's reluctance to take a break at that old cottage, and the way he kept gazing back at it. It must have held so many memories for him.

"So … you found them gone, but you didn't know where. You must have wondered about their safety."

"I did! My father had never been a kind man and I was worried for my sister. Marie always sees the best in people. She thought he was only like that because of the death of our mother, but I'm older and I remember better. Our mother brought out the little good that was inside him but then it vanished when she died."

He swallowed and went back to the catapult, testing the joint that he'd been mending. "I felt guilty too, for abandoning her to an unknown fate. I waited, thinking they must have headed out on an urgent errand, but they didn't return. Not that night or any other. I waited for a full cycle of the moon. I couldn't make sense of it. They couldn't have moved to a new home, for they had taken nothing with them. And there was no sign of a struggle. It was as if they'd disappeared into thin air, or been magicked away."

Magic. The unicorn.

"When did you hear your father had become king?"

"Not until weeks later. I heard of the sad fate of the previous king and queen and that we had a new king. Even when I learned his name was Jacob, and his daughter was Marie, I didn't make the connection. Why would I? They are common names and my father was a poor man, with no links to any royalty. Believe me, had there been even a distant relation, it would have been all we ever heard about."

Woodman went back to his previous task of hammering in the peg, but half-heartedly, swinging the mallet slowly in gaps in the conversation.

"So when did you find out?"

"It was when his likeness began to appear on notices and paintings. The drawings looked like him but different, somehow. He is always shown as a kind, proud man, whereas in reality he had always been cruel and sneering."

Banes had never seen him in real life so she couldn't comment. She shrugged and Woodman continued. "I had a feeling it couldn't be anyone else but still, it made no sense. Like you said to the others, kings don't appear from nowhere. I couldn't be sure until I saw him for myself, so I went to the coronation."

"Did you see him?"

"Yes. I stood at the back of the crowd with my hood up so he wouldn't recognize me, but I needn't have bothered; it was easy to go unnoticed among the throngs of people. As soon as he came out on the balcony, I knew it was him. And Marie too. Yet they looked so strange, as if they were children playing at dressing-up. I was staggered the people saw him as a true king and were bowing down to him."

Woodman had finished with the peg now and wiggled it to see if it was tight. Banes couldn't believe how much he was sharing with her. It must have been so difficult keeping it a secret all this time. No wonder he remained so quiet around the fire in the evenings; the talk so often turned to the king and his selfish ways. He was probably worried he'd say something that gave himself away.

"Weren't you tempted to say something at the coronation? To shout to your father?"

"The crowd was far too noisy; I would have been drowned out by all the people there. Everyone was pushing, shouting, wanting to be heard. Anyway, I didn't want anything to do with my father. His new role as king didn't change my feelings for him and if I'd have made contact, he would have been convinced it was for his money alone."

"I understand that," said Banes. She could see how Woodman could still be angry with his father after all this time. She wondered how she would feel if her parents suddenly became king and queen and had no financial need for her to marry Frederick Fogg. Would she rush home immediately? She wasn't quite sure of the reception she would receive, and, in all honesty, she wasn't sure whether she wanted to go back.

Woodman ran his hands back and forth over the wood of the catapult.

"I hoped the money and power would soften him, change him for the better. My sister once thought it would. She was convinced hardship had made him hard himself and he would change if his circumstances improved. But he didn't. I heard the stories about the way he was treating his people. The high taxes, the irrational rules, the harsh punishments. It made me sick."

Woodman spoke passionately and Banes could relate to his disgust. Indirectly, it was King Jacob who had led her to run away from home. He was the one who had raised the taxes so high they could barely afford to run the inn. But they didn't need to be distracted by another conversation about King Jacob's wrongdoings. Banes wanted to hear the rest of Woodman's story.

"How did you end up here at the camp?"

"I went back to the cottage for a while: made it my home again. I enjoyed the time to think, but the isolation grew too much for me. Then I felt myself growing more and more angry about the way he treated his subjects. When I heard about the rebels, I joined up. Just walked away from the cottage without looking back, as my father did."

Banes leaned against the frame of the catapult. The secret Woodman had been keeping was huge. She tried to imagine what the commander would do with this new information, but she didn't know. She would have to think about whether to share it with Flint or not. Perhaps she would do better to keep it to herself and try to understand Woodman's motives.

"Why didn't you tell anyone?" she asked.

"I didn't want to be treated differently to everyone else. I wasn't sure I would be trusted, or that people would believe I was committed to our cause. From what I've witnessed, I was right. You attacked me with an awl."

"Sorry about that," said Banes, ashamed of herself.

Woodman began stashing the tools away in his toolbox, finished with the catapult for now.

"Also, being the son of the king seemed somewhat far-fetched and I have no proof. I feared I would not be believed." He raised an eyebrow.

Banes smiled. "I believe you. You believed me too – about the unicorn – didn't you?" she asked.

Woodman nodded. "For my father's life to change as it did was more than improbable. It was unbelievable. Only a miracle or magic could be behind it."

"The unicorn."

Their eyes met for a moment.

"It explains everything," he said. "The night I left home, my sister saw something out in the forest, by a waterfall. She was flustered but never told me why. Then my father was acting differently... I knew he was up to some mischief, but I was too angry to ask what. Since then I had often wondered what Marie could possibly have seen to lead to their reversal of fortune. It never made sense until I heard your tale from the dungeon. That night, the night I left, they must have both discovered the unicorn."

Banes finally saw how all the pieces of Woodman's story fitted together. The unicorn had said a young girl had wanted to help her, but ended up helping someone else. That must have been Princess Marie.

Banes was excited there was someone else, along with Commander Flint, who actually believed what she'd seen. Part of her wanted to discuss the unicorn – how King Jacob was getting more than his fair share of wishes – but she still needed to find out more about Woodman.

"This compromises your position here. We are fighting against your father. How can you be on our side? You won't be able to make balanced decisions."

Woodman sighed. "When I left home, I cut all ties with Jacob Woodman, and nothing changes now he is king. Believe me, I have no love left for the man. I want nothing from him. I am going back for my sister alone; I made a promise to her years ago."

"Your sister now lives in an enormous castle with personal guards, a kitten to play with and teeny, tiny boiled eggs. She has servants that do everything for her. What makes you think she wants rescuing?"

"Maybe she doesn't. If she is happy where she is, then I will leave her alone, but I need to hear that from Marie; not from my father or anyone else. I cannot imagine a life with my father would be a good life, no matter what material goods she has."

"You didn't taste the jam tarts."

Woodman smiled. "Even the finest jam tarts in the world would not compensate for my father's tantrums. I feel bad for leaving my sister to deal with them alone. I can't believe Marie would be complicit in my father's wrongdoings. She has a good heart, and a good heart doesn't change."

Banes kept quiet. After the way Marie had helped her, she thought he was probably right, but she didn't know for certain.

Woodman looked pained. "I'm worried other people won't take the time to see that good heart. If there is a successful rebellion and we, or anyone else, manage to overthrow the king, then someone needs to be there to speak up for her."

Banes was touched by Woodman's concern for his sister. This was a side to him she hadn't seen; he seemed like a good brother. Still, she wouldn't know how best to deal with this information until she'd spoken to Commander Flint.

"I agree everyone has a right to be judged on their own merits," she said, jumping off the catapult frame. "I'm glad we had this conversation, Woodman, and sorry about the awl, but next time you shouldn't be quite so reluctant to talk to me."

"Very well," said Woodman, smiling.

Banes began to walk away from the woodpile.

"What are you doing, Banes?"

"I'm off now, to talk to the chickens."

"The chickens?"

"Yes, I'm even more excited now about tonight's mission and I'm going to prepare in my own way. Be ready just after noon."

"Isn't that a bit soon? The commander said not to get there too early."

"The commander also said we should use our intuition and intelligence rather than relying on what other people tell us. It's a couple of hours' ride away, so I suggest we leave the horses by your old cottage and walk the rest of the way, as we'll be less obvious on foot."

"I suppose that's a good idea," Woodman said.

Banes nodded. "It is. Now, I'm off to the weaponry to get as many weapons as we can carry, as requested by Commander Flint."

"As many weapons as we can carry? I do hope this isn't another doomed mission, Banes."

"Of course not. Can you bring a metal file? That was the other thing on the commander's list." Banes tossed a sack to Woodman. "And pack up some supplies from the food store before we leave. We may be gone for a while and I *hate* being hungry."

CHAPTER ELEVEN

BY A WINDOW AT THE TOP OF THE CASTLE

Marie

Marie sat by the window, as she'd done for most of the day, and as she'd done every day since her father locked her in. It had been nearly a week. Fern had brought her meals on trays, and then taken them away again, untouched. Marie had no appetite without her daily morning ride.

Despite her plans to act, and to change her life, she'd found little opportunity. She'd hoped to persuade her father to release her, but she hardly ever saw him. He had checked in on her once or twice but made barely any conversation. Outside, people were hurrying past as they did every day. She'd begun to recognize their faces and to know what time to expect them. But today it had seemed busier. Strangers, country people, heading in the direction of the city square and not returning.

Something was different. Change was in the air.

Now, as twilight neared, the feeling of difference was even stronger. Marie could hear it. A ringing, like a bell, that didn't cease.

"Can you hear that, Twitch?" she asked, but her kitten didn't seem to notice.

Perhaps *hear* was the wrong word. She could *feel* the sound within her. A sound she knew. Since that forest twilight, she'd imagined she'd heard it countless times. But it had always been something else: travelling musicians out in the city streets, or the ringing of a bell in the school yard. She'd dreamed of it, too, but always woke in the morning unable to remember the exact sound. But this was different. This time the unicorn was calling her.

Marie had never heard Blaze from so far away before. She hoped she wasn't hurt, or in trouble. She hoped her father hadn't punished her for helping Banes escape. If he had, then it would have been her fault for telling the truth about the wrap. She wished she'd thought quicker and made up some lie about it, but it was too late for that.

If only there were something she could do to help. She crossed the room and tried the door handle. It was locked. Of course it was. So that was the end of that idea.

Or was it?

If she were a different person, then she wouldn't let something as insignificant as a locked door put her off. She tried to think of someone brave and courageous. Banes. She lived with outlaws in the forest! She'd risked her own personal safety countless times, by attempting to kidnap a princess and by escaping out of a barred window. She wouldn't be deterred by a locked door.

What would Banes do?

The answer was, one way or another, she would get out of this room. Marie looked through the keyhole. She could see very little: it seemed the key was still in the lock. Her father must have turned it and left it there.

Once, a few years ago, Marie had overheard two maids talking about how they were accidentally locked in by one of the footmen. They had pushed the key out of the lock from the inside, then guided the key back under the door with a poker in order to free themselves. Marie took a hairpin and tried pushing the key through the lock but it seemed to be stuck fast.

What would Banes do?

Marie knew Banes wouldn't be put off by one small obstacle. She would find a different idea: bribe a servant, or fake an emergency, or climb out of the window down her bedsheets if she had to. Marie stared at her bedsheets. They were white with sweet briar roses embroidered here and there. Did people really climb down bedsheets? She'd heard about it in stories – the sort of adventures her mother told her at bedtime – but she found it hard to imagine how it might work in real life.

Still, a brave person – Banes – wouldn't stand around asking herself questions like that. She would take decisive action.

The sheets were smoothed across her bed and tucked under at the sides. Marie reached under the coverlet, grabbed a corner of the undersheet and pulled. It was surprisingly hard work. Twitch appeared from wherever he'd been hiding, and danced under the sheet, lifting a paw now and again to swipe at it.

Marie pulled as hard as she could, walking backwards across the expanse of her room. As it came loose, the cushions and coverlet tumbled from the bed into a satisfying heap. *Sorry, Fern – more work for you.*

Marie was left holding the sheet, which was strong, but not long enough to reach the ground outside. It seemed a shame to tear such pretty bedlinen, especially when she knew what it would be worth to a poor family. She rummaged in the pile for another two similar sheets and knotted them together at the corner. She was good at knots. It should be long enough and strong enough.

Her heart began to thump. Was she actually going to do this? What if Fern came into the room now? What if her *father* did? But again, she did her best to ignore these thoughts. If she listened to them, she may as well stay locked up in this room for ever.

CHAPTER TWELVE

BY A WINDOW AT THE BACK OF THE CASTLE

Banes

Banes had not been looking forward to returning to Quessia castle. Last time she had been here, she'd wondered if she would ever escape. But now, as she looked up at the imposing structure in the orange twilight, the thrill of the mission quickened her pulse. She wanted to shout or laugh with excitement. She wondered if Woodman felt the same, but he didn't look like someone who was about to collapse with laughter. His jaw was set and his eyes moved this way and that, as if looking for clues.

Their journey through the forest had been straightforward. They avoided the main roads, favoured by reputable visitors to Quessia, and chose the smaller forest tracks leading to the back of the castle.

Only those who were up to no good would take such a path: poachers, thieves or enemies of the king. Banes's main fear had been that they might meet some guards and be searched. The discovery of their sizeable stash of weapons would soon put an end to the mission. But they didn't meet a guard, or anyone else on their journey.

Once they were through the dense trees, Banes had taken charge, and led Woodman on the same route she'd taken to escape from the dungeons. She'd remembered the way better than she thought she might. Now, under the crescent moon, shining already in the pale blue sky, they stood close to the castle. They ran down the slope into the deep ditch that surrounded the castle and looked up at the dungeon windows. They were all much higher than Banes remembered.

Commander Flint had told her to find the window of the cell in which she'd been held, but she couldn't be sure which window that was. She remembered the unicorn's better, which was around the corner of the building, but she knew the commander wanted them to find her first.

Getting up to any window was going to be more difficult than she'd imagined. Of course it was easier to climb out of a window and drop to the ground rather than climb into it from the outside.

They hid their bags in some nearby bushes, then stood and listened for clues to the cells' occupants. Nothing. Commander Flint had been so sure that all the protesters would be arrested, but what if she'd misjudged it? Flint had been wrong before, when she said the princess always travelled alone. Their comrades couldn't have been released, because they'd have passed them on the way here, but what if the king had sent his army, and killed them all?

"Is everything all right, Banes?" asked Woodman.

She nodded and tried to dismiss any worries and focus on the mission. They followed the external dungeon wall around until she was pretty sure that they were in the right place. Then they assessed which spot would be the best to attempt their climb. At one point, the ground rose in a gentle slope, bringing them closer.

Banes beckoned Woodman over, and he stood next to her, gazing up at the barred openings. The serious look on his face seemed comical to Banes, and once again she felt giggles bubbling up inside her. Excitement, or nerves, or both. Woodman's face remained straight, and she wondered how it must feel to know his father and sister were inside this very castle.

"How do we know where the commander is?" he whispered.

"We don't. We don't even know for certain that she was arrested, but we have to hope that the plan worked. She told me to aim for the cell where I was held. She seemed to think they'd hold female prisoners in the same area. And I'm pretty sure it's one of these two." Banes pointed above the slope.

"We can't reach them – they're about seven feet off the ground!"

Banes had already thought about that. "That may be, but I'm going to sit on your shoulders."

"Great, that should provide at least another foot," he said, drily.

"Very funny, Woodman."

Still, he seemed open to the idea, even if getting on to his shoulders took longer than expected. The first time, Woodman picked her up in a piggy back position. She tried to shift herself up to his shoulders but didn't have the strength in her arms and slid off. The second time, he crouched down so she could climb straight up, but standing proved difficult and they both fell sideways on to the grass. They finally deduced that if Woodman knelt down facing the castle and Banes used the height of the slope, then she could clamber on to his shoulders. He shuffled closer to the castle on his knees, used the wall to pull himself to standing, and Banes steadied herself against the brickwork. Once in position, he let go of the wall, staggering as he did so.

"I'm not too heavy, am I?" she asked.

"Light as a feather," groaned Woodman.

The supressed giggles from earlier began to find their way out. Banes put her hand over her mouth but then lost her balance and grabbed at the nearest thing, which happened to be Woodman's hair.

"Ow!"

"Sorry," whispered Banes, swaying. She was still too far away to see in the window.

"Right a bit," she whispered, and Woodman managed two faltering sidesteps in that direction.

They were finally in position. Banes grabbed on to the bars of the left-hand cell, easing some of her weight off Woodman's shoulders. She peered in. They'd got the wrong cell. This one was much bigger than hers had been and there were a few men in there. The sight of them scared Banes's nervous giggles away. It made it all suddenly real. What if they spotted her and called for the jailer?

She ducked away but then mustered all her bravery for a second glance. This time she recognized one of the men. She could only see the back of his head and an ear but she would recognize those ears anywhere.

"It's Cotter," whispered Banes.

She peeked again. "And Robertson, and a few other familiar faces from the camp."

COTTER

"Cotter," she called quietly, her normal voice seeming impossibly loud after all the whispering.

She felt Woodman's shoulders sag with relief that they'd found someone. Cotter didn't look up at first. She called again and he checked the door hatch before swinging round.

"Banes!" he shouted out, causing Banes and Woodman to put their fingers to their lips in unison. The others followed the direction of his gaze and waved madly when they saw her.

"Shhhhh!" she said.

"Don't worry," grinned Cotter, checking the door hatch again. "The jailer's asleep out in the corridor. Listen – you can hear him snoring!"

Banes could just about hear some faint animal sounds, like a growling guard dog.

"What are you doing here?" asked Robertson.

And how did you get up there?" asked Cotter.

"I'm on Woodman's shoulders. We've come to get you out. There's a plan." whispered Banes, although she didn't mention she had no idea what the plan was.

"Good!" She could see the relief spread across Cotter's face. "I thought we were done for."

Robertson laughed as her words sunk in. "You're on Woodman's shoulders? Say hello from me. I don't suppose you've anything to eat?"

Banes could identify with how he felt. She remembered the gnawing hunger of her first hours in the cell and the wonderful satisfaction of eating Princess Marie's food. She found a hard bread roll in her pocket left over from the meal she and Woodman had packed. She pushed it through the bars and he caught it and tore it into pieces to share. Each of them received little more than a mouthful but no one complained. They all munched away while Cotter and Robertson tried to fill her in with what had happened. "We had barely started the protest... There were guards everywhere... They said we were breaking the law..."

So the mission had worked as Flint had planned. Banes wanted to ask more, but somewhere beneath her knees, Woodman groaned.

"I'm sorry but I don't think my shoulders are up to chitchat," he said. "Can we *please* move on and do what we've come here to do?"

In the cell, they couldn't hear Woodman, and Cotter continued with his mumbled commentary. "They arrested dozens of us ... took us down to these cells. The jailer stole all my food—"

"—Look, I'm sorry to interrupt," said Banes, "but we've got to be quick. We'll get you out soon, I promise, but at the moment we're looking for the commander."

Cotter stopped munching for a moment. "Oh. She's in the cell next door. That way." He pointed. "Ford and some of the others are across the corridor from us."

Banes couldn't believe their luck. "Great, thanks!" she said to Cotter and then, in Woodman's ear, "Commander Flint's in the cell to the right."

They drew up to the next cell window and Banes peeped through, holding on to the bars as she'd done at Cotter's window. Down below, the commander was alone in Banes's old cell, curled up on the floor as she herself had been, but without a princess's soft wrap draped over her. She looked vulnerable, in a way Banes hadn't seen before. Banes remembered her own feelings of cold and loneliness after she'd been arrested and spoke softly to arouse the commander's attention.

"Commander Flint?"

COMMANDER FLINT

Unlike Cotter, Flint looked straight up at the window, without an ounce of surprise. She was immediately back to her confident and authoritative self.

"Banes! Well done. You made it. At twilight too, as we'd agreed. I knew I could count on you."

"And me," murmured Woodman, out of earshot.

Banes realized then how much faith Commander Flint had placed in her. Without her (and Woodman), the commander and the entire camp would be facing their fates in the dungeons with no hope of escape.

"Did you find the cell easily enough?" she asked.

"Yes, I have a good memory for those sorts of details," said Banes, not confessing it was partly a lucky guess.

Woodman snorted at this but the commander didn't seem to hear. Banes kicked her heel back into his chest and he wobbled. She had to grab the bars at the window to prevent herself from toppling. The commander frowned. "What are you standing on up there?"

"Woodman."

"Oh!" said the commander. "In that case, I'd better make this brief. As I'd hoped, you've come at the right time."

"We have?"

"Yes. The jailer is out cold, thanks to your information. You told me he ate stolen food from your bag, so before we left camp, I hid a delectable fruit tart in mine, that happened to be laced with sleeping nightshade. Unfortunately, he ate it much more quickly than I imagined, so I was concerned he might awaken before help arrived."

"But here we are!"

"Indeed. Unfortunately, he is asleep on the other side of the door. My plan was to keep him talking for so long he fell asleep in my cell. I could have then taken the keys from his belt and unlocked all the doors."

Banes was surprised to hear the commander say this. She'd told her the jailer didn't talk much. Yet Flint was acting surprised he didn't speak. Maybe she thought that she had some kind of charm Banes was lacking. Banes felt secretly smug that the commander hadn't succeeded where she had failed. She tried not to let it show.

"So what do we do now, Commander Flint?"

The commander set her jaw in familiar fashion. "I have been thinking about this long and hard and I think the best way is for the two of you to try different approaches." She stopped for a moment. "Can Woodman hear me down there?"

Banes looked down. "Can you hear her?"

"It's muffled, but just about," he said.

Banes nodded to the commander.

"Good," she said. "First, pass the weapons you've brought with you through these bars. You do have the weapons?" Banes nodded again. She climbed off Woodman's shoulders to retrieve the bags, then resumed her position, with the first bag slung across her shoulder. The extra weight made it even tougher on Woodman, but the swords and knives fitted through easily, so they were able to empty the bag quickly and repeat. Soon, all the weapons were inside.

Flint seemed satisfied.

"Woodman, I need you to get into the castle by some cunning means – bribe them to visit a prisoner or say you are bringing a delivery or anything. Get yourself down to the dungeons, on the other side of this door, and take the keys before the jailer wakes up. If you can do this, we will be able to let everyone out. Our army will be inside the castle – the closest they have ever been."

"Why me?" he said, in a high voice. Now she knew his secret, Banes could understand why he was panicking. Inside the castle, his chances of bumping into his long-lost father were much higher than out here.

The commander hadn't heard his question, so Banes asked her now. "What about me? Aren't I going with Woodman?"

"I need you here, Banes."

"What for?"

"As the back-up plan. Did you bring the file, as I asked?"

"Yes, but I think it should be the other way around," said Banes.

The commander looked irritated. When she issued instructions, she expected people to follow them. "What do you mean?"

"I think I should head into the castle and Woodman should file through the bars."

"The plan was that you were going to stay away from anyone who might recognize you."

"I know, but I will keep my hood up. Only a handful of guards and the princess saw me anyway. The jailer's the only one who would know me and he's fast asleep. I don't think I'll be recognized. Besides, Woodman's been a carpenter for years. He knows what he's doing with a file and he has the height too. I can't reach."

The commander nodded impatiently. "Fine, the other way around then. Banes, you head into the castle; Woodman, you start filing."

Woodman groaned. "Anything as long as I can shift this weight from my shoulders."

"Oi!" joked Banes. "One more thing," she said to Flint in a lowered voice, "why don't I try the other side of the castle. And get in the way I got out?" Surely the unicorn would let her in again?

"No." The commander raised her hand to put an end to that idea. "It's too risky. The king will no doubt be watching that area. Follow the orders given, Banes."

Banes nodded. "Yes, Commander Flint."

"Are you finished now?" asked Woodman.

"Yes," said Banes, and he lowered her down.

When they'd both straightened up, Woodman rolled his shoulders in a circular motion and mouthed the words "Thank you" to Banes. He'd noticed she'd saved him from going into the castle.

Banes passed him the iron file from her bag and Woodman assessed the bars. The commander thrust some of the straw from the floor of her cell through the bars. They stuffed it tightly into the empty weapons bag to give Woodman an inch or two of extra height.

"This is likely to take me all night," he said.

"Better start now then," said Banes, with a wink.

It was going to be strange undertaking the next part of the mission without Woodman, after getting used to working together. But, if all went well, she would be back with her comrades before long.

"See you soon," she whispered, and headed back in the

direction of the forest. It would take longer than walking around the castle, but she didn't want to arouse suspicion by appearing from the back. Instead, she would cut through wooded area and arrive from the front, like anyone else. She hadn't planned out how she was going to get in, but she knew she needed to do it before the jailer awoke.

THE WASHING BASKET

Banes hurried along the forest paths. She emerged on to the main road and walked straight through the city gates. The sun was low in the sky and stallholders in the marketplace had all packed up and gone home, evidence of the market strewn over the cobbles. It looked like any other city square, with no sign that a great protest had taken place just hours before, although a number of guards patrolled the streets.

Most folk seemed to be rushing home to their families or off to the city taverns but Banes passed a pair of women having a low conversation.

"They say it was near a hundred people he arrested this afternoon," said one, who was wide and short with a stained apron.

"Not all from outside, neither," said the other, taller one. "My neighbour's son was taken away just for standing with 'em in the crowd."

The first woman tutted, but when they noticed Banes, they stopped talking and waited for her to go past. She strode by, walking with purpose and her chin up, trying to show she hadn't been listening.

Two guards were positioned at the entrance to the castle. Banes would have to get past them. She steeled herself, thinking of all the other things she'd achieved in recent weeks that proved she was capable. She had left the inn weeks ago with a small bundle of possessions on her back. She had talked her way into the camp and convinced Commander Flint she was someone worth listening to. She had kidnapped the princess. It might have been a failed attempt, but at least she'd been brave enough to do it. So she should be able to convince a couple of dim-witted guards to let her into the castle. The commander had said she could get in *by some cunning means.* Banes decided to play on her strengths and do this the way she did everything else. She would talk her way in.

Banes found an old basket in the marketplace. The scraps of onion skin caught in the weave suggested it had once been used to transport vegetables. It was broken and rotting on one side, but for Banes's purposes, it would work well. She bundled up her bag and cloak, tucking them into the basket so they looked like a pile of washing. She held the basket close, with the broken weave close to her body to hide it. Then she strode boldly up to the gates.

As she approached, she assessed the two guards. The one on the right looked alert, and was standing with a straight back and his eyes set dead ahead. The other was scuffing the toe of his boot back and forth in the dusty ground, making a wide mark, scratching absent-mindedly at his upper arm as he did so.

Banes picked the daydreaming one. She walked in a straight, confident line towards him, waving cheerily. It took him a while to notice her, and as soon as he did, he glanced to his left and then his right to check she was waving at him.

"Good evenin'," she said, in a voice she hoped sounded local.

"Evenin'," he replied.

"It's Bert, isn't it?" she said, as if they were old friends.

He shook his head slowly. "Maurice."

"Maurice, of course! I'm Cassie. I know your cousin."

He thought for a moment. "Annabel?"

She breathed out. The risk seemed to be paying off. "Yes, good old Annie."

"She's only ten."

"Yes, but an old head on young shoulders, I've always said."

He stared blankly. "You know her from the village?"

"That's right. Anyway, I can't stay here all evenin' and chat – must get these linens to the servants' quarters before they have me strung up on the washing line myself! Hahaha!" She moved towards the doors with an expectant look and he opened them up for her.

"Thanks, Bert! I'll tell Annie you said hello!"

"It's Maurice," he reminded her. Banes waved a hand in the air and turned to stride into the castle. But another voice stopped her.

"You – where are you going?"

Banes turned with a smile, ready to relay her story once again, but she realized with horror that she recognized the other guard. It was one of the ones who had arrested Banes at the kidnapping: the younger one.

She lowered her head and began to fake a fit of coughing, keeping her face shielded from view. "Maurice … can you … explain?" she asked, between coughs.

The second guard narrowed his eyes suspiciously. Banes considered turning and running, but some more guards appeared from inside the castle, distracting both of those at the door.

"What are you doing here?" the younger guard asked.

"We've been told to watch the entrance with you," said one of the new guards. "Orders of King Jacob…"

An argument began about how there were only ever two guards on the gate, not four, and how they should go back to the dungeons. But Banes didn't wait around to find out how it would end. She slipped through the doorway, muttering, "Thank you very much," and marched as briskly as she could towards the servants' quarters.

As soon as she was out of sight, she turned off the main hall and looked for a staircase leading down.

BACK IN THE DUNGEONS

It didn't take Banes long to find her way down to the dungeons. Along the way, she discarded the broken basket, which had served its purpose, and pulled her hood back up over her face.

There was no one on duty at the top of the stairs. It seemed that those guards arguing at the door had left their posts and replacements had yet to arrive. What a stroke of luck. She raced down the dark stone staircase. Since leaving Woodman and the commander, she'd been as quick as she could, but she didn't know if it was quick enough. How long did a sleeping draught last? What if the jailer had awoken and discovered the weapons in Commander Flint's cell? Before she reached the bottom of the stairs, she stopped and listened. She could hear loud grunts and snorts, which informed her the jailer was still asleep. She followed the sound through the maze of corridors, as she knew he was outside the commander's door.

It was colder and darker down here than in the rest of the castle: a damp, forgotten place. Torches flickered in sconces at regular intervals, but the light was dim. And it was noisier. Unlike her previous trip here, the cells all seemed to be full now.

She passed the unicorn's cell. Was she still down here? Would anyone hear her cry? She was tempted to check but knew she must follow the commander's orders first.

The prisoners realized something was going on and most of their faces were at the door hatches, hands gripping the bars. In some places the cells seemed to be overflowing and numerous pairs of eyes peered out of individual hatches.

Some faces were unfamiliar, with blackened teeth and scars.

"'Ere! Lady! Where are you going? I'm 'ungry! Got any bread?"

It reminded her of the chickens squawking for their food that morning. She didn't reply, which made her feel bad, but she had no time to strike up a conversation. She would help them later. She tried not to make eye-contact but kept her head down as she hurried past. She recognized most of the faces from the camp but still didn't stop. With her hood pulled up, they didn't recognize her.

She reached the jailer on the floor – thankfully still motionless – and then she heard Ford's voice above the others. He was on the other side of the corridor to the commander.

"Banes! Banes!" Now that she'd stopped, he'd got a better look at her than the others. She turned to look at his door hatch. She'd only seen him the day before, but he looked different: desperation in his eyes. "Get me out of here, Banes, will you?"

"There's a plan – I promise," she said. "Let me find the commander and then I'll help."

Flint's face was at the door hatch. She looked so much more composed than all the other prisoners.

"Banes. You made it. Well done." She sounded pleased, but

not surprised, and once again, Banes felt a thrill that Commander Flint had faith in her.

A screeching, scraping sound echoed from behind the commander. Banes could see Woodman's hands and the file working away at the window bars. It must have been exhausting having his arms stretched above his head like that and it didn't look as though he'd made much progress.

"Shall we tell Woodman to stop now?" asked Banes.

The commander glanced over her shoulder and shook her head. "No. Until we are all free, it makes sense to have a back-up plan. Don't worry about Woodman. You find the key to my cell and get me out of here first."

Banes nodded and bent down beside the jailer. He grunted and shifted over on to his side and she sprang back in alarm.

"He's still asleep," said the commander, a little impatiently. "Get the keys."

Two iron rings, each holding multiple keys, hung off the jailer's belt and Banes's heart sank at the sight of them. There were so many – how would she ever know which was the right one?

"It's one of those smaller ones on the left-hand ring," said the commander, who must have been observing the jailer very closely. Banes tentatively unbuckled his belt and removed both keyrings. She approached Flint's door and tried the first couple of smaller keys in the lock, with no success. She wasn't sure if they were the wrong ones or if she was turning them the wrong way. Her hands were shaking, which didn't help. The commander tutted.

Banes tried the third key. "It won't budge," she cried, jiggling at the lock in frustration. She couldn't think any more. Her senses were overwhelmed: the smell of rusty iron, the loud squeaking of the file, and the prisoners shouting. She might hear footsteps in the corridor at any minute.

"Banes," said the commander, sharply. "Look at me."

Banes looked through the hatch.

"Keep calm. One of these keys will open this door. You just have to find it."

Banes nodded.

"Turn the key clockwise."

Banes took a deep breath, and inserted the fourth key in the lock, gently this time. To her great relief, the lock sprang open. She'd done it.

The commander smiled. "Well done, Banes," she said.

Banes opened the door, letting Flint out into the corridor.

To her surprise, the commander hugged her, pulling her to her briefly, then releasing her. "Well done," she repeated. "You are proving yourself to be my right-hand woman."

But the congratulations couldn't last long – they had to act. The commander brought out the pile of weapons Banes had passed through the bars and dropped them at her feet with a clatter. Then she knelt by the jailer. He had stopped snoring, which Banes hoped wasn't a sign he was about to wake up. She also hoped it wasn't a sign he was about to die.

"Will he wake up eventually?" asked Banes.

"He should do," said the commander indifferently. She unthreaded his belt and tied it around his wrists, then rummaged through his pockets. She removed two knives, which must have been confiscated from prisoners, and added them to the pile. "Choose a weapon," she instructed Banes.

Banes stared at the mismatched pile of swords and knives. Some were as long as her arm. She wouldn't know what to do with them and instead picked a small dagger with a carved hilt, which she tucked into her belt. She hoped she wouldn't have to use it.

"In which cell is the king's secret weapon? Do you remember?" asked Flint.

She meant the unicorn. Banes pointed to the cell at the other end of the corridor that she'd passed. "There is no lock or handle on the door, though. I don't know how we'll open it."

Commander Flint glanced towards the door. "We'll deal with it once everyone's free. Pass me the larger keyring."

Banes passed her the keys, her heart sinking a little, as she'd been looking forward to seeing the unicorn again. Still, she knew that Flint's plan made sense.

"Let's get to work," said the commander. "You have the smaller keys, which open the doors on the right-hand side. Mine are for those on the left. As you release people, send them here to choose a weapon."

Banes nodded.

"Over here," called Ford from inside his cell, which irritated Banes. She would have gone to his cell first anyway, as he was opposite. He didn't need to call out. She went through the same process as she had with the commander's padlock, but this time she had more faith in the keys to work. She tried to keep calm, which was difficult when Ford was so agitated. He had sweat on his forehead and was red in the face.

"Quickly!" he said.

Banes gritted her teeth. "I'm doing it as quickly as I can."

Luckily, it worked on the second attempt, and soon Ford and all his cellmates were out in the corridor choosing swords from the pile. Banes recognized most of them from the camp but there were one or two new faces. City folk, maybe.

When Ford had picked a suitable weapon, he walked straight to the door where the unicorn was held. He must have heard them talking about it. He pushed at the door and kicked it, puzzled to find no lock or handle. He gave up and walked away and Banes was pleased. She wasn't sure she liked the idea of him setting eyes on the unicorn, even if it would prove she hadn't been lying.

"There's no one in that cell. Here," she said, unthreading a couple of keys from the ring. "See which doors these fit. They will be on the right."

Ford did as she suggested. With three of them unlocking the doors, the corridor soon began to fill with rebels, delighting at their release and trying out weapons.

The commander called out instructions. "Once you have a weapon, move back so that others can reach the pile. There won't be enough for everyone. Pair up so that you're protected. When we're all free, I'll inform you of the next steps."

Banes moved on to the next cell, where Cobb was held. She'd

barely put the first key in the lock when she heard something, behind the shouting of the prisoners and the scraping of the file, that made her stop. The sound of footsteps on the stairs. Someone was coming.

CHAPTER THIRTEEN

BEDSHEETS

Marie

Marie's four poster was solid and heavy: it wasn't moving anywhere. She tied one end of the sheet-rope around a bed leg, and then gathered the rest of its length up in her arms, tugging it out of Twitch's grasp. She headed to the window and looked out. Apart from Blaze's call, which still reverberated through her, it was quiet out there. It usually was at this time, when everyone was settling down for the evening. But the streets seemed emptier than usual. She would have to trust they stayed that way.

If she threw the sheets as they were, they might blow about in the breeze or get caught on something. She looked around for something heavy to weigh them down. Her hairbrush was too light. The chair was too big. Twitch was now playing in Marie's bed, tangling himself in her covers, and that gave her an idea. The bedwarmer was still at the foot of her bed from the night before and it would be perfect. Twitch had pulled off the soft blanket Fern wrapped it in to keep Marie from burning her feet. It was no longer hot, of course. The domed copper pan, about the diameter of a dinner plate, had an iron handle on top. It was still full of coals, which made it heavy for its size.

Marie knotted the last bedsheet through the handle, and threw it from her window. There was a distant clang as it hit something – hopefully the ground. It was hard to see from her position quite where it had ended up.

She took a deep breath through her nose. She was committed now and she should act quickly before anyone appeared outside. Guards did occasionally walk past on patrol. If one of them did see her, she would have to have an excuse ready. What, exactly, she wasn't sure: she'd figure that out on the climb down.

THE DESCENT

Marie wasn't scared of heights. She had climbed plenty of trees in her forest days. Still, dangling out of a second-storey castle window held only by some knotted bedsheets was scarier than she'd imagined. She should have tested the knots with more than a quick tug. She hoped they held her weight until she'd at least crossed the second storey. A fall from halfway down might mean broken bones, whereas from up here, it was likely to mean death.

She squeezed her eyes shut, hanging there. Her heavy dress billowed out below her. Perhaps she should have changed into something more practical, but it was too late now. She'd made her decision and there was only one way to go. As she inched her way down, she kept her gaze up, counting the rows of brickwork above.

Somewhere in the middle of the descent, she began to find a rhythm – one hand under the other, feet bouncing against the castle wall, and she knew she had done it. She'd at least reached a height where it wouldn't be disastrous if she fell. She glanced down to the ground.

That was a mistake. She might have managed half the descent, but the ground was still a long way away. Her vision swam wildly and she had the unnerving feeling she was spinning, like one of the balls of thread she dangled in front of Twitch. For a moment, she felt she might let go, and jump, or fall, just to stop the sensation.

But she didn't fall. She shut her eyes again and waited for the worst to pass, then opened them and looked straight at the wall, careful not to glance down. Somehow she managed to find the bouncing rhythm that she had before, and climbed down the remaining length of the bedsheets. The makeshift rope didn't quite reach the ground. The clang she'd heard must have been the bed warmer hitting the castle wall. She swung there, a few feet up, the warming pan knotted at her feet.

The ground below looked reassuringly solid and she felt an overwhelming urge to be standing on its safe, flat surface. She would jump.

She'd seen Twitch perform similar manoeuvres from the shutters to the bedroom floor. She pictured her kitten, the way he sprang and landed lightly on his feet. Marie let go of the sheets and leaped to the ground like a cat.

The reality was much less graceful, with a more surprising impact than Marie had expected. Humans clearly didn't spring as well as kittens. Luckily, she hit the grass, but it was still with some force. She cried out, tumbled over on to her side and lay there for a moment.

When she'd recovered from the shock, she sat up, worried someone must have seen or heard her. But there was nobody around. She looked back up at her bedroom window and, for a moment, thought she saw someone there, but then the shadow vanished. She brushed herself down and raised herself, unsteadily, to her feet. Miraculously, she was unhurt. Better than that, she was free. But she wasn't going to head for the forest, the carpenter's cottage or run off into the fields.

While she'd been concentrating on her descent, the ringing sound had grown faint. But now, as she stood in the twilight and listened, it became clear. She shivered a little. The poor unicorn. Princess Marie knew she would do whatever it took to help. And she knew where to find the unicorn, forbidden or not. She set off straightaway to the dungeons.

CHAPTER FOURTEEN

FOOTSTEPS IN THE CORRIDOR

Banes

"Someone's coming!" Banes said, in a loud whisper. "Be quiet, all of you!"

Ford looked so panicked, Banes wondered if he might run, or do something else unwise to put them all at risk.

"Take your weapons and get back in the cells," ordered Commander Flint. Groups of men retreated as quickly as they'd flooded out, dozens packing into the bigger cells.

Flint ushered those nearest to her towards her own cell so that maybe ten of them stood together in the tiny room. Banes was between Ford and Flint, who pulled the door of the cell nearly shut and gripped her knife tightly, at shoulder height. Banes reluctantly copied the action.

The footsteps grew nearer, and Flint peeped around the door. "The princess!" she whispered, whipping herself back to safety. The blade of her knife flashed silver in the torchlight.

Banes gave the commander a silent, panicky look. The princess was not their enemy! She thought she'd made that clear to the commander that night in her tent. But Flint tensed, eyes focusing on the princess like a hawk eyeing its prey.

Marie was a few paces away down the corridor, staring into one of the cells. Her guard was down and she wouldn't stand a chance against a surprise attack. There would be no chance for her to call for help. And the commander was getting ready to spring out at her. Banes's heart thumped wildly as Flint began to push the door open. Without thinking too much about it, Banes shot out a hand and grabbed the commander's knife arm. "No, we can't!"

The commander shook off Banes's hand with such a look of outrage that Banes thought she might turn the knife on her.

"Why can't we?"

"The princess… She helped me. She's on our side, I think. And … she's Woodman's sister!"

Banes had never seen the commander look surprised and this moment was no exception. She paused, and lowered her knife.

"I see. Go on, then. Speak to her, Banes. But believe me, I will be listening, and if I have any suspicions whatsoever about this princess's loyalties then I won't hesitate to act."

Banes stepped out into the corridor, into Princess Marie's path.

"Oh!" cried the princess, stepping back, before stopping and realizing who it was. "Banes? I thought you'd gone – long ago."

Banes shrugged. "I had. But I'm back." There was no time for proper explanations. "What are you doing here, Princess?"

She smiled sheepishly and glanced towards the locked door – the unicorn's door. "I had a … feeling, I suppose." Her eyes were wide. Not for the first time, Banes thought how she looked young for her age.

"You can hear it too, can't you?" she asked. But Banes couldn't hear anything, apart from the sound of iron bars being filed.

Banes shook her head. "I can't hear anything presently. But I did – before." She felt strangely disappointed. Marie's connection to the unicorn must be stronger than her own.

But Marie put a hand on Banes's shoulder. "There is too much going on now. It has faded for me too. It only comes when you can listen – really listen." She glanced at the jailer's motionless body with a look of concern. "Is he...?"

"Sleeping," said Banes.

Then the princess noticed the open cell door. She stared at it and the door opened. Commander Flint stepped out towards them, and the princess gasped again. At least she wasn't brandishing her knife. She must have heard enough of their conversation to satisfy herself the princess was an ally.

"Princess Marie, please let me introduce my commander, Commander Flint."

The princess offered her hand, but as the commander was about to take it, something strange happened.

The filing stopped.

GUARDS

Woodman's filing had been going on for so long Banes had almost become used to the sound, and its sudden absence startled her almost as much as a loud bang. Then came Woodman's voice, somewhere between a whisper and a panicked shout. "Commander? Commander! Someone's coming out here!"

Flint tutted, then turned and called out to him. "Don't worry, Woodman. Keep your head down – they shouldn't see you—"

But her words were interrupted by a scuffle and a shout: Woodman's shout.

"Got you!" shouted another voice.

The commander dashed back into the cell and a cold feeling of dread ran through Banes like a shiver. Her eyes met Marie's, who was looking equally as concerned.

"Did the commander say Woodman?" she whispered.

Banes nodded.

"It's Wyll, isn't it? I think I recognized his voice."

Banes nodded again. "He told me," she whispered. "That he's your brother."

The princess's mouth fell open, and she shouted out, "Wyll!" in a piercing shriek that rang through the hollow corridors.

A SAFE PLACE

The guards had Woodman. One peered through the window into the commander's cell, her eyes and the top of her head just visible.

"You in there! What are you up to? The king is going to hear about this!"

It was unclear how much she could see from out there as it was growing dark, but the commander, as always, appeared completely unruffled.

"Listen," she said coolly, ignoring the guard. Marie seemed to be doing anything but listening, looking all around her and twisting her hands together. "Now they have Woodman, it will be a matter of minutes before they're down here. Ford, you get a move on and release anyone left in the cells." She threw him the keys. "Cotter, you tell everyone else to mobilize ready for an attack. The guards are coming and they need to be ready for them."

Banes thought suddenly of Maurice, the guard at the gate. He had seemed like a reasonable, not too frightening type. "What's the penalty for breaking a prisoner out of their cell?" she asked the commander.

"King Jacob will decide that, but given his past sentences, it's probably death."

"No, no, he couldn't..." whispered Marie. Banes patted her on the arm, partly to make herself feel better, but Flint looked at the princess as though she were an inconvenience. "Let's hope not," she said shortly, then she turned to Banes. "You, Banes, must escape with Princess Marie to a safe place."

"Why? I want to fight by your side!"

The commander lowered her voice, so that only Banes could hear. "Believe me, the time will come for fighting. Once we have freed as many prisoners as we can, we will find the unicorn and then face the king. At that point, we might find it beneficial to have the princess with us. We don't want to risk any harm coming to her in the meantime, and I trust you to keep her safe."

As usual, the commander's words made sense, and Banes felt flattered to have an important job.

"Very well," she agreed, "But where shall we find you afterwards? And when?"

"I can't know that, Banes. But we will be looking for King Jacob and the unicorn. You must do the same. Do you know where we are likely to find him, Princess?"

Princess Marie shook her head slowly. "On a normal day, the Great Hall, or his Strategy Room up in our private quarters, but with all this unrest, I don't know…"

The princess trailed off and Commander Flint turned away from her to check on the others. Ford was doing well with the locks (better than Banes had done herself). The corridor filled with the last of the comrades, all looking more stunned than the last time she'd seen them. Cotter was trying to make sure everyone was armed, or at least partnered with someone who was. There were enough of them, perhaps, to take on the king's guards. This was a good thing, because the narrow corridor was suddenly filled with the sound of many boots stomping down the stairs.

The commander turned and issued her order once again.

"Princess Marie, Banes, go now! We will hold the guards here."

The commander and Ford raced down the corridor and around the corner in the direction of the stairs, gathering the others with them as they went. Banes didn't know what their aim was. Perhaps they would hide in one of the now-empty cells and ambush the guards as the commander had tried to do with the princess.

Banes's only responsibility was to get herself and the princess to safety. This had sounded like the easy option, but now Banes looked around, she saw that escape routes were limited. They could get out via the stairs by which Banes had come, which would mean passing the guards. The alternative was to hide in one of the cells in the hope they could sneak out later, but Banes wasn't sure she wanted to risk that. Unless there was another way out, of course. Luckily, Banes was with one of the few people who knew the castle well enough to tell her that.

Marie was staring through the commander's cell, up at the iron bars. It was as if she was expecting her brother to appear there at any second. She must know that it wasn't to be. They had heard him, shouting at the guards, struggling, and then nothing. Wherever Woodman was, he wouldn't be coming to their rescue any time soon.

"I can't go without seeing my brother," whispered the princess. "It has been so many years. Now he is so close... What if they hurt him, Banes?"

Banes held her by the shoulders and spoke to her directly. "Princess Marie, we are of no use to Woodman here. If the guards find you with me, if they suspect that you are helping us, then you ... we ... could be in big trouble, do you understand?"

Marie nodded. "We can help him later," she said. "Maybe I can speak to my father..."

"Yes!" said Banes, pleased she was beginning to see sense.

Someone shouted around the corner. There was the clash of steel on steel. The guards had arrived.

Banes's heart raced. "We need to get out of the dungeons now. Is there any other way out, to save us going past the guards?

A secret doorway … or a tunnel or anything?"

Marie blinked and spoke clearly, as if she'd been listening all along.

"Of course there is. Stop. Listen, Banes. Can't you hear it?"

Banes couldn't hear anything other than the sound of fighting and shouting coming from further down the hallway. It didn't seem the time to stop and listen. But now she really tried, she wondered if she could hear something. A familiar, distant sound, like a bell.

"There is no secret passageway," said Marie. "This castle only holds one secret, which you discovered on your last visit."

Banes's heart leaped at the mention of the unicorn. She had helped Banes to escape before. Maybe she would do so again. "Do you think she will help us now?"

"There is only one way to find out," said Marie, and she took Banes by the hand.

BLAZE

Banes and Marie stood together in front of the impenetrable door, palms flat against it.

"How will we get in?" asked Banes. Last time she had followed the music, and found all the doors open for her. This time, the door appeared to be locked and Banes wasn't entirely sure she could hear the tune after all. Perhaps it was wishful thinking.

"It is the right time," said Marie. "Her magic is always at its most powerful at twilight."

"Is it?" Banes had barely thought about the time of day, but she supposed it had been twilight when she escaped. She'd been contemplating her first lonely night in the cell.

"Think about the unicorn. Try to hear her song."

Banes was still a little preoccupied with what was going on around the corner. The sound of swords clashing: metal on metal. A shout. A cry. The guards had arrived, but who was winning the fight?

But Marie had her eyes closed, listening, smiling, concentrating only on the unicorn. If the princess could hear her, then it must be possible for Banes too. She tried to block out all the other sounds from her mind and thought maybe she could hear a ringing sound. It was faint, but most definitely there.

"Blaze," whispered the princess, "please let us in."

"Blaze. Is that her name?" asked Banes. She'd never thought

to ask. Marie nodded as something inside the door clunked open and released beneath their hands. They pushed it open and stepped through into the cell.

A small part of Banes had wondered if she'd imagined the unicorn. When everyone had laughed at her and dismissed her story as fiction, she'd half-wondered if she'd invented the whole thing. Her encounter had felt like a dream, after all. Even when the commander and Woodman believed her, even when Marie had led her back to the cell door, it still felt like a beautiful daydream.

But now, as the door clicked shut behind them and she gazed into the blue eyes of the Blazing Unicorn, nothing had ever felt more real. There she stood, surrounded by flames, like the first time Banes saw her. Her black forehead mark contrasted with her bright white coat, her long horn glowed orange in the firelight, and her lips were parted as she sang her pitiful cry.

She and Marie exchanged excited glances. Banes stood back by the door, as she had done the last time, watching the flames flutter around the unicorn like a butterfly's wings. Marie displayed no such reticence. She walked right up to the unicorn, and, without flinching, reached her arms through the flames. She wrapped her arms around its neck, bringing her nose close to the creature's forehead. Then she stayed like that, as the fire died away.

"Blaze," she murmured, "how I've missed you."

Banes felt a little jealous at the sight. Something – not just the flames – had held her back before, but she wished she hadn't been so cautious. She joined Marie and put her hand on the unicorn's side. It felt warm and soft.

They rested like that for a moment, until Marie stood back to take a good look at the creature. "Oh, Blaze," she said. "What has he done to you?"

Banes followed her gaze and saw the poor creature was shackled by an iron chain from its foreleg to the wall of the cell. It was a long chain so she could move around the whole cell, but still, it was cruel. Banes wanted to rip it from the wall.

"My master was displeased with me and made his anger clear," said the unicorn.

Marie gasped. "Oh, I'm so sorry, it was all my fault." She turned to Banes to explain. "My woollen wrap was discovered here and I told my father I had given it to you."

"Oh no! I dropped it when I was climbing out ... so it was my fault."

"No, I should have come up with a cover story. It wouldn't

have been hard, but I'm not always the quickest thinker."

The unicorn looked from Marie to Banes, her silky mane rippling as her head swayed. "Neither of you have anything to feel guilty about. Nobody but my master put these shackles on my legs."

"Melt them away!" said Banes. "Like you did with the window bars. The magic dissolved them, didn't it?"

They all looked towards the bars which were solid and sturdy as ever, and the unicorn shook her head. "If my master wants me to be bound in irons then that is the way it must be."

Marie closed her eyes. "But I can't bear to see you this way. He is mistreating you."

Banes could see what Marie meant. As well as the shackles, the unicorn was thinner than the last time Banes had seen her. Now the bright flames had died away, it was clear her eyes and coat were duller. The same could also be said for Princess Marie.

"He will never treat me too badly," said the unicorn, in a reassuring tone. "He needs my magic too much for that. Yet I sometimes wonder if it might be better for everyone, for the people of Quessia, if I were to die and take his power with me."

"No!" cried Marie, and she flung her arms back around Blaze's neck.

A sudden loud thud on the door made them all jump. Fists, or feet knocking against the door, trying to get in.

"Where's the key?" asked a man's voice, muffled through the door. Ford, or one of the guards, Banes couldn't tell. She wondered what had happened out there, whether the rebels had defeated the guards, or the other way around.

There was a jangling and some hard-to-decipher muttering as the man searched for the key. He would soon discover the door had no lock, and no handle, even. As far as Banes knew, the only one who had ever opened it was the Blazing Unicorn, with her magic.

After a short while, the banging sound came again. This time, it sounded as if someone was throwing their whole weight at the door, trying to break it down.

Every time the thump came, the sparse contents of the cell shook. Banes looked at Marie in alarm and saw her expression mirrored in her eyes, although the unicorn stood still and proud as ever before.

"Blaze, we need your help," said Marie. "Father locked me in my chambers and he will be so angry if he finds I am here.

I think that is the guards outside now, after us. My brother is out there somewhere, too, and he's in trouble. Please help us to escape."

The unicorn bowed her head. "I would love to help you, but I may grant only the wishes of my master."

Banes and Marie both nodded. They understood that. But still, Banes's heart sank a little. The unicorn had rescued her before and her hopes had been high that she would do so again.

"However, it is not safe for me in this cell," said the unicorn. "My master told me if ever I sense his enemies approach, then I must get myself to safety."

"If it's the rebels, they don't mean you any harm," said Banes.

"They mean to take me and use me for their own purposes," said the unicorn.

"No, not this time. They only want to stop you helping the king."

"They may say that, but in the end, people always want me for their own purposes. Besides, the only way to stop me helping the king is to take my life or his."

Marie winced and Banes wasn't sure if she was reacting to the thought of the rebels killing her father or the unicorn. Both, perhaps.

"I am sure they mean me harm," said the unicorn, "and I must find a way to keep myself safe."

Without warning, the blaze began around the unicorn once again. From within the flames, she stretched out her left foreleg, and lowered the point of her horn to the iron band secured above her fetlock. Blaze's horn shone brightly and the black iron ring glowed white and red as if it had been plunged into the blacksmith's forge. Banes stared as it dissolved away before her, as the bars of the cell had done on the evening of her escape.

Blaze shook her leg. The flames disappeared and the chain clinked on to the floor like a discarded necklace.

The banging on the door continued. Banes looked up at the window and wondered if Blaze was going to dissolve the bars as she had before.

But instead, Blaze moved to the wall on the opposite side to the door. Starting at the floor, she drew a large oblong shape with the point of her horn. A line of fire followed and cut through the stone itself. Inside the blazing line, the stone shifted and swung open into the cell, as if it were a door.

And in front of them, a doorway leading to a staircase emerged. This staircase was unlike any other that Banes had ever seen. It appeared to be made from fire, each step blazing in the way the unicorn had done.

"I must find my master now," said Blaze, and she stepped through the door, on to the stairs.

Banes and Marie both peered at the fiery staircase, and at each other.

"May we follow you, Blaze?" asked Marie.

The unicorn blinked. "If you choose to follow me, then I cannot stop you."

Now Banes understood. The unicorn was providing them with an escape route after all but without breaking her ties of loyalty to her master.

Marie went first, seemingly not worried about her long gown on the flaming steps, just as when she'd put her arms into the fire to embrace the unicorn. She was braver than one would expect. Banes swallowed, looking cautiously at her feet. A few weeks ago, stepping on to a staircase made of fire would have seemed preposterous. But things had changed, and she was beginning to get a sense of the unicorn's magic. Besides, Marie was climbing the stairs quite happily, as though they were made of marble.

Banes stepped through the opening. The stone wall began to close behind her, at exactly the same time as the door to the cell banged open. In that split second before the stone became wall again, she saw a group of figures crash into the room, but not for long enough to identify them. She had no idea if Woodman was in their number, or the commander.

Then the wall closed fully behind her and it was just Banes, a magic unicorn, a princess, and some stairs made of fire.

THE FIERY STAIRCASE

Although the stairs looked insubstantial, like flames blazing in a hearth, they were reassuringly solid beneath her feet. They were not even hot. This was the unicorn's magic. Blaze had helped her before and Banes trusted now that she wouldn't be leading them into danger.

The steps led up, for long enough that Banes, who normally had boundless energy, grew out of breath. She didn't talk to Marie, just followed her footsteps and tried to concentrate on the stairs themselves, which were a constantly changing mass of colour: orange, red and yellow. Shapes danced in them, as they would in a real fire, and they crackled and spat as if logs were burning beneath. Other than that, there was a soft silence.

The stairs twisted to the left and then seemed to turn back on themselves. The three climbed steadily until Banes guessed they must have reached the top floor of the castle. Finally, there were no more stairs and Blaze stopped at a stone wall. Once again, she bent her head and traced a fiery shape with her horn. Another magic doorway, this time leading into the castle itself.

THE PLAYROOM

They emerged from the opening into a strange room, lined with shelves and models. Miniature houses, trees and even Quessia castle itself. Banes had no idea what such a room was for, but it couldn't be the servants' area. Unless Banes was mistaken, they were inside the royal family's private quarters. Behind her, the opening closed shut, as it had done down in the dungeons.

Marie paled. "We're in Father's Strategy Room."

"*Strategy* Room? It looks more like a playroom," said Banes, although she couldn't help but feel a little impressed by the room's high ceiling and the thick drapes at the window. She ran her hand along one of the counters and picked up a little soldier figure.

"Don't touch that!" The look of horror on Marie's face made Banes put the model straight back. "Don't touch *anything*," she exclaimed. Then she turned to the unicorn, who in this room was looking somehow smaller.

"We can't be found in here. My father would kill us both." Marie said this as though it were fact, not an exaggeration.

The unicorn lifted her head and fixed her blue eyes on the princess. "Don't worry, Mistress Marie. King Jacob is elsewhere. But I advise you to go to your bedchamber as quickly as possible before he returns."

"Won't you come with us?"

The unicorn bowed her head towards them. "No. I must await my master. But I wish you well and I know we will see each other again soon."

Marie flung her arms around the unicorn's neck and whispered her goodbyes. Banes still didn't feel she knew the creature well enough to do that, so she simply lifted a hand in farewell.

They left the room, Banes careful not to touch or knock into anything on the way out, and exited at one end of a long corridor.

"This way," said Marie, setting off at some speed. Banes raced down the corridor after her. It had stone walls, stone floor with scarlet runner, and a few royal portraits on the walls. Banes noted that there were no other doors. If the king, or anyone else they wanted to avoid, came in the other direction, then there was nowhere to hide. They turned a corner into another corridor: one with numerous doors.

"It's like the dungeons all over again up here," whispered Banes. "Just nicer, and cleaner."

Marie took her lightly by the arm. "My rooms are down here."

MARIE'S ROOM

"Thank goodness the key is in the lock," said Marie as they reached the brass-handled door.

Banes nodded. It had to be a good sign, for if anyone had discovered Marie's absence, they would surely have left the door unlocked. Marie turned the key and left it in the keyhole as she opened the door. "I don't seem to have been found out. Even if my father returns now, he won't realize I escaped."

"You were really locked in?" Banes had heard Marie tell the unicorn earlier but she could hardly believe it. Whatever her own family had been like, and they had been difficult at times, they would never have locked her away.

"Yes," said Marie. "Father suspected I had sympathies for the rebels." She gave a wry smile.

"So how did you get down to the dungeons?"

"I took a different route."

Marie began to open the door very slowly and carefully. Banes wasn't sure why, as she thought they were in a hurry, but then she saw a little white paw snaking its way around the door as if to pull it open.

"Twitch!" said Marie, then she turned to Banes. "Get ready to grab him if he runs out – my father will be furious if he escapes."

Banes adopted a kitten-catching position, crouching with arms outstretched, but luckily it wasn't necessary. Marie was able to sidle in, scooping up Twitch as she went. Banes followed, gazing around at the bedchamber. It was an enormous space – you could have fitted ten of her tents in it. The bed itself was a heavy four-poster, five times the size of her own, with soft cushions and pillows piled upon it.

Banes threw herself down on to the bed and stretched out her arms, enjoying the feeling of the soft mattress catching her. She'd never slept on a featherbed like this one. Even back at the inn, where she'd lived in relative comfort, her mattress was filled with straw.

"Wow! When you said you had been locked in your bedroom, I felt almost sorry for you, but this is quite something. I could be locked in here for a few months without getting too unhappy."

Marie looked around, as if seeing the place for the first time.

"Yes, I am very lucky." Her voice was joyless. She nuzzled Twitch's fur and he wriggled to be set free, so she released him on to the soft rug. He rubbed around Banes's legs, interested to meet a new person, and Banes sat up and stroked his back gently. She looked around. On the dresser by the window stood a silver tea tray, set with a teapot and a light meal.

"Is that a tea tray I spy? Are there any of those little bread rolls or jam tarts going spare?"

Marie span around. "Oh no! It *is* the tea tray."

"This is a problem?"

"Yes! No! Perhaps. It means Fern has been here."

"Fern?"

"My maid. She has made the bed, too!"

"Is she trustworthy?"

"I think so, but she is frightened of my father. If he asked her about me then I don't know what she'd say."

Marie hurried to the window, where a whole bundle of bedsheets were discarded in the corner. Untidy behaviour from the maid, thought Banes. Twitch followed and crawled under the sheets, rolling and tumbling beneath them so just the shapes of his paws were visible as ever-shifting bumps. Banes laughed but Marie seemed to be distracted by the sheets, lifting them up from the floor and running her hands along their length.

"What are you doing?" she asked Marie.

"Somebody untied them from the bed," she said, her face pale.

"Untied them?"

"Yes, this end was tied to the bedpost and the other end was draped out of the window."

Banes didn't know what she was talking about, unless the princess had been drying her sheets out of the window, which was a job she would have expected the staff to do. Then she saw Marie was untying a large, tight knot. She looked at the crumpled bed and back to the tied-together sheets, and something clicked.

Banes's eyes widened. "Was that your ... escape rope?"

Princess Marie nodded. She was certainly not a typical princess.

"I was going to pull it in before anyone had a chance to see it, but someone has done that already. I do hope it was Fern and not Father."

"I'm sure it would have been your maid. The tea tray is proof she was here, after all."

Marie perched on the end of the bed. "I suppose you're right."

"So, about that tea…" said Banes.

"Help yourself, although it is likely to be cold by now."

Banes didn't need to be asked twice. She jumped up and poured a cup of cold tea into the glass beaker on the tray. "Would you like some?" she asked, but the princess declined. Banes took a sip. It was sweet: barley tea with honey, and she drank it in thirsty gulps. Banes was used to drinking from a wooden or leather cup but she liked this glass; the water tasted cleaner. She also helped herself to some slices of cheese, oatcakes and grapes. Delicious. Not quite as tasty as the jam tarts but she decided not to mention that.

Banes finished the tea and put the glass on the bedside cabinet, picking crumbs from her lap. The princess was deep in thought. It was funny, but the longer Banes looked at Marie, the more she saw the family resemblance to her older brother. She and Woodman looked different but they shared some features and mannerisms: their colouring, the way they raised their eyebrows. Banes could hardly believe she hadn't made the connection when she'd first set eyes on Marie.

"You are worrying about him – about Woodman – aren't you?"

The princess nodded. "I knew the guards had him. I shouldn't have run away. I should have revealed myself and told them who he was."

"But then the guards might have taken him to your father. The whole mission would have been compromised."

"Better than hurting him. He could be dead. If he's dead then it's my fault."

"Of course it isn't your fault." If anything, Banes thought, it was her fault. Originally the commander had wanted Woodman to come into the castle and Banes to file away at the bars. If they'd done it that way around then she would be the one captured now, but she'd made him swap. Still, thinking like that was unhelpful. They had to be positive. "We have no reason to suspect he is dead," said Banes. "We don't know what is happening down there."

The princess sighed. "I know. It's just been so long since I've seen him." There was a pause. "He told you about me? About our father?"

"Well, yes, but only because I was holding an awl to his throat at the time."

"You tried to kill him?"

"No! Just threaten him. I knew he was up to something. It was the only way I could get him to speak."

"But you're friends again now?"

"*Friends?*" spluttered Banes. She thought about how he'd opened up to her about his carpentry (before the awl incident), about their walk to the castle from the cottage, about laughing and joking as she climbed on his back to get through the window. Then she thought how she'd feel if she never saw him again. Tears pricked sharply at her eyes. "Yes, Woodman and I are friends," she said.

She and Marie smiled at each other, but a sudden rattling sound in the lock shocked the smiles from their faces.

Someone was at the door.

It sounded as though they were trying to unlock it, but actually locking it by mistake.

Marie grabbed hold of Banes by the upper arms, panic in her eyes.

"It could be anyone. It could be my father! Quick – hide!"

"Where?"

"In here." Marie pulled her into her dimly-lit dressing room. Banes barely had time to notice what was in there, although she saw a bathtub in one corner and clothes everywhere. "Hurry!" said Marie. She parted some dresses hanging on a rail and pushed Banes into the gap. It smelled of old perfume and dust. Banes coughed. Then Marie pulled the dresses back across, fluffing out the long skirts so Banes was in the dark.

"Marie? Marie?" boomed a man's voice from the bedroom area.

"Coming, Father," said the princess, the shake in her voice noticeable.

So it was King Jacob. The commander had told her to find the king and here he was, in the room next door. Banes edged forward a little in her hiding spot so she could hear what they were saying. She didn't want to miss a thing.

CHAPTER FIFTEEN

DRESSING UP

Marie

"Coming!" called Marie, stepping out of the dressing area into the bedroom. "Hello, Father. I was … tidying up."

The king stood by her dressing table, looking awkward and out-of-place amongst her beautiful things. Twitch retreated under the bed, remembering this was a person he didn't trust.

Marie tried to read her father's face but it was neutral. She hoped her hunch was right and this was the first time he'd checked in on her since locking her in.

"Why was your door unlocked?" he asked, abruptly.

Marie felt herself flush. "Oh, was it? Fern came to my room earlier with some tea. She was confused to find the door locked. She must have forgotten to lock it on her way out."

The king made a nondescript grunting sound and Marie added, "It's nearly time for the supper tray now," as an afterthought, just for something to say.

King Jacob paced around her room, looking vaguely at various items and fully opening her shutters at the window. Marie tried very hard not to look towards her dressing room. She hoped Banes had stayed in her hiding place.

"I am not here to discuss supper trays," said the king, still pacing. "Some prisoners have escaped and I was checking on your safety."

"Oh dear," said Marie. She swallowed and trying to appear concerned. He knew about the prisoners, then, but did he know about Wyll? She thought not. He would surely be angrier and confront her on the matter. "I am quite well. I have seen nothing."

"I wonder if that is true," said the king, looking out of the window. Marie eyed the crumpled pile of bedsheets in alarm, hoping her father didn't notice them and realize what she'd been doing.

Suddenly, from the direction of the dressing room came a crash, which sounded like a wagon had driven into it. What was Banes doing in there?

"What was that?" asked the king, turning sharply.

"The ... cat..." said Marie, glancing inadvertently at Twitch, who was still under the bed, eyes bright. "My fault. I was tidying up my shoes and I left the storage chests in a wobbly tower—"

"—Very well," said the king, interrupting her talk of shoes. "I am going to see what else the guards can tell me about these escaped prisoners. Stay here for your own safety. I will be back. Keep your eye on what is happening outside and you can report back to me when I return."

He left, closing the door firmly behind him.

"You can trust me – you don't have to lock the door," she called. "If you leave it open then I can find you if I see anything suspicious."

But her father seemed not to hear, and she heard the key turning in its lock. She was trapped again, although this time she had company.

Marie ran to the dressing room. It did look as though a wagon had crashed in there. At least three chests had been knocked over, scattering an assortment of hats, gloves and masquerade masks.

Banes stood in the midst of the chaos, in a pair of buttoned boots that looked about three sizes too big, and a green velvet gown that drowned her in fabric. She swished the fabric around her and held her arms over her head. "What do you think?"

Marie couldn't believe Banes's audacity. "What are you doing? My father could have found you."

"I couldn't hear properly behind those dresses. Besides, he'd never have found me in here." Banes held up an elegant butterfly masquerade mask in front of her and peeped through the eyeholes. "There are too many disguises!"

In spite of herself, Marie laughed and tied on a black cat mask of her own. She made some cat noises and Twitch soon came in to see what all the noise was about. He jumped straight into the interesting pile on the floor, in search of ribbons and sequins.

Marie eyed the clothes Banes was wearing. "You know, you could wear something of mine – something a little less extravagant than that frock. It might help you blend in. If you were discovered, then you could claim to be a member of court or a servant. My father has so many staff he'd never know them all."

"Ooh, good idea. How about this … or these?" Banes picked

up another mask, this one with giant feathers, and some crushed velvet gloves.

Marie raised an eyebrow. "*Less* extravagant, I said!"

She pushed her dresses along the rail and lifted out a plain blue one with a simple skirt, similar to the one she was wearing herself.

"This one's a little short for me and you could gather it with an apron to make it fit around the middle. Here, let me help."

They wrestled Banes from the velvet green gown and into the more practical frock. She smoothed it down and Marie found an almost matching ribbon in the pile on the floor.

"Here," she said, sweeping back Banes's hair from her face with the ribbon, and tying it in a bow at her temple. "You have lovely thick hair," she said, not commenting on its short and unruly style.

"That's what Frederick Fogg thought," said Banes.

Marie raised a quizzical eyebrow but Banes just laughed. "A story for another time."

They checked in the looking glass together and decided that Banes could blend in well enough. Then they picked up the scattered garments and began putting them back into some kind of order.

"When do you wear all these things, anyway?" asked Banes.

"I don't," said Marie, looking wistfully at a deep red dress with beading on its bodice. "I stick to the same three or four plain gowns. We never have balls or banquets as other royal families do. I never see anyone at all, apart from my father and the castle staff."

"Can't you request a royal ball? Demand one! You are a princess, after all."

Marie shook her head. "My father would never allow it."

Banes couldn't understand the princess. On the one hand she seemed so brave. She barely registered shock when Banes had tried to kidnap her, and she'd climbed down the castle wall on her bedsheets. But on the other hand, she seemed so frightened of her father, and so unable to stand up for herself.

"If life with the king is so difficult, then why didn't you leave? Before you were locked up, I mean. You must have had so many opportunities."

Princess Marie picked up the red dress and twisted the velvet in her hands, crushing and uncrushing it repeatedly. "I kept … keep hoping Wyll will return. I thought if he did, and Father could forgive him, then there was a chance for us to be happy together as a family. Like before, when my mother was alive."

Banes felt unexpected tears pricking at her eyes, and turned away. According to Woodman, Jacob had never been a pleasant man, even in those old days that Marie remembered. But Banes knew what it was like to look back on those happy times – to want to go back to when life seemed simple. But that was impossible. For Marie and for her.

"Those times have gone now," said Banes gently. "If you are planning to live a full life then it cannot be in the past. There is only the future and you choose what that looks like."

They left the dressing room in some sort of order and returned to the main bedroom. This time, Marie sat on the bed and Banes stood by the dressing table, twisting at the waist and holding her new skirt out at the sides.

"My father is too powerful," said Marie, sadly. "Also, I can't leave Blaze. You saw her. He is mistreating her. She is already a changed animal and if it goes on like this, she will fade away to nothing."

Banes stopped swishing. "That is why you have to help us. Don't you see? The commander wants to take the unicorn away from your father. That way, his source of power will be weakened."

Marie could see why the rebels wanted to do this. She too

was worried about her father's actions. But she wasn't sure they were going about things the right way.

"Are you sure your commander knows what she is doing? We can't just take Blaze away. She is not a treasure to be stolen."

Banes smiled. "Commander Flint knows exactly what she is doing. Your brother trusts and respects her. We all do. Blaze will be safe."

Marie sighed. She wanted to help but she was worried the rebels were deluded in their mission, especially the commander.

"It will never work, you know. Whatever you do to Blaze – lock her up – hide her away – she will be loyal to him. It doesn't matter what she wants for herself; she is controlled by the magic."

Banes sat down next to Marie. "But wasn't she once loyal to *you*? Weren't you the one that found her?"

"I was, but I was foolish: I wished the unicorn would help my father, and in doing so, I gave away my powers."

Banes nodded. "Then that's what we have to do. We must somehow persuade your father to give his powers away. And you are the perfect person to do it."

THE BRASS HAIRPIN

Banes was right. If anyone could talk her father around or trick him into giving Blaze's power away, it was her, his own daughter. This way, nobody, not even her father, needed to get hurt and they could find Wyll, and everything would be well. Surely that would be better than trying to take Blaze by force, as Commander Flint planned.

But that was easier said than done when they were trapped away in a locked room with the rebels and the guards fighting downstairs. Marie and Banes sat in silence for a little while, both trying to think of the best thing to do next.

"I like your cat," said Banes, stroking Twitch from head to tail and laughing as he arched his little back in response.

Marie unpinned her brooch and handed it to Banes, wiggling it this way and that, sending a beam of light up to the ceiling. "Try this," she said. "It's his favourite game."

"You mentioned this brooch out in the forest," said Banes.

Twitch recognized it and was on alert, eyes wide, little paws stretched out. Banes directed the light on to the floor, and he pounced on it instantly. She laughed and did it again. Marie tried to smile with her, but found she couldn't, and that the tears were welling up again. All she could think about was Wyll and Blaze and the mess they were all in.

"I'm sorry," she said, her voice shaky, "but I can't sit here and pretend that everything's normal. We need to find my father, and Blaze. I need to talk to him."

Banes handed back the brooch. "Commander Flint did tell me to keep you safe for now."

Marie blinked back her tears. "It's not safe to keep me in a locked room, and it will be even less safe if my father realizes we've been collaborating. You need to help me get out of here."

Banes thought for a moment and smiled. "That's what we'd better do, then!" She glanced to the pile of crumpled sheets by the window. "How did you find the bedsheet rope method?"

Marie remembered the lurch of her stomach when she'd been foolish enough to look down. "I don't think I'd like to repeat the experience unless absolutely necessary."

Banes jumped up and paced around the room. "What other options do we have?"

Marie shrugged. Banes tried the door, then felt her way around the room, presumably searching for loose floorboards, secret doors and who knows what else. She even looked up the chimney.

"What are you hoping to find up there?" asked Marie.

"A way out," said Banes, "but I'm not sure we'd both fit."

Banes would, thought Marie. Banes was tiny. But it would never work anyway. "All the fires will be lit at this time," she said.

Banes went back to the door again, rattling the handle and looking through the keyhole. "I know what to do!" she announced.

Marie brightened. "What?" She was so glad that this time she was not on her own. Escaping was much more fun with two, and there were so many new ideas.

"Do you have a hairpin, or anything like that?"

Marie removed the hairpin from her hair. She had a feeling she knew what Banes was going to suggest.

"We can push the key out of the lock, catch it on something flat, and bring it back through the gap under the door," Banes announced, in the voice of a genius. She went looking for a flat item and returned with the silver tea tray.

Marie frowned. She didn't like to tell Banes this plan had already failed once.

"What's wrong with my spectacular idea?"

"Nothing. It's just I tried it earlier and it didn't work."

Banes grinned. "You didn't have *me* here earlier." She slid the tray under the large gap at the bottom of the door. "Now hand over the hairpin."

Marie passed her the hairpin without much hope.

"Are you sure I should use this?" asked Banes, examining the shining bronze pin, which had some greenish stone, possibly emerald, clasped in a clawlike fitting at its head. "It looks rather ornate."

Marie shrugged. "It's all I have."

Banes bent down so the keyhole was at eye-level and wiggled the pin in the lock, in much the same way as Marie had done earlier. But, this time, after a few seconds, a clunk sounded from the other side of the door as the key hit the tray. Banes straightened up triumphantly, holding half a hairpin. "Sorry," she said, but Marie shrugged and smiled. Banes crouched down and wiggled her fingers under the gap at the bottom of the door.

"Now, all we have to do is bring the tray back…"

Banes moved her hand in the way Twitch did when he was pawing at the carpet, and the tray duly appeared through the gap.

It was empty.

"Oh," she said.

"But I heard it hit the tray. It must have bounced off." Marie joined Banes at floor-level, then lay down on her stomach, so she could get a good look under the door.

The two of them lay like that for a few moments, their legs stretched out behind them.

Through the large gap, they could see torchlight reflecting off the tiny brass key, which was a good arm's length away: tantalisingly out of reach.

"There must be a way," said Banes.

"The poker! That was what I was going to use before." Marie sprang up to her feet and ran to the fireplace to fetch it.

She examined the weight and length of it as she walked back towards the door. "I'm not sure it's going to reach," she said. "It will fit through the gap but will it—"

Marie stopped when she saw Banes was sitting up, pointing to the gap under the door, with wide, urgent eyes. "Feet!" she whispered.

FEET

Banes rushed back to her hiding place in the dressing room. Marie returned the poker to its stand by the hearth, then smoothed her skirts down, attempting to look natural. She couldn't remember what she was usually doing when people arrived unexpectedly at the door.

The key rattled in the lock, pushing out the hairpin-half, which fell to the floor inside the room. *Please not Father again*, thought Marie. She had no idea how she'd explain away the key on the floor or the tea tray.

But when the door swung open, she saw it was Fern. Lovely Fern. Marie had never been so happy to see her.

Fern wasn't looking quite so happy herself.

"Your 'ighness," she said, bobbing her usual curtsey. "There was a key, and a tray, on the floor outside your door, Ma'am."

"How peculiar," said Marie, raising her eyebrows high.

Fern raised her eyebrows back at the princess, in an expression that suggested she wasn't that easily fooled. "Yes. I put the key back in the lock. 'Ere's the tray." She waved it at Marie, and it was only then the princess realized Fern didn't have her supper tray. At this time of the evening she would usually lay out another light meal, but she had nothing with her at all. She shifted restlessly from foot to foot and kept looking over her shoulder.

"Is everything well with you, Fern?" asked Marie.

Fern shook her head. "There is some unrest down in the castle, Ma'am."

Marie's heart beat fast. "Unrest. Is there?"

The maid nodded. "A group of protestors were arrested today. Some outlaws from the forest but some locals, too. Some'ow, they've all managed to escape from the dungeons. Like your kidnapper did," she added, knowingly. "They're saying it's a rebellion, against the king, Ma'am."

There was a lot Marie wanted to know, but she wasn't sure which question to ask first. "The rebels – have you seen them? Is there a young man with them, with sandy hair?"

Fern wrinkled her brow. "I'm not sure you quite understand, Ma'am. There are a lot of people down there. I wouldn't know if they had sandy or sky-coloured hair – I tried to give 'em as wide a berth as possible."

Marie nodded. "I'm sorry – the servants – I should have asked. Are they all safe in their quarters?"

"They've gone, Ma'am. Most of them. Some fled the castle as soon as things got 'eated. Others … well, they're fighting, Ma'am. Against the guards."

So it was really happening. Marie wondered if Banes could hear this from her hiding place. Was she pleased? Marie didn't know how she felt herself; all she could think about was Wyll.

Fern's anxious face seemed to be looking to her for answers. "What about you, Fern? You didn't fight or flee."

"No, Ma'am. I was worried about you. I knew you were locked in up 'ere ... or I thought you were ... and I worried for your safety."

"Thank you, Fern, for being a true friend." Marie reached out and hugged the maid, leaving her flushed in the face. "If things are dangerous out there for you, then you can wait here in my dressing room."

"Thank you, Ma'am. Much appreciated."

"You will be alone, though. We have to go and speak to the king."

"*We*, Ma'am?"

"My kidnapper is here with us. Banes!" called Marie, and Banes looked cheerfully around the doorframe of the dressing room.

Fern nearly leaped out of her shoes. "Your *kidnapper*, Your 'ighness?"

Banes laughed and walked into the main room. "Don't worry, you're all safe with me!"

"Banes is a friend, Fern. There's no time to explain, but she's on our side. Now, you hang on to the key, but lock it from the inside this time. Only open it for us. I'll call through the keyhole on our return. We should be back before too long. I hope."

Fern looked at Marie with wide eyes and shook her head. "No, Ma'am."

"I'm sorry?" Marie looked quizzically at her maid. This was the first time in five years she'd responded with anything other than a curtsey and a nod of her head.

"It's kind of you to allow me to stay here, Ma'am, but I don't want to be on my own. I'd rather come with you, wherev'r you're going. And to help, if I can."

Marie studied Fern's expression. Her chin jutted out defiantly. She looked proud and determined. Marie had always thought there was more to her than might first be apparent. "Very well, Fern. Banes, Fern will accompany us."

"The more the merrier," said Banes with a grin.

Marie opened the door a crack and checked to see if anyone was about. "The corridor's clear," she said.

Fern smiled shyly. "Where are we going?"

"To King Jacob's Strategy Room." said Marie. "We're going to take my father's powers away before anyone else gets hurt, and then we're going to find my brother."

All three left Marie's room. Banes, unlike the other two, didn't live in a castle, and was less used to the concept of doors and closing them behind her. Her current accommodation was a tent in the forest, after all. So she swung the door semi-closed but didn't push it shut. Marie had so much on her mind, she didn't think to check behind her as she always did. So they headed down the corridor, with a shaft of light shining out after them from behind the open door.

CHAPTER SIXTEEN

LISTENING FROM THE CORRIDOR

Banes

Banes walked along the corridor for the second time, this time taking in her surroundings as they walked. The deep red runner lining the stone floor provided softness and warmth beneath her feet. The thick wall-hangings too, made the place feel cushioned from the outside world. One could stay cocooned in this place for ever, and ignore any suffering outside the castle walls. That seemed to be King Jacob's method, yet his daughter had chosen to open her eyes. Banes respected her for that.

They turned left at the end of one corridor and then walked

all the way to the end of the next and stopped outside the door to the Strategy Room.

Marie turned and spoke in a low voice. "If there is unrest downstairs then I believe my father will have fled back up here."

"Shall we come with you?" offered Banes, but the princess shook her head.

"I will do this alone. But be ready! If I need you, I will call."

Marie knocked three times on the door, her knuckles making a sharp rapping sound which echoed through the quiet corridor.

A deep voice called out from within. "Who is it?"

So Marie was right. Her father was inside.

"It's Marie, Father. May I come in?" Marie's voice was higher than usual.

"Are you alone?"

There was a pause. Marie glanced at Banes and Fern. Fern shrank back against the wall as if to make herself invisible. Banes nodded towards her, silently willing her on.

"Yes, Father," said Marie in the same high, strained voice.

"Enter," came the response.

Marie looked once more at the two of them waiting and Banes mouthed, "Good luck." Then, with a rustle of skirts, Marie walked through the doorway of the Strategy Room. She closed the door behind her, leaving the pair of them waiting outside.

Banes listened.

"Can you hear anything?" she whispered to Fern. The maid shook her head. Eyes wide, cheeks pale, she looked petrified and Banes felt for her. Banes wasn't sure herself how Marie planned to take Blaze from the king. She liked Marie, but the princess seemed so completely under the influence of her father, Banes wasn't sure she would find the strength to stand up to him.

Banes tiptoed to the door and pressed her ear against it.

"Careful! We don't want His Majesty to hear us," whispered Fern. Banes gave her a reassuring smile. She was going to be very careful not to alert anyone to her presence. Banes closed her eyes and strained to hear what was taking place inside the room.

"Hello, Father." Marie's voice rang out clearly and Banes wondered if she was speaking extra-loudly for her benefit.

"What are you doing here? I told you to stay in your quarters." The king's voice was also loud, with a threatening edge to it. Banes had never seen the king but she pictured him as tall and strong-jawed, sitting on a throne with a heavy jewel-laden crown.

"I ... one of the servants let me out..."

Outside, Fern's eyes widened. "No!"

Marie continued, "...but you mustn't be angry. She did it for my own safety. This is why I am here, Father. There is unrest within the castle. Those escaped prisoners are fighting the guards."

"I am perfectly aware of that!" exclaimed the king.

"Yes, Father."

"You think I don't *know* what is happening within the walls of my own castle?"

"No, Father. I mean, I'm sure you do. But there was one more thing I thought I should tell you…"

"Yes? Out with it!"

Marie lowered her voice so Banes could only just hear. For a minute Banes thought she was going to turn them both in. Surely not! She trusted the princess. Still, Banes's hand closed around the handle of her knife, tucked away in the pocket of her dress. She was ready to … she didn't quite know what. Her one weapon, a dagger with a stubby blade, was not going to be much protection against an all-powerful king with endless wishes.

But she didn't have to test out the theory. The princess said, "The unicorn. I went down to the dungeons and the unicorn is not in its cell."

Fern's eyes widened again, like Marie's kitten. Confirmation that the unicorn's presence was not well-known throughout the castle. Banes gave a small nod, to tell her, yes, it was true, and

Fern looked up and down the corridor, perhaps expecting the unicorn to emerge from one of the doorways. Banes wondered why Marie was saying this. She knew where Blaze had gone: they had walked up the fiery steps together not even an hour before.

From inside the room, came the king's voice again. "I thought I told you not to go down there."

Banes listened, her heart beating fast. She clutched the knife again.

"I know, Father." Marie's voice was still small. "But I was worried about Blaze. I know how important she is to you and I had a terrible feeling something had happened to her. I wanted to keep her safe."

Now Banes understood what Princess Marie was doing, or she thought she did. She couldn't see Blaze in the room, and was trying to establish her whereabouts without asking directly.

Very clever, Princess, thought Banes to herself.

"I see, so you had a *feeling,*" said King Jacob. "I thought I had already told you the danger of you having *thoughts* and *feelings.* I am the king and I have it all under control. The unicorn is perfectly safe and closer than you think." He chuckled a little. "If you promise to keep it to yourself, then I will show you where."

DO YOU EVER WISH...?

So the princess's plan seemed to have worked. King Jacob couldn't resist showing off the unicorn.

After a moment, Marie cried out, "Blaze!" from inside the room, and Banes guessed that the king had brought out the unicorn from wherever she'd been hidden. From the little room around the corner, perhaps.

"You see, Marie, the so-called rebels in my castle can do whatever they like. They can destroy my fine furniture, they can kill my servants. I can always find more furniture and servants. But while I have this magical creature under my control, no one can touch me; my power is too strong. Let them come to me; let them try. They will be walking to their deaths."

At the word death, Fern stepped back, looked panicky once again, but Banes gave her a smile she hoped was reassuring.

"The unicorn is so very beautiful," said Marie.

"Beautiful, yes, and very useful." Banes could hear the sneer in King Jacob's voice. Her mouth was dry. Swallowing, she listened to Princess Marie's response.

"What a shame she has to be kept locked away, hidden from sight. Even from you, Father. Do you ever wish you had used your powers differently?"

Now Banes thought she fully understood what Marie was doing. *Don't you ever wish...* She was trying to trick the king. He might say something to give his wishes away, as she herself had done, all those years ago.

King Jacob laughed deeply. "No, I do not wish for anything to be different. I am the most powerful man in the land. I own riches beyond compare. There are many who want to stand in my place and yet they cannot defeat me. I am invincible. What could I possibly wish for that would be better than that?"

"You could wish life were better for everyone and not just us. You could wish you had your son back, that we were a family again." Marie's voice rose with every word. "You could wish for a little love or laughter in your life, or for this poor unicorn to have a life of her own; to be free to gallop through the fields."

Banes held her breath. From what she knew, Marie had never spoken up to her father like this before. How would the king react?

There was silence for a little while and then King Jacob laughed again. It was not a pleasant sound.

"So, the time has come. You think you know better than everyone, like your brother before you. You think you can influence my wishes. You don't seem to realize I am *incredibly careful* what I wish for. And I cannot afford to have a daughter who doesn't abide by my wishes. A daughter who is making trouble for me."

"I am not trying to make trouble for you."

"So you say, and yet I am not a stupid man. Many have accused me of that in the past, and do you see how wrong they were? Would a stupid man become leader of a powerful kingdom? No, I see quite clearly you are disloyal to me. I have seen you going to visit our enemies in the dungeon. I have seen you speaking to my magic unicorn. Now I see you coming here and questioning my authority. I begin to wonder whether your presence here in the castle is necessary."

Banes exchanged a worried look with Fern. Things were not sounding good for Princess Marie.

NEW ARRIVALS

Banes's heart pounded in her chest. She didn't know whether they should rush in to help, or whether the princess was more in control of the situation than it seemed. Charging into the room with a two-inch blade and a quivering maid servant might do more harm than good. She couldn't even discuss it with Fern, because they were both trying to be quiet.

A noise in the corridor made her jump.

Footsteps. And voices.

"Down here!" one said, and the footsteps grew louder.

Fern grasped hold of Banes's arm as Cotter appeared around the corner, followed by Commander Flint. They looked sweaty and dishevelled, but unharmed.

"Banes!" called Cotter, with a big grin. Commander Flint nodded a swift greeting.

Banes brought her finger to her lips to indicate quiet. *They're friends*, she mouthed to Fern, and the maid's grip on her arm relaxed a little. Banes kept her eye on the corner from where they'd emerged, in case anyone was following. But there was no one else.

"Where's Ford?" whispered Banes to Cotter, seeing as they normally came in a pair. Cotter shook his head slightly, his expression pained. Banes knew what that meant. They'd lost Ford. Banes couldn't quite believe it and, although she'd never particularly liked Ford, he was still a comrade: someone she'd shared her supper with around the campfire. Tears began to rise up and she swallowed them down. She steeled herself to ask the next question. About Woodman. Surely they would tell her if they'd found him? But then Flint stepped forward and she missed her chance to ask.

"Who's this?" the commander whispered, pointing at Fern.

"This is Fern. She is maidservant to—" began Banes, although Fern's uniform gave a good indication to who she was.

"Is the king in there?" the commander interrupted, mouthing her words, having already lost interest in the maid. She pointed to the door of the Strategy Room.

Banes nodded. "And the princess," she mouthed back. "And the unicorn."

The commander's eyes narrowed, and she too joined Banes at the door, listening and waiting until the time was right.

CHAPTER SEVENTEEN

TINY WOODEN GIRLS

Marie

Inside the Strategy Room, the king strode towards the model of Quessia castle. He leaned across the table on which it stood and lifted out one of the wooden figures. He held it aloft. "Do you recognize this figure?"

Marie was some distance away, still standing near the door, but she instantly recognized the wide skirt of the dress, the hair flicking out at the shoulders, and the fixed, wooden smile. She nodded, feeling a little faint.

The king smiled. "Yes, it's you. My daughter, the princess.

How I have loved and cherished these figures."

He looked at the models with real affection. How strange it was that he'd spent all this time with her wooden likeness while ignoring her in person.

Holding the princess figure in one hand, he moved to the shelves where Marie had discovered the box of death. She hoped this wasn't what he was about to fetch now, but he brought down a different, smaller wooden box and opened the clasp. "I have made new figures to reflect how you have changed at different stages of your life. Look, here is a baby Marie, then you as a tottering infant and you as a young girl. Your entire life is here." He took out the figures and laid them in a line on the table. She recognized one of them as the figure he'd brought out the night she'd met the unicorn. The night everything changed. She couldn't identify with the baby and child figures in the same way as the princess doll. Seeing multiple versions of herself made Marie feel a little queasy. She glanced at Blaze for support, just to know that someone in the room was on her side, but the unicorn stood motionless, eyes lowered.

King Jacob prodded one of the figures of her aged seven or eight. "See how ragged your clothes were then. How poor we were. No royal finery."

Marie looked at the figure with its bare feet and simple pinafore. She'd loved that dress. She had gathered little treasures in its large pockets. Feathers and pinecones, her mother listening to her chatter. She remembered handing over nutshells to her father, who had filed away the rough edges so she could use them as bowls for her dolls. Maybe she'd played with this exact figure, although she couldn't remember. She touched it gently. "We may have been poor, but we were happy. We had Mother then." She spoke hesitantly, as she so rarely mentioned her mother, and didn't know how he would react. She knew he still loved his wife, still kept her likeness in this room.

"Happy? Happy, you say? Happiness didn't keep her with us, did it? Happiness didn't pay for medicine to make your mother better or for food to get her strong. If we had lived as we do now, with endless riches, then we would not have lost her."

She reached out to touch his arm. Maybe if they could talk about this some more, then she wouldn't have to trick him. Maybe there was still some good in him, somewhere.

He met her gaze and his eyes were filled with tears.

"Father—" She searched for any words that might reach him, but before she could speak, the door to the room swung open. They both turned at once. It was Banes and Fern! What a time to pick to come and rescue her, just as she'd been getting through to him.

"Not now!" she said. "Give us a few moments."

The king looked sharply at Marie. She wondered if he was going to ask her who Banes was, and she quickly tried to think of a cover story. But then she saw that it wasn't only Banes and Fern in the doorway. Behind her were two more: one of the rebels Marie recognized from down in the dungeons and Commander Flint. They were armed with knives and swords, and they were gaping at Blaze. The only one not looking at the unicorn was Banes, who was gazing at her father, King Jacob, chin raised, as if ready for a fight.

CHAPTER EIGHTEEN

OUTNUMBERED AND UNARMED

Banes

From the sound of the voice she'd heard through the door, Banes had expected King Jacob to be a menacing figure. In real life he looked much less threatening. He was pale, with the look of someone who didn't go outside very often. Despite his crown, he looked more like one of the gamblers she encountered each night back at the inn, than a king. He was one of those people who would never be satisfied with his lot. Although there was a physical resemblance between him and Marie, Marie's dreamy half-smile was much more pleasant than his sneer.

Before they had walked into the room, the king had sounded measured and calm, but now this calm turned to fury. King Jacob's eyes bulged and his pale cheeks reddened. His ire seemed to be directed less at the rebels breaking into his private quarters, and more at his daughter.

"Just as I thought! You are scheming and duplicitous: you are no daughter of mine."

"No ... I hadn't planned this. I..." Marie lifted her hands in a pose of surrender and stood helplessly, seemingly unsure whether to move nearer to her father or back towards Banes and the others.

But the king wasn't listening. He turned his back and began taking some objects down from his shelves. Some little figures and a wooden box. Blaze stood as still as the figures themselves, gazing at the floor. A rope hung around her neck. King Jacob obviously couldn't shackle her in irons up here but still wanted her tied up.

Commander Flint strode forward and addressed his turned back, loudly and formally.

"King Jacob, you may not remember me, but I am Commander Flint. I used to lead your army but I left when I saw your cruelty in action."

The king turned. "So you call yourself *Commander* now?" he

scoffed. "And are these the troops you command?" He laughed and walked towards the model of Quessia castle, holding the wooden figures and the box. He silently lined up four soldiers in one of the rooms.

Flint continued. "Your guards have been defeated. Your castle is surrounded. The people of Quessia have spoken and they no longer want you as their ruler. You cannot hide away up here. We are offering you a choice. Leave now, peacefully, or die at our hand."

Banes flinched at the talk of death. She'd known that it was why they were there, and that it would come to this, but she still didn't want to see it. This was Marie's father, after all.

King Jacob didn't react to the news. Banes wasn't even sure he'd heard. He removed a piece of string from the box and tied it tightly around the wooden soldiers.

"So, the people of Quessia have spoken, have they? And who is going to enforce this? You, I suppose?" He looked the commander up and down, his expression a mix of amusement and antipathy.

Commander Flint narrowed her eyes and took two steps further into the room. "Yes, you are outnumbered, unarmed, and we are guarding the only exit from this room."

He paused for a moment and picked up a little wooden maid from the servants' quarters, and a figure in a dress and crown that must represent Princess Marie. Three soldiers, a maid and a princess, all in a room which looked very much like this one. Banes shivered.

The king stared into the model castle. "Ha! You think me unarmed? Defenceless? You are wrong! I have powerful weapons in this room that will defeat you all in an instant. Isn't that so, Unicorn?"

Once again, all eyes in the room turned to Blaze, who, with her head bowed meekly, looked mild and gentle. In the dim light, she appeared more grey than white, and her mane and tail were stringy and lank.

Blaze blinked, her long lashes batting up and down. "Yes, Master. This is true."

Behind Banes, Cotter and Fern gasped. They hadn't yet heard the unicorn speak. King Jacob looked around, checking everyone was impressed. The commander leaned forward a little, as if she wanted to reach out and touch the unicorn. Perhaps she would have done, had she been nearer. Then she seemed to remember herself and drew her sword. But as she lunged towards the king, he laughed.

"I have made my move, Unicorn!" he declared.

"Then it is so, Master," said the unicorn sadly, and a bright light shone around her as if a fire had been lit. For a second, she looked whiter, brighter than before. Banes recognized this blaze, although the others looked shocked all over again.

Banes felt her arms snap to her sides, as if someone or something had squeezed them there. From the looks of things, the same thing had happened to Cotter and Fern. And the commander. All of them stood suddenly straight with their arms at their sides. Commander Flint's sword clattered to the floor.

The king laughed loudly. Banes felt as though someone was pushing her back towards the doorway, her feet scuffling on the floor to keep up. Soon all four of them – Banes, Flint, Cotter and Fern – stood back-to-back as if tied together. Like the wooden soldiers in the king's little castle but with no visible rope.

"Now do you see how my weapons work?" asked King Jacob.

POWERFUL WEAPONS

The four of them could only move their lower arms, hands and feet. Banes and Flint looked into the room, whereas Fern and

Cotter were facing the corridor. Only Marie was free and she seemed unsure what to do – her gaze darting from her father, to Banes, to the unicorn and back again.

Banes was so close to Flint that she could feel her shoulders moving in time to her short angry breaths. But when the commander spoke, her voice was as calm as usual.

"Now I see the power you wield, King Jacob, but you cannot defeat us all."

"There are more of you?"

The commander nodded. "Our rebels are overpowering your guards. They will soon be up here to rescue us. Also, there is something you do not yet know."

The king raised a single, questioning eyebrow. "Which is?"

"Your son – the next in line to the throne – is in the castle now," she replied.

The king's son. Woodman. Relief flooded through Banes. Woodman was still alive – unless the commander was using a clever choice of words. Banes exchanged a quick glance with Marie, whose hopeful expression mirrored her own.

King Jacob walked back to the shelves and selected another figure. A young man. He examined it. "My son? I might have known he was behind all this. Where is he now? Hiding away and letting you do his work for him?"

"Not at all. If you release us, we can take you to him," said the commander.

King Jacob laid the figure on the table by the castle and looked up at Commander Flint.

"Take me to him? So he can steal my crown? That boy will never be king! I am the one living a life of luxury, whereas he is living in the forest with a bunch of criminals and ne'er-do-wells. Surely that tells you something about how different we are." King Jacob was talking as if he'd earned his right to the throne, rather than wished upon a magic unicorn. He seemed to think he was invincible. "No, I won't release you, *Commander*," he said snidely. "Aren't you interested to see my full power in action?"

"Astound us," said Commander Flint, shortly. She put on a good impression of nonchalance, but Banes knew she wanted to know. She'd wanted to know for a long time.

The king knew, too. He smiled.

"There has been much speculation about how I remain invincible and keep armies away from Quessia castle. For many years, I have kept this secret hidden. However, you have taken the trouble to visit me in my private quarters. That makes you the first lucky people to witness the secret of how I am the most powerful king that ever lived. It is standing right here in the room, as you have seen." King Jacob swung into full performance mode, flinging one arm out to the side to indicate Blaze.

"Three wishes, this creature granted me. Three little wishes! An ordinary man might wish for treasures or a palace, yet I knew I could make those three wishes give me *everything*! This room, and these figures, hold the answer. My first wish was, of course, to be king. My second wish was the clever one. I wished for all the moves I make in this miniature kingdom to become real, forevermore. All I have to do is to declare my move, and it is so."

King Jacob grinned at his own cleverness.

"And the third wish?" asked Flint.

"I never made a third wish!" exclaimed the king. "And I never will. Why would I, when that would send the unicorn trotting off to find its next master? No, the unicorn stays with me, making each move real. I have so much power! You see how a simple piece of string binds you all, but I have created more interesting weapons than that. Isn't that right, Unicorn?"

"Yes, Master," said Blaze, her eyes lowered to the floor.

"Which weapons are you talking about?" asked the princess,

in a low voice. The fear in her eyes was clear as she looked towards the wooden box in front of King Jacob.

The king slowly opened the lid as if he were about to perform a trick. He took out a small hammer, no bigger than the palm of his hand, and a couple of wrought iron nails the size of his thumbnail. If it hadn't been for the sinister atmosphere in the room, then Banes might have laughed: these didn't look like the powerful weapons he'd described. But she had a dreadful feeling there was more to them than met the eye.

The king held the hammer in one hand and a nail in the other. He drew himself up tall as if he were an actor, about to put on a show.

There was a strange moment of stillness.

"You – the tall solider. How is your head?" asked the king, projecting his voice.

"Me?" asked Cotter, confusion clear in his knitted brows. "It feels well," he muttered.

"Do you feel an ache in your temples?" asked the king, with a cruel smile.

"No," said Cotter.

"What's 'e doing?" whispered Fern, but Cotter shrugged. From their positions, neither of them could see King Jacob selecting the tallest wooden soldier in the group. But Banes, Flint and Marie had a good view and they watched in horror as, with a few taps of the tiny hammer, he drove the nail into the side of the figure's head.

"I have made my move, Unicorn!" he declared.

"Then it is so, Master."

Flames sprang up around Blaze like before, then the light died away and Cotter cried out. He lowered his head and hunched his great shoulders forwards. "My head!" he cried. "Stop, stop! make it stop!"

Banes winced and turned to look at Cotter. It was awful to hear him in so much pain and be powerless to help. Marie and the commander gasped in unison. Fern, beside Cotter, turned pale and struggled in a bid to help him, but there was nothing she could do. She was held tight as if by some invisible rope and there was no mark on Cotter. No bloody wound. Magic was at work. The king was doing this, with the help of the unicorn.

Jacob held the figure aloft and flamboyantly removed the nail.

"I have made my move, Unicorn!" he shouted once again.

The unicorn replied, "Then it is so," and in a blaze of fire, the magic worked like before. Cotter stopped moaning and breathed slowly with relief.

"Who next, I wonder…" said the king. He pulled another figure out from the string and smiled. "Commander Flint."

Flint sprang towards her sword, but the king kicked it away.

"Careful!" he said. "Take another step further and you might feel a crushing pain in your chest." He flashed them a glimpse of a simple-looking tool from the box: two blocks of wood secured together with screws. He put the figure between the wooden blocks with another smile. Banes felt sick. It was easy to see what would happen to the soldier if he tightened the screws.

They all exchanged glances, questions in their eyes.

The king had spared Cotter, but would he be as lenient with Commander Flint? He seemed to be enjoying himself.

The commander stood very still, appearing composed despite the fact the king held her life in his right hand. But Princess Marie looked a lot less calm. Tears streamed down her face and she was shaking her head as though she couldn't believe her father's actions. After everything Marie had told her, Banes found this difficult to understand.

Banes just hoped she didn't do anything foolish.

TRAITOROUS CHILDREN

Marie moved towards King Jacob with outstretched arms. "Father, you must stop this," she said. "The unicorn cannot keep making this magic. Look at her! She is fading away. If she dies, then your power dies with her."

The king looked first at the unicorn, then at his daughter, as if seeing them both for the first time.

Marie continued. "You can change! You can still be a good king. Your people only want a fair chance at a happy life." She nodded towards the rebels. "They have reasonable requests. Surely you can talk to them." She was rambling a little and Banes was surprised to hear these suggestions coming from her. Did she really still believe the king was capable of change?

King Jacob himself looked surprised to hear Marie talking so much, and for a moment he froze, watching her.

"Mother would say the same if she were here," continued Marie. "She was so kind; she always wanted the best for everyone—"

"Stop!" The king raised a hand to Marie. "Look at you: like your brother before you, siding with the enemy over your own father. You know nothing of what your mother would have wanted. She would have been ashamed."

The king put the commander figure back under the string with the others and watched Flint shuffle back to the doorway with satisfaction. He picked up the figure of Woodman that he'd laid on the table earlier. He held it in his left hand and, with his right hand, plucked the figure of Princess Marie from the castle.

"You children have been a curse to me. I should have turned you both out of the house when your mother died. I always knew your brother was a troublemaker, but I expected more of you, Marie. You were always so much more obedient. I thought you would act like a princess and support me as king but now I see you are like him."

"No, Father, you can't mean that—"

"—Oh, but I do mean exactly that. You are a traitor. I should have seen it years ago. You want my unicorn for yourself—"

"It's not true—"

"Of course it's true!" he bellowed. Spittle ran from his lips, down his chin. He held the two tiny figures up in front of his face. "Two traitorous children. I must now decide what to do with you both."

Horrified, Banes watched the king's face as he examined the wooden figures. She had seen that expression before: a calm assessment of the damage he was about to cause. He was looking at them in the same way the fox had considered the hen house that morning.

The king had shown them all what he was capable of, and who knew what he had in store for his children? They had to do something to help Marie. She'd stepped forward to protect them and put herself at risk. But from the way their shoulders sagged against her back, Banes could tell that Fern, Cotter and Flint were relieved their figures weren't in the vice. None of them could save the princess: they needed back-up.

But then Banes felt a familiar swishing around her legs and she realized she was not alone after all. Twitch had joined them.

$\mathcal{C}$HAPTER NINETEEN

DECISIONS

Marie

Marie watched her father in desperation. The commander's sword lay on the floor but she couldn't reach it without him seeing.

He was roaming around the room, moving the figures across the model land as he spoke, as if he were playing some childhood game.

"I could lock you away here, in a high tower, in these far-off woods, with bats all around."

He moved to a different table.

"Or I could put you here, by the slopes of this fiery volcano."

There was nothing anyone could do to help her. Even though they outnumbered the king, as always, her father was the one with the power.

The king continued, crossing over to the edge of the room. "Maybe I could cast you out on to this deserted island. Then you could wish and wish all you liked, but there would be no one to hear you."

He put the figures of Marie and Wyll on to a scrubby circle that represented an island, far out in the ocean.

"I am a compassionate man. This would be the best place for you. You could live for a long time here. You would have each other for company, and plenty of fish to eat, but I wouldn't have to put up with your traitorous behaviour."

Marie's heart began to thump. A remote island was better than a volcano or a windowless tower, but only marginally. She was scared, but not only for herself. If he sent her there, then what would it mean for those she was leaving behind? For Banes? For the people of Quessia? For poor Blaze? The only comfort would be seeing her brother again after all these years, but she wasn't sure he was still alive.

"No, Father. Don't send us there. Please." She tried to appeal to that spark within him that was good, but now even she was beginning to doubt it was there.

He glared at her and her heart sunk. He was unreachable now; all goodness had disappeared. He looked down at the little figures instead of replying to her pleas. The models were real to him in a way she would never be. She'd done everything she could to help him, but it hadn't worked. She had to save herself, and the others.

A familiar rubbing around her ankles made her look down. A little black tail twitched. Twitch had escaped. They must have left the door to her bedchamber open. She would normally have feared for Twitch's safety but this time the king had other things on his mind, and she was comforted by her kitten's presence.

Marie used her foot to respond to Twitch's rubbing without drawing attention to him. She looked around the Strategy Room for anything that might help defend her against her father. Banes's head was cocked and her eyes darted around the room too, landing on Twitch before flitting up to Marie's throat. Banes's eyes widened for a moment, before locking on to Marie's. "Your brooch," she mouthed.

Marie frowned. Why would Banes be interested in her brooch? Perhaps she was planning to use it as a weapon, although the pin at the back was short and blunt. Still, she trusted Banes.

With her gaze glued to her father, she undid the clasp at the back. The king was still playing with the figures.

She fumbled for a moment, then threw the brooch to Banes. It was a good throw, straight towards her hand and Banes caught it with ease despite only being able to move her arms at the elbow. The sudden movement distracted the king momentarily but when he saw nobody had moved, he went straight back to his figures.

Meanwhile, Banes angled the brooch this way and that, catching the light from a nearby candle, reflecting a tiny flickering diamond. Why was she doing this? Marie normally played this game in the daytime when the light was brighter, but the candlelight still had an effect. The light danced on the floor and the lower part of the wall. Twitch immediately recognized the game. His eyes followed the mysterious shape. His favourite prey.

Marie saw then what was Banes was doing.

She was taking the dancing light on a deliberate path, leading Twitch straight to the strategy table.

The king, who had been moving the figures of his children from the high tower to the island and back again, stopped and placed the tips of his fingers together.

"I just can't decide," he said. "I think, after all, I will keep my precious unicorn with me and put you down in the dungeons in its place while I make up my mind." He dropped her figure and Wyll's in a cell.

"There!" he announced.

From that point, everything seemed to slow down. Marie wanted to scream, to cry, to protest, but she found she could no longer speak, as if she were stuck in a bad dream where every movement is impossible. The king didn't look at his daughter. His eyes were glazed over as if he were somewhere else.

"Unicorn, I have made my move!" he declared.

As he spoke, Banes tilted the brooch in her hand so the diamond of light fell on the strategy table. And, as if chasing a butterfly, Twitch pounced.

The little kitten sprang up, paws outstretched. He landed in the middle of the table, batting his paw from side to side as he chased the mysterious light. One paw caught the figure of the king, which toppled from its place and went rolling across the table. It kept rolling and then the finely carved figure fell straight off the table, head first. It landed on the floor with a crack.

At exactly the same moment, the unicorn lifted her head and blinked twice.

"As you say, Master. It is so," she said in her cool, clear voice, as bright flames blazed around her.

And for Marie, everything went black.

A COLD, DARK, PLACE

Marie awoke in a cold, dark place, feeling bruised and stiff, as if she'd fallen from her horse. Her head ached and she was shaking. It took her a few moments to raise herself to a seated position. Fear clutched at her insides. Was she on a deserted island or locked in a tower?

She blinked. She was indoors. The floor was cold stone with a rectangle of pale moonlight falling from the window. Then, suddenly, the place was flooded with a bright orange light and she saw she was somehow down in the dungeons, in the unicorn's cell. Of course. He had decided to send her down here after all.

The light came from the blazing fire that had sprung up in the corner of the room. It took her a couple of moments for her to recognize those light, yet heatless flames. Blaze was with her.

The sight of the unicorn brought joy to Marie, despite the

aches in her body and the confusion in her mind. For the unicorn was no longer cowed and withdrawn as she had been in the Strategy Room. Blaze stood proudly, her chin held high, her blue eyes bright and the flames flickering around her like a mane. She still had the rope around her neck, but it hung limp, no longer fixed to anything.

"Blaze!" called Marie. "You're here!"

"Yes, Mistress Marie," replied Blaze.

"My father...?" asked Marie, unable to form the whole question. In her heart she knew why the unicorn was by her side, and why she looked different.

Blaze moved her muzzle close to Marie's shoulder, as the bright flames died away.

"The king – my master – is dead," she said, softly. "His figure fell and was broken, just as he made his wish."

Marie closed her eyes, replaying the events of the Strategy Room in her mind. Her father's wish. He had rejected her, wished her harm. The expression on his face. The wooden figure rolling and falling, breaking on the ground. His wish had finally backfired. Marie took a large gulp of air, making a sound that was somewhere between a sigh and a cry. Her father was dead.

She shook her head slowly. "If only I could have helped him."

The unicorn nuzzled her shoulder. "You tried, Mistress Marie. You tried for longer and harder than anyone else would have done."

And Marie nodded, wondering if that were true.

She closed her eyes, feeling the softness of the unicorn's coat under her hand and cheek.

"There is another here, with us," said the unicorn, mysteriously. Marie turned around, still shaking from the shock of it all. There was indeed a figure curled up in the shadows. A dead body? But no, it moved, struggling to sit up as she had done a few moments before. She couldn't see the person's face, and Marie's first thought was of Banes, who had helped her escape her father's cruel punishment.

But then she remembered: her father had put two figures in the dungeons, not just her own.

It was a man. Much taller than Banes. And when she saw the sandy-coloured hair, she knew straightaway who it was. Even after five years, he hadn't changed that much. A bit broader across the shoulders, darker stubble on his cheeks, but it was him: her brother Wyll.

"Wyll!" she cried, and ran to him, sinking back down to the floor and putting her arms around him.

"Ow," he said, flinching away from her. She saw then he was hurt: a deep wound in his arm that was covered with a makeshift bandage. The blood seeped copiously through the white of the cloth.

"Marie?" Wyll lifted his head. Frowning, he looked around the room, as if searching for answers. "Where are we? Is this real?" His confusion wasn't helped by the sight of a blazing unicorn.

Marie laughed a little. "I think it's real." She pictured the strategy room again, the figure of their father rolling across the table. "We're down in the castle dungeons."

"Father...?"

"He's gone, Wyll. Dead. I will tell you everything, but try not to speak for now. You're hurt and I need to fetch help."

He sighed in response and sunk back down to the stone floor of the cell. Marie stood, her dress stained and sticky from her brother's blood. She made her way to the door. "Is it open?"

"Yes, but be careful who you invite to help, Mistress Marie," warned Blaze.

REUNION

Marie pushed open the door, looking out into the dim corridor, past the open doors and the flaming torches. Bunches of keys lay abandoned and dark smears stained the floor and walls. Blood, Marie guessed. Wyll's blood and perhaps others'. She shuddered. There must have been a terrible fight after Banes and Marie had left.

Footsteps echoed in a distant corridor and she heard voices, shouting "Marie? Princess?" It was Banes, Fern, and the others from the Strategy Room.

"I'm here!" she called, and the sound of the boots on the stone floor grew louder.

In a moment, they were all there with her, their faces lit eerily by the torches, shadows distorting their features.

Banes threw herself at Marie and enveloped her in a hug. "You're all right," she said, with a grin. "I knew you would be. I mean, I hoped. But I knew."

A mew sounded and Fern laughed, reached under her cloak and retrieved Twitch. She passed him to Marie, who cuddled the kitten close. He soon wriggled free and began rubbing around everyone's legs in delight at discovering a brand new place *and* new people.

"Fern insisted on bringing him with her," said Cotter, stroking the kitten. Flint rolled her eyes.

"Well he did save you," said Banes.

Marie shook her head. "No, you saved me, by acting so quickly."

Twitch stalked off into the inviting shadows, no doubt hunting for mice. Marie let him go. She supposed she didn't have to worry about keeping her kitten close any more.

"How did you get out of the room?" she asked.

"The king's magic seemed to stop the minute he—" began Cotter, but Banes gave him a sharp look and he trailed off.

"Did the unicorn tell you ... about your father?" Banes asked.

Marie nodded, her eyes filling with tears. How kind of Banes to recognize that, despite all the cruel things he'd done, he'd still been her father.

"The wooden figure didn't stand a chance. It was more intricately carved than the others and so delicate. The head snapped off as soon as it hit the floor. But your father ... he looked happy, you know, as if he was sleeping," said Banes. "Happier than when he'd been alive, perhaps—"

The commander stepped forward and cleared her throat,

putting an end to any sentimental conversation. "We knew you'd be here after he put your figures in the dungeons," she explained.

"And Woodman's figure too," added Banes, her voice a little wobbly. "Is he here?"

Marie nodded. "He's inside this cell. He's hurt. I hoped you might be able to help him."

She led them into the cell. Banes ran immediately to Woodman and the commander strode up to Blaze.

"The unicorn is here too, thank goodness," Flint said, as if to herself.

The others shuffled in behind her. The cell seemed very cramped with so many people inside and the flames around the unicorn had died away, so there was little light. Fern brought a torch from the corridor and placed it in a sconce in the wall. Banes rushed straight to Wyll and knelt at his side.

"Woodman," she whispered.

He opened his eyes and struggled to raise himself up on his elbows as he had before.

"Banes. You look different," he said, registering her new gown and hair.

Banes's cheeks flushed pink and she rubbed at a dusty patch

on her skirt. "So do you!" she said, indicating his wounded arm and torn clothes.

He tried to smile.

"Not planning to finish me off with any woodworking tools this time?"

Banes shook her head. "I'm sorry about that," she said. "And for thinking you weren't brave. I know you are really."

He smiled, but didn't reply. Marie wondered what they were talking about. He looked pleased to see Banes, she thought. More pleased than he'd even been to see his own sister, but she didn't mind. She was glad he'd found people that cared about him.

He closed his eyes again, as if worn out by the effort of speaking.

"Can we do anything for him?" asked Banes.

Cotter took out a small hip flask from his pocket and passed it to her. "Here, give him some of this."

She poured a little of the amber liquid into the lid and brought it to his lips. He took a sip.

"We should bandage that arm properly as well," said Fern, offering up a large clean handkerchief.

"I don't know how," said Banes, standing up. "I've never treated anything more serious than my brothers' and sisters' cuts and grazes." She moved away, and Fern took her position beside Wyll, tearing the handkerchief into strips and efficiently tending to the wound.

The only one who ignored Woodman completely was the commander. She seemed mesmerized by the unicorn. This was unsurprising; Blaze had the same effect on Marie, especially when she looked as beautiful and proud as she did now. The commander stood close to Blaze with one hand on her back and a strange smile on her face, as if she'd just discovered a secret. She brought her face down very close to the blaze on her nose, but the unicorn didn't nuzzle her back or respond in any way. She stood motionless, her large eyes fixed on Marie, blinking steadily.

Then the commander spoke, murmuring something into the velvety skin near the unicorn's nose. Her voice was quiet, and Marie wasn't quite sure, but from where she was standing, it sounded like,

"Now you are mine."

CHAPTER TWENTY

THE UNICORN IS MINE

Banes had been entirely focused on Woodman, but since Fern had taken over the bandaging, she had a chance to look around the cell. Both Marie and Cotter looked a little uncomfortable. They were watching Commander Flint, who was acting strangely, like a young girl with her first pony. She whispered to Blaze, and stroked her back. Then, when she realized all eyes were upon her, she straightened up and stood with a proprietorial hand on the rope around the unicorn's neck. She looked around the room as if assessing each one of them, then spoke in a loud voice that echoed in the small cell.

"The unicorn is mine."

Everyone stared at her, open-mouthed. Banes hadn't expected this from the commander, although perhaps she should have. Flint was clever, calculating and highly motivated. She'd told Banes herself to be ruthless, and Banes realized suddenly that, with the power of the unicorn, Flint could be dangerous indeed.

The commander continued in a voice that was worryingly reminiscent of King Jacob.

"We killed the king and thus the magic and the wishes transfer to us. As commander, that means I claim ownership and control of the unicorn."

Blaze had told Banes how two different sorts of people reacted when faced with the power of wishes. The unicorn's words played in her mind.

The other sort of people know straightaway how they can get the most from my magic. They are not content with three wishes but want more. They want power and wealth and fame, and they want it at any cost.

Banes looked at the others in the room. Cotter stood rigid, glancing this way and that. He was never going to challenge the commander, whether or not he agreed with her. Fern stopped tending to Woodman for a moment and gaped. There was nothing she could do to help.

Marie stood near to the unicorn, blinking. She'd already been through enough. Banes was the only one who could challenge this. She took a deep breath and faced the commander, who had been her mentor and inspiration for so many weeks. Flint had told Banes she was her righthand woman and now she was about to undo all of that.

"With all due respect, Commander Flint, you didn't kill the king. It was an accident. The kitten knocked over the playing pieces. If anything, *I* was the one responsible, for encouraging the kitten on to the table."

Banes only claimed responsibility to absolve Marie of any guilt, but the commander seemed to interpret it as a challenge. She narrowed her eyes and fixed them on Banes, her expression stony.

"I see. So you think you have more of a right to control this creature than I?"

"No..." said Banes, her cheeks hot. "I feel we shouldn't decide anything yet. We have seen how power can corrupt—"

"—It is not up to you! Either of you!" This came from Princess Marie, her voice high and strained. "Blaze is not a toy in the nursery to be fought over – she has feelings of her own and she knows the rules of her own enchantment. If we can wait in civilized silence then she will tell us what happens next."

There was a moment of silence. Blaze breathed softly through her nose.

"Good idea, Princess," said the commander in a low voice. "Let us hear what the animal has to say." She sounded calm, but Banes noticed she didn't loosen her grip on the rope.

The unicorn lifted her chin, blue eyes flashing, and turned her head a touch so she was looking the commander in the eye. "My power does not belong to you, Commander Flint," she said. "But nor does it belong to Cassie Banes."

For the first time Banes had seen, the commander looked a little flustered, angry even.

"What do you mean?" she asked. "I thought killing the king was the only way to release your power. *'Unless he bequeaths my power to another, then I serve him until his death or mine.'* That's what Banes told me. Unless she got it wrong." She stared daggers at Banes again.

"Banes informed you correctly," said the unicorn. "But now my master is dead, my power reverts to another. My previous owner has not yet spent all her wishes."

Previous owner?

Banes knew straightaway who that was.

"Princess Marie!" she cried. "It's you, isn't it?"

CHAPTER TWENTY-ONE

A NEW MISTRESS

Marie

"Oh," said Marie. Her head spun. Her 'fall' from the Strategy Room to the dungeon, her father's death, the confusion of all these people. It was overwhelming and she could barely focus on the faces in the room, let alone think straight.

One more wish. Of course. Back by the waterfall, all those years ago, she'd wished first to hear more about the unicorn, and then that the unicorn could help her father. Two wishes out of three. She'd thought by handing power over to the unicorn then she'd forfeited her third wish, but no. After all these years, the power belonged to her.

Banes stepped forward, a worried look on her face. "Don't be hasty, Princess. You don't have to wish straight away. Think for a little while. Plan what it is you want. Don't waste this opportunity."

The commander looked across at her and nodded her agreement. "Think strategically. Your father made his three wishes last for many years. If you are shrewd, then you can do the same."

Flint's smiling face was at odds with her aggressive challenges. And she was still holding on to the rope around the unicorn's neck. Marie didn't trust her. But it didn't matter, because Marie wasn't going to listen to anyone's advice or their warnings. She had planned out her third wish five years ago by that waterfall. Ever since, she'd regretted not being able to make it.

She glanced at Wyll. He was hurt, bleeding. Should she change her wish to help him? No, Wyll was strong. She would take him to the best healers and he would survive. She couldn't look at Banes in case she changed her mind.

"I know what I shall wish for," she said, looking deep into the unicorn's eyes and smiling. Now was the time. The only time.

"I wish..." she began, but then the commander suddenly leaped towards the torch in the sconce. She ripped it free and then stood over Wyll, holding the flames close to his face. Fern gasped and pulled away. Wyll had been resting, eyes closed, but now he opened them in horror. He tried to back up against the stone wall but was too weak.

"No," whispered Marie.

Cotter raised both hands. "Commander Flint—" he began, but she swung the torch wildly towards him and he stopped mid-sentence. The commander, usually so controlled, had lost all sense of reason.

She swung the torch back so the fire blazed by Wyll's chin. Marie saw the flames reflected in his eyes and her arms felt shaky.

Keeping the torch where it was, Flint turned her head to face Marie. "I'm sorry if I didn't make myself clear, but I am not advising you; I am *ordering* you. You will make exactly the wish I tell you to make."

Her eyes had the same look as her father's before he wished her away. "If you do not, then I will have to explain to everyone how poor Prince Wyll met with an unfortunate accident before he could claim the throne."

"I – I," Marie swallowed. She'd never trusted that woman. She knew what she had to do.

"Please leave my brother alone, and I will do as you ask."

ℰHAPTER TWENTY-TWO

THE LAST WISH

Banes

Banes closed her eyes for just a moment. Not Woodman. She'd thought they'd lost him once before and now they had him back, injured and defenceless, but alive. They couldn't lose him. Princess Marie stood, shaky and pale, before the commander, looking almost as vulnerable as her brother. Banes was cross with herself. How could she have trusted the commander? She'd seen the look in Flint's eye and should have known she would stop at nothing. Now all she could only appeal to her good nature.

"Commander! Woodman is on our side. Don't hurt him."

The commander kept the torch in position. "He will not get hurt if the princess does as I ask." Banes stepped forward, but, without turning, the commander shouted out an order. "Hold her back, Cotter."

Cotter hesitated for a moment and then stepped forwards and grabbed Banes's upper arms. She struggled against his hold but he was too strong, like when she'd been tied by the magic in the Strategy Room.

Flint looked in her direction, eyes flashing. "That was a mistake, Banes. I suggest you think carefully about where your loyalties lie."

"The princess sided with us against her father! She nearly ended up banished from her own kingdom! You can't—"

"I can, Banes, and I will do whatever is necessary. Now be quiet before I silence you too." She swung the torch towards Banes and back again, long shadows looming over the unicorn.

"Do as she says, Banes, then nobody will get hurt," Cotter whispered, in a voice that was not unkind. But he continued to grip her tightly, leaving her powerless to help Marie.

Banes watched the commander in disbelief. She had admired

her, respected her, wanted to be like her, yet now she saw she was scheming and deceitful. Banes had thought she was a good judge of character. How was it possible to be so wrong about a person?

"No!" shouted Banes. "I will *not* be quiet. I have a right to speak! And Marie has a right to wish! Her wish won't harm anyone – she isn't like her father."

"Don't worry, Banes," Marie said, her voice barely audible as she looked down at her clasped hands. "I will do this. For Wyll. What is it you want me to wish, Commander?"

Banes closed her eyes. Why did the princess have to be so compliant? She'd hoped Marie might have developed some self-confidence after standing up to her father at long last. But maybe it was unfair to judge her. It was hard to say what Banes herself would do if she found herself in the same position.

Commander Flint took one step away from Woodman and lowered the torch. The room darkened. She glanced at the unicorn with a satisfied smile.

"I want you to bequeath the unicorn's power to me, as you did for your father. You will know the precise words you used. Wish for me, Commander Flint, to have an unending supply of wishes."

Cotter gasped, surprised perhaps at the commander's ruthless ambition, but Flint turned and narrowed her eyes at him.

"This is for the good of us all. I will not use my wishes to cause harm as King Jacob did. My wishes will be for the good of all of Quessia, and my people."

My people? From the way she spoke, one would think Commander Flint already held the throne.

Marie nodded and kept her gaze down.

She sighed, as if this were a difficult thing for her to do. Then she began to speak in a timid, but rapid voice.

"I wish that you, the Blazing Unicorn, should be free from the magic that binds you. You should take your original form and never again be enslaved to another."

FREEDOM

Marie had looked so compliant, it took Banes a couple of moments to realize she had said the wrong words. Or rather the right words, but not the ones the commander had demanded.

There was a moment's silence and then the unicorn spoke.

"Your wish is granted. A thousand thank yous, Mistress

Marie," she said, her voice as clear as crystal. The rope around her neck began to dissolve.

A happy laugh escaped from Banes, sounding odd in the taut atmosphere. By the look on the commander's face, she too had only just realized Marie had tricked her. The look of greed dropped away from her face and was replaced by a look of total dismay and then anger.

She raised the torch and swung towards Marie.

But Blaze reared up on her hind legs, front hooves skimming the commander's face. Flint staggered back.

As the unicorn's hooves clattered down to the floor, a blaze of light rose up around her. She shook her mane and flicked her tail, and flames licked around as though she was on fire.

Fern sprang away from Woodman and backed into the corner, mouth agape. Cotter loosened his grip on Banes, who took advantage and leaped from his grasp. In the mayhem, Banes made a grab for the commander. She knocked the torch from her hand. It went spinning to the floor, catching the filthy straw on fire. Flames blazed up, rivalling those of the unicorn, and moving dangerously close to Woodman. Marie and Fern stamped the fire out. Banes coughed as smoke filled the room. She struggled to hold the commander and then Cotter was there to help, pinning the commander's arms as he had done with Banes before.

The flames around Blaze reached the ceiling, obscuring her from view. They all recoiled, shielding their eyes. Even though Banes was familiar with this magic blaze, she still felt they might be consumed by flames. The unicorn's fire would travel through the dungeons, burning everything in its path. But it did not happen. As ever, the fire was devoid of heat, and it blazed brightly without burning, like the light from a faraway sun.

In moments, the bright light died away and they all brought their arms and hands away from their faces.

There, in the place of the unicorn, was a woman with long hair the colour of fire.

She was older than them – the age of Banes's mother. She wore a green dress and had a tired, but kind face. Banes caught the scent of rosewater.

"Y-You're a person, like us?" Banes asked.

"Yes. I've been trapped in this form for so many years," she said, in a familiar clear voice. "All I ever needed was someone unselfish enough to free me." She turned to Marie and smiled.

Marie stepped forward and embraced the woman as if she were an old friend. The others watched, amazed.

When the cell door swung open once again, they all turned.

For some reason, Banes expected to see the unicorn, or even the king, alive after all. But it was not the king. It was the big, burly form of the jailer, looking groggy, as if he'd awoken from a deep sleep, which Banes supposed he had.

He looked from person to person, surprised all his prisoners had ended up in the same cell. On seeing the princess, he looked expectantly towards her, and she obliged with an order. "Lock this woman up," she said, inclining her head in the direction of Commander Flint. "The others may go free."

CHAPTER TWENTY-THREE

ANNOUNCEMENTS

The king's death was announced. It seemed he had suffered an accidental death, fallen and hit his head, perhaps, although there was no tell-tale mark. The court physician could offer no further explanation. It seemed he had somehow ... broken.

Afterwards, there was a lot to organize.

The rules stated that Marie would automatically be queen, but she knew that could never be so. She had come a long way in confidence and courage but she could still not see herself in that position, and above all, she didn't want to be. To her, Quessia castle had been a prison, and not somewhere she could ever call home.

Which meant there was a big question mark over who should succeed. There was no bringing back the old royal family – they had long gone.

Wyll didn't want to be king, either. Besides, how would they have explained the absence and sudden reappearance of King Jacob's only son?

Marie had wanted to tell everyone the whole truth, about the unicorn, about her father's abuse of his wishes, why he (and she) had no real right to the throne, but Banes persuaded her against it. She thought of the incredulous faces at the camp when she'd told them all about the blazing unicorn. "Sometimes, the truth is the most difficult thing to believe. When that is the case, it's best you weave them a tale. Not a lie, but something truer than the truth."

So Marie looked inside herself for the truest truth. Who did she know who was wise and strong, capable of leading a kingdom? Someone honest and empathic, who would understand the needs of the people? And she realized she did know someone:

someone who had been on a great journey, someone from humble beginnings who had known great suffering and would be kind and fair.

And she told the council that, thankfully, she had remembered another living relative: a distant cousin, who would now be first in line to the throne.

And this was a "truth" the council was happy to accept.

As for Marie, she had to decide what it was she did want for her future. She, Wyll and Banes discussed it on one of those in-between days, when they were waiting for the new queen to take the throne. They had been strolling in the castle gardens, Wyll and Banes amazed by the splendour of it all, Marie amazed she'd never noticed the beauty all around her. She'd always been too concerned about her father, that he might disapprove of what she was doing.

They had strolled through the main grounds and ended up in the kitchen gardens, close to the castle.

"What will you do now?" asked Banes. "Think of all that gold stuffed into the treasuries – you could have anything you ever wanted."

"It's not my gold," said Marie, trailing her hand along the spiky thyme plants in the herb planter.

"It wasn't his gold, either," said Wyll, referring to their father. "Nothing he had was real. It doesn't belong to anyone."

"Maybe you could take just enough, for whatever it is you want," suggested Banes.

Marie sighed. They had reached the pear tree arch where the king had placed the model of himself and her mother. Despite everything she'd been through and everything she'd experienced, she would still give anything to be back there, to be part of a happy family once again.

"I want to go back," she said.

"You can never go back," said Wyll.

"Life isn't like that. Nothing lasts for ever," agreed Banes.

Marie raised her chin. "Then I will go forward. I know where I want to be if I can. But I don't want to be on my own. Will you come with me?"

There was a pause, then Banes and Wyll both answered, "yes," at exactly the same time.

Banes turned a little pink. "I'm sorry, I thought you were speaking to me."

Marie smiled. "I was speaking to you both."

QUEEN MAYBETH

On her coronation, Queen Maybeth looked the part: her blue eyes steely and her hair ablaze around her. Her crown was silver, in the shape of flames, with a black stripe down its centre. The crowd gazed in wonder at the very sight of her. There was music – such music! – and laughter in the air.

For a brief time, there were some questions about her background: a hazy question mark over her right to the throne. But soon, when it became apparent she was a strong and benevolent leader, the questions died away. She had family, too, a daughter from another kingdom. A beautiful princess, as strong as her mother.

Within a generation, the people of Quessia had virtually forgotten there had ever been a King Jacob, let alone a Princess Marie.

FIVE YEARS LATER

BRUME FOREST, IN THE

RULE OF QUEEN MAYBETH

THE WOODMAN'S ARMS

Deep in Brume Forest, where two roads met, stood a warm and inviting inn called The Woodman's Arms. A carpenter's cottage had once stood on the site, but it had fallen into disrepair when King Jacob was on the throne. That old cottage was long gone. The inn that had taken its place was a sturdy, two storey building with dark beams, white walls and dormer windows in the thatched roof. Ivy climbed over the walls and fat happy chickens scratched around outside.

People sometimes wondered how a business survived, hidden away in the forest as it was. It was true that in the old days, not many travellers passed this way, but now Quessia was a thriving city once more. Merchants and entertainers and visitors flocked to visit, and the inn had such a good reputation that people took the forest track rather than the main road, just to call in.

Cassie the innkeeper could tell tales that would put froth on your ale, whereas Fern the barmaid was a sympathetic ear to those in need. Marie, the cook, made simple, comforting fare and there were fresh eggs from the chickens every morning. Out the back, an old pole lathe hummed away as Wyll, the innkeeper's husband, worked away, with the little ones getting under his feet.

It wasn't unusual for travellers on their way to Quessia to stop for three nights rather than one. You couldn't find that feeling of home just anywhere.

"The secret," said Banes (or Cassie, as Marie now called her) "is old fashioned hard work, but remembering to stop sometimes, to relax and enjoy the life we're living."

It was at one of those relaxing times, as the daylight hours were dwindling, but the night had yet to begin, that Marie and Cassie were putting the chickens away for the night.

"Come on Cotter, come on Ford," called Cassie. "Oh dear, has Flint been pecking away at you again?" She secured the hen house and smiled at Marie, who was gazing up at the pink sky.

Marie had that dreamy look about her that seemed to overtake her at odd moments. "It's a magical time, isn't it?" she said.

"Twilight?" Cassie thought back to the magical twilights she'd known. She found herself listening for a distant ringing sound. She shared a look with Marie, who was listening too. But there was no ringing to be heard. Just the usual dusk song of the wood warbler. She sat on the grass and Marie joined her, looking into the legions of slender tree trunks.

"It was near here you first saw her, wasn't it?" asked Cassie. She didn't have to say who.

"Yes," said Marie. "By the waterfall." She'd told Cassie the story many times, but she kept asking and Marie never tired of telling it.

"Do you ever think of how life might have been, if you hadn't squandered those first wishes – if your father had never become king?"

Marie studied the backs of her hands for a moment. "Ten years ago, all I wanted to do was to go back in time. I wanted my mother, and my father the way he used to be. I knew it was impossible but could picture no other happy future." She paused and Cassie let her think for another moment. "I think, if I'd have known you back then, and Fern, then this is what I'd have wished for. All of this, exactly as it is now."

Cassie smiled, looked around and nodded. She thought not of what she'd lost over the years, but of everything she'd gained. "It is what I'd have wished for too," she said.

And for a moment they sat together, with their backs to the chickens and their faces to the sky, watching the sun go down together.

THE END

Acknowledgements

Thanks to:

Fiz Osborne, Pete Matthews, Liam Drane, Harriet Dunlea, Laila Dickson, Lucy Page, Tina Miller and to the wider Scholastic team for making this book happen and getting it out into the world despite the unbelievable challenges of 2020.

Emma Young for pointing me in the right direction once again.

Jodi Carmichael for valuable advice and support, including excellent suggestions for gruesome details.

Clara for Twitch, Tom for the wooden soldiers and to Simon for helping me reflect candlelight around the house using a variety of household objects.

Also available:

The
Midnight
Unicorn

ALICE HEMMING

An evil threat. A fight like no other.

Also available:

Also available: